# THE RAREST ROSE

# By the Author

Sanctuary

The Rarest Rose

# THE RAREST ROSE

*by*

I. Beacham

2013

# THE RAREST ROSE

ISBN 10: 1-60282-884-9
ISBN 13: 978-1-60282-884-1

THIS TRADE PAPERBACK ORIGINAL IS PUBLISHED BY
BOLD STROKES BOOKS, INC.
P.O. BOX 249
VALLEY FALLS, NY 12185

FIRST EDITION: JULY 2013

---

**CREDITS**
EDITOR: CINDY CRESAP
PRODUCTION DESIGN: SUSAN RAMUNDO
COVER DESIGN BY SHERI (GRAPHICARTIST2020@HOTMAIL.COM)

# Acknowledgments

I am indebted, as always, to BSB publisher, Len Barot, for continuing to trust in my abilities, imagination, and dreams. You are the best.

Huge thanks also to Cindy Cresap, my editor, for her excellent guidance, patience, and outstanding sense of humor. I have learned much and feel a better writer.

Finally, but never least, to the entire BSB team for their continued support.

# Dedication

To Jan and VKP

For your time, encouragement, and dogged support.
You are both treasured beyond any words.

## PROLOGUE

He passed each window, peering into the depths of the house. No sign of her. When he approached the large front door, he stopped and stared, willing it to open, needing to see her. She wasn't home. He returned the way he had come, back along the windows and across the drive. She was not here. He waited.

## CHAPTER ONE

The winding road seemed longer as Ele Teal negotiated the bends and slight inclines of the English lane that led home. Dusk was falling, and with it, a rapidly thickening fog that licked the grassy meadows on either side of her. It wrapped itself like an unwanted passionate embrace around unresponsive, insensitive farm buildings. Fields of sheep in wet, green grass grazed contentedly, penned in behind miles of traditional country iron railings, oblivious to the miserable weather.

Ele applied more pressure on the accelerator than was wise on country lanes like this. If an approaching driver took a bend too wide, the outcome would be something neither of them wanted. She reduced her speed and accepted that "slow but sure" was the safest way home this evening in such weather.

She turned left and onto her graveled drive, completing the final 800 yards through a short wooded area that led to an opening, to her Georgian home set in the lower half of the Oxfordshire Cotswolds.

She breathed a sigh of relief to be at her journey's end. Ele switched off the engine and allowed herself a few moments of simple indulgence as she let the peace of this place wash over her—as it always did, always had. Memories of laughter and love immediately seeped, for the trillionth time, back into her veins and she let a small smile rest on her lips. Would there ever be a day when she would sell this place? Not while oxygen nourished the planet.

Drops of rain appeared on her windscreen, pulling Ele back to the present. With a chill in the air increasing, she dashed to the rear of her eight-year-old Land Rover and pulled open the back. The door hinges creaked. She grinned. Still faithful and ever reliable, her car had never let her down, but was now past its glory days, and it felt obliged to bellyache now and then to remind her.

She leaned in and began gathering her weekly shop of groceries, pulling plastic bags together and throwing escapee apples that had rolled in every direction, back into them. It was a routine, mundane action, like every other week for so many years, and it should have progressed in its customary fashion. But it didn't. Not this time. Something made Ele stop. Stop immediately. She held her breath, and as she did so, her fingers froze around the bright orange plastic bags she now clutched tightly. In the passing of a second, what had always been repetitively monotonous, at once became unusual and abnormal.

Her hearing ached for sound, but found none. She jerked back and stepped away from the car to look around. Something—not a noise, not a movement—had grabbed her attention.

She swept her eyes left and right like a windscreen wiper in a rainstorm, searching for whatever had forced its way into her comfort zone and now made the hairs on the back of her neck stand up like sentries outside Buckingham Palace. Her heart pounded in her chest, her breath quickened. She scanned her surroundings and saw nothing, just the trees in the driveway, the little orchard down to her right, and the acre of lawn and garden in front of her. Everything was still. Everything was as it should be. Nothing moved except the thick, creeping fog that rolled over her home. She felt and saw only its heaviness, its clinging dampness, like a life force.

Ele wasn't a nervous woman. When she grew scared, there was always a damn good reason. Why then did she feel like this?

Her strange sense of alarm had nothing to do with the weather conditions. She was English for heaven's sake and born to the vagaries of its climate. Fogs and mist were as common as politicians' broken promises. But she knew enough to trust her instincts, and right now, they were telling her that something was not right.

After a final glance, she resumed gathering her shopping and slammed the car shut. She heard nothing, but the sound of her feet on gravel as she dashed to the house. Her discomfort scarcely lifted once she stepped inside and shut the door behind her, throwing the locks and bolts.

Her heart continued to race and only calmed when Featherstone, her three-year-old black cat with a bushy tail like a squirrel, tore down the stairs and bounced toward her. He wrapped himself around her legs with wild abandon and purred as if his life depended on it.

"Oh, so now I'm your best friend again, eh?" She bent and stroked him. "Where were you when I went out?" His purring became louder. "You're so fickle, Feathers. I can see through you like clear river water. You just love me because I bring you tinned tuna." Featherstone meowed and gave his true intentions away as he stared toward the bags of shopping at her feet with the focus he might give to a mouse about to be slaughtered.

"If you knew how to use a can opener, I'd be history." She stroked him once more before lifting the shopping. "Come on then. Let's go unpack." As she watched him run ahead of her down the hallway and into the kitchen, she felt a welcomed lightness. Perhaps she was being stupid, but just knowing that Featherstone was at ease made her feel better. This was a cat that growled at the wind and arched his back when a leaf moved unexpectedly across his path. If he was mellow and more interested in his stomach, then all was well with the world—or at least her little part of it. If anything was wrong, Featherstone would have told her.

## CHAPTER TWO

Kiernan Foyle flicked her shoulder-length hair back off her face as she heaved camera equipment onto her shoulder and simultaneously hit the lock button on her car key fob. Straightening her back, she glanced up at the house.

Very nice, she thought. Not too big, not too small, it was a typical, well-designed Georgian-style house that she guessed was built out of period around the 1870s. She admired its elegance and clean-cut simplicity. It had a square, symmetrical look with paired chimneys, pillared door, and the distinctive sash windows. Set in the middle of about an acre of land, Kiernan liked that it wasn't built in the usual Cotswold stone that lent the area so much uniformity. Not that she didn't love consistency, but it was satisfying to find something different every now and then. This was a delightful place that looked cared for and loved.

As she moved toward the center-paneled front door with its slim stone pillars either side, it opened, and the unmistakable figure of Eleanor Teal appeared. Though older, she was still instantly recognizable. She seemed taller than Kiernan remembered, but her elegant poise remained. This was the attractive woman whose early morning TV breakfast show once dominated the ratings. Natural honey blond hair fell in waves past shoulder length, encasing pale skin. On anyone else, that complexion might have implied some fragility, but her rosy cheeks suggested health. Conservative and model-like in her movement, she still possessed a subtle hint of boundless energy in her step.

Ele had retired suddenly from everything public about ten years ago, and Kiernan calculated that she was somewhere in her mid to late thirties, not much younger than herself. Although the fresh, alluring brush of youth that had so enamored her to the British public was gone, Ele retained her natural, English rose appeal that was enhanced by the way she was dressed this morning. She was in a stylishly cut, plain navy blue dress that emphasized a petite waist and long, slim legs. Her narrowness of build somehow made her appear taller than she was. Kiernan grinned as she wondered if the woman ever suffered from altitude sickness—something she would never be accused of at just under five and a half feet tall.

However, as always, it was Ele's eyes Kiernan noticed. From the minute she'd first seen her on screen all those years ago, she'd been drawn to them like dowsing rods to water. They were unusual, an intense radiant green reminiscent of an emerald gem reflecting light, or some sea grotto that mesmerized tourists. It was no wonder TV had grabbed her as a presenter and front woman as a way to wake up the nation and increase their ratings. Even now, the years past, Kiernan considered Ele's eyes still breathtaking.

Kiernan raised her hand to shake Ele's already outstretched one. "Good morning. I'm Kiernan Foyle, the photographer from *Oxfordshire Countryways Magazine*," she said as she handed over her business card.

Ele broke into an easy smile. "It certainly *is* a good morning." Her refined BBC classic English voice shone through, her diction clear and precise. Kiernan thought how old-world it sounded, like someone speaking in a 1940s movie. Ele's style of speech was becoming an unusual commodity these days. Everybody seemed to have an accent, almost wearing it with pride. She guessed it was a finger's up to the old class system. But it made Kiernan feel nostalgic. It was nice to hear that crispness, and she found herself thinking how it contrasted with her own lilting Irish brogue.

"I was worried last night's fog would hang around, but I see you've brought the sunshine with you."

"Oh, that?" Kiernan looked up at the sun with cavalier mockery. "It's just something we photographers like to arrange for our photo shoots. That way we can capture our subjects in the best that nature can offer. Rain, fog, snow, it's all fine, but you can't beat a good ray of sunshine."

"Well, I thank you for bringing it." The response oozed genuine warmth. "Now, what do you want to do? Where do you want to start?" Politeness acknowledged, Kiernan suspected her subject was keen to get the photo session over. "How long will all this take?" Ele asked as if reading Kiernan's mind.

She was already preparing her camera. "I'm afraid I'm one of those awful photographers who likes to have too many shots so I can pick the good few that will best sell the article and do you true justice."

Kiernan didn't know why she said that. No shot in heaven would do this woman an injustice. She could tell before the camera even clicked that Ele Teal would be loved by the lens. She was a Grace Kelly type, and certain things were just given. "I may be here for a good hour, but I promise to make it as painless as possible." Kiernan arched a brow in humor.

"To begin with, I'd like to get a few shots of you outside this beautiful house, maybe some here and then a few over there." She directed her eyes across the driveway to a corner of the garden where an old wrought iron gazebo stood. "After that, some in the house, Mrs. Teal, if you don't mind. The readers love to see people in their natural environment—where they nest, where they eat—"

"You make me sound like some rare species of bird," Ele quipped before adding, "and for heaven's sake, Kiernan, call me Ele. You make me sound like my mother."

Kiernan caught the grin as she nodded her head in acknowledgement. She also thought on Ele's confident use of her first name. Normally, clients either called her Miss Foyle or just avoided her name altogether. The former always made her wonder if they saw her as a spinster, the type unlikely to be married, or if their instincts tagged her as a lesbian. Not being called anything made her feel invisible. As she set her tripod, she noted that she liked the way Ele said her name. There was friendliness in it and a sense of connection. She maneuvered Ele so she was facing the sun, and began taking her first shots.

"I don't see the attraction of an article on me. I mean, I've been out of the limelight for ages," she said. "The request from your magazine stunned me."

"Not actually my magazine," Kiernan said from behind the camera as she clicked away. "I'm freelance, but I've done quite a bit of work for them over the years. Move left a bit," she directed her, preoccupied with her task. "I think your appearance at the opening of the Swan Centre mall raised your profile. When the editor learned you'd also written a book, well, you've become someone the magazine would like to do an article on for the 'Then and Now' pages."

Ele gave a tense laugh. "I think the readers are going to be very disappointed." Her tone was diffident and spoken in a way that hinted of uncertainty.

Kiernan surfaced from behind her camera, all action temporarily on hold. That self-effacing voice had taken her by surprise. She felt compelled to balance it. "Doubtful. You were very popular. When you left the breakfast show, I think you threw half the men in the UK into therapy."

Ele seemed to hesitate for a moment. Kiernan thought she registered gratitude in her eyes as she lightened up a little. "Only half?" Large eyes sparkled, their intensity focused on Kiernan.

"Not all men confess to seeing a therapist," Kiernan bantered back, her eyes drawn to Ele's.

"Oh, that's all right then." Ele's face lit up with friendly eagerness, and as Kiernan returned her attention to the job at hand, she found herself thinking how much she was enjoying this particular assignment. Too many of the people she photographed were walking egos on legs and puffed up with their own self-importance. It was rare to meet someone who was different.

"My book has just been accepted by the publisher. It may not sell. An illustrated study of British woodpeckers isn't exactly the competitive alternative to Harry Potter. A bit dull, don't you think?"

Kiernan straightened from behind her camera again. Working with Ele Teal was exasperating, for the woman never shut up. "Well, like it or not, you've been unearthed by Tom Mitchell, the editor, and if he decides you'll make good reading, well, you could have written the sequel to Alvin and the Chipmunks. He knows you'll make good reading."

Ele shrugged. "I don't share his enthusiasm," she said matter-of-factly. "I think your photos are going to have to be spectacular."

"They will be, if I can get you to stop talking," Kiernan said as she hooked a hand on her hip and deliberately displayed a look of patient amusement. Ele dipped her head in mock guilt.

"Sorry. Believe it or not, it was my chattiness that landed me the job on TV. I could hold a conversation with a Trappist monk."

Kiernan frowned.

"Their vows forbid them to talk," Ele clarified.

"I believe you," Kiernan whispered back, though she doubted Ele was hired only for her verbal skills. Every woman in the UK must have secretly yearned for a figure and looks like hers. There would also have been much jealousy as they watched their husbands drool. And all that during breakfast!

She was done with these photos, and with a gentle touch to Ele's elbow, indicated that they move toward the gazebo. She chatted about the house as they cut across the lawn. "I've driven past your place a few times, but never seen it because it's hidden by the trees. I'm amazed what's here...all the garden and the house. So unexpected. This is a fine place."

"Yes, it is now, but it wasn't when we bought it. Frankly, it was a nightmare. Rafters falling in, woodworm, rotten wood, dry rot, wet rot. We hoped the latter two would cancel each other out when they met in the middle." Ele rolled her eyes theatrically. "You name it, we had it. It had been empty a long time. The owner didn't live in it, but wouldn't sell. It never takes a property long to run to seed if it's neglected."

Kiernan wondered who the *we* was, as she was under the impression that Ele lived alone. She knew very little about her other than her previous professional life. Ele had managed to keep her private life *private* and away from the ever-intrusive press. It had been a mystery—and still was—why Ele had walked away from a very successful and lucrative career. Kiernan found it intriguing, but of course, none of her business. "How old is the place? Eighteen seventies?"

Ele responded with an obvious haste to Kiernan's show of interest and spoke with enthusiasm. "No, it's a little older than that. I think eighteen fifties. It started out life as a vicarage, and people still refer to it as that."

"Lucky vicar," Kiernan said and caught an expression of amusement from Ele.

"This used to be a wealthy area with a lot of manufacturing that grew out of the industrial revolution during the eighteen hundreds. I guess the area employed a lot of people, and the vicar would have had quite a congregation, but times change. Much of the industry has dried up, and the people have left to find work elsewhere. The church eventually sold the place. The church is still here of course, in the village."

Kiernan nodded. She had driven through Pegmire village at the bottom of the hill and seen the church. At the time, she had pondered why an unremarkable place would have such an imposing ecclesiastical building.

"When can I expect the article to appear?"

Ele broke her chain of thought. "I don't know, but usually at least a few months after I've done photos. I'm guessing early spring. They plan these things well ahead. I can ask for you, if you'd like?"

Ele casually shook her head as if it wasn't important before looking at her wristwatch. It was done in an understated way that wasn't meant to attract attention, but it did, and it made Kiernan forge forward with her job. She had promised the photo session would take no longer than an hour, and she would stay true to her word.

After a few shots by the gazebo, they moved to a small outbuilding that had recently been converted into a studio. It was where Ele produced her watercolor illustrations of varied colorful and handsome woodpeckers.

She showed Kiernan some of her work, announcing that most of it was in the soon to be published book. While the drawings were very precise and delicate, Kiernan's attention focused on the slim, well-manicured fingers that pointed out particular feathered subjects. She insisted on a photo of Ele holding one. Readers of the magazine would love those hands, too, for they were like fine sculptured marble, such human artwork at its best.

When they moved into the house, Kiernan found it as impressive as the outside. The inner rooms reflected grand Georgian proportions, yet simplicity in design. The owner of the house had added color and a sense of hominess to the imposing structural integrity.

She chose simple shots showing Ele stood in her hallway with an impressive wooden stairs behind her and with old-fashioned mosaic tiling on the floor. Then they moved to the warm, cozy sitting room. There was a burr elm desk in the corner by a window where Ele mentioned she sat and wrote about the indigenous bird life in the surrounding countryside. All this was photo recorded for the readers.

When Kiernan's task was complete and she left Ele, she felt content that she had all the photographs she needed, and that Tom Mitchell would be a happy man.

Everything had gone well.

## CHAPTER THREE

E verything had not gone well.
Ele's Sunday morning was not turning out as expected.
Not that she had any great plans, just a lazy morning in bed and some quality time with Featherstone.

He was a cat with routines. Mornings were where he allowed her to lavish him with affection; a hug, an ear massage and perhaps some gentle teasing along the length of his whiskers. For this, he would trill. It was a sort of high-pitched purr reserved for special moments. When he grew tired with this sumptuousness, Ele would *have* to get up and feed him; there was never any discussion or negotiation. He would then disappear for the day to embark on a ritual hunting regime, only occasionally returning home for energy snacks.

She would rise and shower, dress, and move downstairs to read the Sunday newspaper. After lunch, she might do a little watercolor painting in her studio.

But none of this was going to happen this morning. She had received a call last night from a very apologetic, upset Kiernan Foyle. The photographer had stated that none of her photographs had come out, and that—again, very apologetically—she hoped Ele might allow her to come back and repeat the photo shoot that day?

Ele had agreed. What else could she do? While she was genuinely ambivalent regarding the article, she liked Kiernan. The woman with the lovely auburn colored hair and soft Irish accent had a straightforward, no-nonsense way about her, a strong sense of purpose. Wiry and athletic, not too tall, she was the type of person you might discover climbing the Himalayas, a rope over her shoulder, an ice pick in her hand with a snow shovel in the other.

She was charming too, with a welcome sense of dry humor that had made the morning enjoyable. Not that Ele sought out compliments, but she quietly enjoyed hearing the pleasant remarks Kiernan made about her old media life. It had been a while since anyone massaged her ego. She guessed that Kiernan's editor would not be impressed if the article was delayed. Although she was freelance, Ele suspected all employment was well received in these hard economic times.

Ele checked her watch and, realizing she had a few minutes until Kiernan arrived, she moved to the hallway and inspected her appearance in a full-length mirror. She made a few minor adjustments. If the magazine's readers really did want to know about her boring life, she could at least put the effort in to look nice.

As she fluffed her hair out to give it body, she felt a chill run down her spine. She *knew* she was being watched. A noticeable shadow cut across a beam of sunlight that fell in the hallway from a window behind. Ele turned sharply. There was no one there, and despite crossing to the window rapidly, she still saw no one. She felt uneasy.

It didn't reassure her when she opened the front door for Feathers who demanded to go out. He took two steps forward and froze. His back bristled, and the fur on his body puffed out. He growled, and then with slow, feral movements, his stomach low, his haunches high, he backed back into the house, refusing resolutely to go out.

Relief flooded through her when she heard Kiernan's car approaching up the graveled driveway. As she moved to the still open door, she saw Kiernan slam her car shut and walk toward her. She couldn't help but admire her petite, lean physique and the way she looked so comfortable in what she was wearing. She was no sharp dresser, but everything about her looked crisp and clean, and spoke of someone who cared for her appearance.

Ele chuckled as she noted the stone-bleached jeans with sharp creases down the legs. Who irons jeans? Even the waxed dark green jacket, the type favored by country types and notorious for the distressed look, intimated it was clothing hung up when not in use. Most of the time, and at best, Ele's was thrown over the back of a kitchen chair. Maybe it was her old-fashioned values, but it appealed to her that Kiernan took such pride in how she looked. She liked cleanliness and self-respect in people; it was a clue to how they might deal with others.

As Kiernan approached, Ele could see her agitation, and once inside the hallway, it didn't take her long to voice its cause. She held up two cameras as she spoke. "I am so sorry. I can't believe it. When I downloaded the file, every single shot I'd taken was ruined. It was as if I'd had a lens cover on all the time."

"You hadn't, had you?" Ele teased. She could see the stress Kiernan was under and didn't want to add to it. Narrowed blue-gray eyes stared back at her, and she wondered if Kiernan resented her comment.

"I did that as a young apprentice when I worked for a local newspaper in Ireland. It's one of those mistakes you only ever make once."

Ele grinned. "Well, that's reassuring. I hope you appreciate I've had to dress up again," she joked as she pirouetted. "This isn't my usual Sunday potter-around-the-house garb." It wasn't. Sundays were for trainers and sloppy sweats. Here she was dressed in a charcoal gray long sleeved satin blouse that hugged her body and a pencil slim, dark gray skirt with a wide shiny black belt. Her pumps were bright patent red, like her lipstick. "I feel like a dog's dinner," she declared.

"Well, you don't look it," said Kiernan emphatically. "You're very smart. The readers will love your look, and if I may say so, it's even better than yesterday, if that's possible."

Ele fought a surge of delight. She didn't want the unexpected compliment to make her appear vain, but it pleased her that Kiernan appreciated her efforts to dress up. Her discomfort evaporated, which was more than could be said for Kiernan.

"I really *am* sorry. I used my new camera, a Canon EOS ID Mark III." Kiernan looked at it lovingly. "Works like a dream. Well, it did. Cost a fortune too. I just don't understand it. The last time I used it the shots were spectacular. Anyway, I've brought old faithful with me this time." She held up another Canon. "Bit older, but the stuff of legends. I promise you, it won't let us down."

*The stuff of legends?* Ele groaned to herself as she regarded how some of these professionals were so attached to their equipment, it almost became a living entity. She thought back to one of the film crew on the morning show who used to talk to a huge wheeled camera he pushed around the studio floor as if it were alive, and called it "my darling."

She was grateful that the morning progressed well, but for one strange exception.

When they were retaking photos over by the gazebo, Ele focused on the camera, posing for a shot. She suddenly spun around, expecting to see someone. It felt like someone was creeping up behind to surprise her. But when she turned, no one was there. Not seeing anyone disturbed her more than if she had. It was creepy and sent shivers through her, like someone walking across her grave.

"Is everything okay?" Kiernan looked concerned, and Ele could see she didn't understand what had upset her.

"I thought I heard something…maybe someone in the bushes behind." It was a lie. Ele hadn't heard anything. It was an inner sense that made her turn. She prayed Kiernan would say she saw something, but she looked none the wiser despite bothering to walk behind the gazebo and check no one was hiding there. The absence of evidence made Ele more anxious, a feeling she couldn't shake for the remainder of her time outside. She was glad when Kiernan announced they should move into the house.

When Kiernan left, Ele felt a strange tinge of sadness. She probably wouldn't see the rather charismatic and kind photographer again. Somehow that thought depressed her.

## CHAPTER FOUR

Normally a rational and level-headed woman, Kiernan had not been calm since she looked at the digital photos of the previous day's reshoot at Ele's.

Her mind would not accept what she saw. At first, convinced her computer was playing up, she had spent the evening transferring all the shots onto other equipment. When that hadn't worked, she had processed the photos through alternate software. No matter what she did, how many times she loaded and reloaded the photos, the outcome was always the same, and it continued to defy her reasoning. What she saw was not possible.

All night, her nerves were on edge as she thought about the photos and what they meant. Consequently, here she was on Ele's doorstep—again—and out of breath. Though the weather was damp and chilly, a typical November day, Kiernan was hot and bothered. There was no question that she was out of her comfort zone, and her hands felt sweaty as she tightly grasped her laptop to her body. When Ele opened the door, Kiernan realized how much her agitation showed, for she saw the instant look of concern on Ele's usually serene classic features.

"Something's wrong." Ele stated the obvious.

"You have no idea," Kiernan breathed as she moved into the house without waiting for an invitation.

"But you said all the photos came out." Frowning, Ele referred to the phone call she'd received from Kiernan that morning.

Kiernan had tried to sound composed and reassuring. That hadn't worked. She had ended up sounding like an alarmist trying not to sound like an alarmist, which of course, had alarmed Ele. Kiernan then insisted she might be allowed to *show* Ele the photos, that she might then understand what it was she wanted to bring to her attention, what it was that couldn't wait.

"Go into the sitting room," Ele said. "Do you want a drink or something?"

Behind the politeness, Kiernan thought she heard the birth of unbridled interest. Ele was hooked on whatever had brought her back for a third time.

*A drink?* Oh Jesus, yes, she thought. Would it be too soon in the day for a large neat whiskey? But she said nothing, not even bothering to answer Ele's question. Instead, she scanned the room for a suitable area to place her laptop, to show Ele what had made her drive over here at some ungodly speed and then sprint to the door.

She moved to a small baby grand piano with an attractive embroidered cloth draped over the far end of it that Kiernan assumed was to protect its high polished veneer from sunlight. There she removed a silver photo frame from its top. The photo displayed two women stood together, their arms draped around each other and smiling into the camera. Normally, Kiernan might have given the picture more scrutiny, but right now, she only wanted to switch on her laptop and let the setup program run.

Ele placed an outstretched arm on the piano, leaning casually into it, a mixture of amusement and kind tolerance in her eyes, a warm smile on her full lips. "Okay, you now have my full, unabated attention. What's this all about? What's so intriguing about these photographs?"

Kiernan rubbed the bridge of her nose, something she always did when faced with a thought provoking problem, something she couldn't solve easily. She stared straight into Ele's eyes, registering how long her eyelashes were. Her demeanor and voice took on gravitas, her desire to explain the seriousness of what her photos exposed. "I knew I couldn't tell you this over the phone. This is something you have to see, to try to make some damn sense of, because I surely can't." Kiernan looked at the screen and began opening the file she needed to show Ele.

She revealed one photo, then another, then a third. All photos were taken by the gazebo and looked as they should, but for one exception. There was a stranger—a man—in the background of them all.

The man stood as solid as any Kiernan might meet in the street. He appeared of average height and slight build, and was neatly dressed—one might almost say impeccably. He wore an overcoat that was either black or very dark gray, and Kiernan could see the white shirt and a dark tie contrasting beneath. His shoes were polished leather, and she considered he looked every inch a gentleman. This mystery man was good-looking with appealing chiseled features. He seemed to be in his mid twenties, with an old-fashioned thin moustache, well groomed dark hair swept back and tight to his head.

However, it was his eyes that frightened Kiernan. They made her think of her mother's ancestral Irish roots and all the folklore, myths, and legends she'd grown up with. Every macabre, nightmarish, unearthly banshee, troll, and demon had become part of her Irish inheritance. Kiernan had, until now, banished all these from her mind, until she had looked into this man's eyes. They were dark and intense, so piercing and penetrating…and so focused on Ele in every shot.

Kiernan studied Ele as she stared hard at each of the three photographs, absorbed by what she saw. She moved closer to Kiernan, tight at her side, and with her own fingers now on the keys, moved back and forth between shots, trying to make sense of them. It was a closeness that sparked an unexpected response in Kiernan, one she momentarily delighted in and yet did not want. She forced herself to remain professional and mentally chastised herself for allowing personal feeling to surface. Had she forgotten the pain of recent years so soon?

"Where'd he come from?" Ele asked the golden question that had plagued Kiernan for most of the night. "No one was there when these were taken," Ele quietly stated.

"No, they were not," Kiernan whispered. "There are others, too." She took over the keyboard and brought up more photos, all ones in the garden. Again, the man was present. "Every outside shot, our mystery man's in them."

"None inside the house?" Ele asked, her voice suggesting she didn't want to know the answer.

"No." Kiernan hoped that fact would be reassuring. Something like this in your garden was one thing, but in the house? Not good.

Ele leaned over the laptop, captivated with each photo. Kiernan stepped back to give her the space she needed to scrutinize what she herself had examined in every minute detail since yesterday.

Ele swept hair back off her face, and long, delicate fingers tried to poke it behind an ear, but it fell back again. This time Kiernan noticed a ring on Ele's wedding finger. For a brief moment, she thought again of the *we* and who that person might be. There didn't appear to be any evidence of another person living in the house. Just a cat, and that didn't count.

Her straying thoughts were interrupted as Ele drummed her fingernails on the piano to some unheard beat. What would Ele make of everything before her? Would she come to the same disturbing deduction Kiernan eventually had?

When Ele's conclusion came, it wasn't what Kiernan expected. Ele went rigid as if frozen at the keyboard before straightening her body in an unnatural slow movement. It was like watching someone trying to protect a back injury, except Kiernan knew there was no impairment. Ele stepped away from the piano and turned to face her.

Kiernan noticed the change instantly, a tangible alteration in Ele's warm demeanor. Her body language now spoke of detachment, an unseen barrier of distance being erected.

Drawing herself up to full height, Ele looked down on Kiernan, her jaw firm. "Tell me, how long have you been a photographer?"

Kiernan contemplated the strange turn of question. One minute they were studying sinister photos before them, and now this? But maybe it was a line of questioning that required Ele's attention, to help her make sense of what was happening.

"All my life," Kiernan answered. "I entered the profession when I was about twenty."

Ele nodded, but said nothing. A long, uncomfortable silence cut across the room, and though Kiernan longed to fill it, to break its somber heaviness, she could think of nothing to say. She let the emptiness hang there for a while before being compelled to chase it. "My father was an amateur photographer. It was his all-consuming hobby. I caught the bug from him and ended up studying photography at college and working Saturdays in a camera shop. Long story made very short, I've had a pretty varied career, but I'm now freelance."

"Freelance…" Ele repeated with slow deliberation. "You must be very good to be able to cut a living that way. I can't imagine it pays well, but I suppose *Oxfordshire Countryways Magazine* only contracts out to the best."

At face value, the comment should have been a compliment, but Kiernan knew it wasn't. There was a heavy implication behind the words, and Kiernan didn't like their tone. She took several deep breaths, girding herself for the unpleasantness that was steam rolling her way. "Freelance can pay, if you work hard," she said. "And yes, I guess I am considered well in the industry. You're right, magazines contract out to those who they know can deliver. I have a reputation for not letting people down." Kiernan could hear herself getting defensive. She wished she knew why.

"And you process all your own shots," Ele added casually as if she already knew.

Now Kiernan was getting rattled and considered the comment ignorant. "Of course I do!" Her restraint was slipping. "I'm hardly going to pop down to the local drug store and let them do my work, am I? Who does these days? I edit all my own material, straight from the camera to the computer. Any artistic interpretation or creative judgment is mine. I'm the professional photographer."

Now it was her turn to ask the questions. "Why the sudden interest in my technical abilities?"

"Because I think your *artistic interpretation* borders on the criminal."

The acerbic comment caught Kiernan full blast. Where had the relaxed, warmhearted woman gone? She felt her absence as she drew breath and analyzed the way Ele was looking at her, with contempt. The sour spoken words made her feel insulted, as if everything she was, honest and a consummate professional, were being called into question, but over what? What was happening here that she wasn't seeing?

"What's your point?" Her voice was low, no longer hiding her irritation. "I'm not sure what you're getting at, but I know I don't like it."

Ele shook her head in what looked like disbelief. "You must take me for a complete fool," she said with an unnatural calm. "Do I look like such an easy target for a confidence trick?"

"Confidence trick?"

"I wasn't born yesterday." Kiernan heard the controlled journalistic authority that Ele once used on her morning shows, her steel when she was chasing revelation. "And I certainly know when I'm being deceived. I can see through your photographic trickery, Miss. Foyle. I'm not sure where this particular scam is leading, but I can tell you, it's not going any further with me. I want you and your laptop out of my house, now."

Kiernan was struck dumb. It took a while to find her voice. "Scam? You think all of this"—she waved her hand over her laptop—"is trickery? That I'm doing this for some fraudulent gain? I can assure you that every photo I have shown you is genuine. There are no trick shots here."

"Well, I'm sure you'll have every opportunity to explain that to your editor when I tell him what's happened."

When Kiernan failed to move, Ele rounded off with a warning. "If you don't move, I'll also be alerting the police. Your decision; act fast."

In all her professional life—no, in *all* her life—this bizarre outcome had never happened to Kiernan, and because it was beyond her scope of experience, she didn't know how to handle it. It was pointless telling her that she'd done many jobs for the magazine and, if she'd been remotely criminal, didn't Ele think that would have come to the editor's attention sooner? But there was no reasoning with this woman. She had made her mind up that the photos were some illusion conjured by a masterful computer program. How could Kiernan convince her that it wasn't when she couldn't believe what she was seeing herself?

Moments later, Kiernan sat in her car and turned the engine. *Oh damn!* How was she going to explain this to Tom Mitchell?

❖

Ele threw the latches and bolts across her door making sure it was secure. She didn't want Kiernan trying to reenter. Did she consider that a possibility? Damn right she did. Anyone who would go to so much trouble to produce such a ruse was capable of that. She was just grateful Kiernan left quickly, and with minimum fuss.

She sat back exhausted on the bottom of her stairs, her emotions in tatters. Her hands hung limp between her knees as she contemplated what happened. It was a horrible experience. She felt angry and raw—raw because someone, a complete stranger, had almost managed to dupe her into…God knows what? Ele let this person into her home and had been gracious and welcoming. This was the result, and she considered herself a stupid fool. Was this what her self-enforced solitary existence meant, that she was now the easiest of pickings for the criminal fraternity of this world?

She looked down at her shaking hands and fumed as tears ran down her face. She cursed Kiernan as she roughly wiped them away. "Damn it," she muttered. The ridiculousness of the whole thing was that she had liked Kiernan. Liked her a lot. There had been an instant connection, and she had warmed to her wry, gentle humor. Despite her remonstrations about dressing up, she had looked forward to seeing her again. The latter point was a surprise and it shook Ele. Not many people evoked that level of interest from her, not in years. Of course, most successful con artists were the type that people liked; that was how they drew in victims. *Oh damn. She's a crook.*

"Oh, Beth," she whispered, "I wish you were here. I miss you so much." She hung her head. Would she ever stop missing her? Sometimes the pain cut through her like a razor, its sharpness not blunted by the years. Maybe this was Ele's punishment for liking someone a little too much. For even thinking beyond Beth?

She remained on her stairs for a while before moving. She wanted to find Kiernan's business card, and also the letter she'd received from the magazine. Ele was going to phone the editor. She was not going to let that woman get away with this, to survive and inveigle others with her dishonesty.

However, she didn't make the call. Perhaps it was because of the shock, but she chose to retire early, thinking sleep would give her a clear head in the morning when she spoke to Tom Mitchell.

The ploy worked. When she arose the next day, her thoughts were again rational, and the emotional sway of yesterday, gone. She reasoned that a magazine as well established and renowned as *Oxfordshire Countryways* would only contract those well known, and with good credentials.

But it irritated Ele that her first impressions of Kiernan had been so way off base. She was a good judge of character. Had she suddenly lost that ability? Instead, she tried something different. She grabbed her digital camera and went outside. She took a handful of photos before returning and loading them onto her computer.

What she saw made her step away from the desk. She clasped her hand over her mouth in fear. There, in every photo she had taken, was the same strange man in the background, the strange man whose eyes were focused on her.

## CHAPTER FIVE

Only a day later, Kiernan doggedly pulled onto the driveway of Ele's house. She'd returned to her car after a photographic shoot for the National Trust in Banbury to find her cell phone had a missed call. It was from Ele. Her message was simple. Ele had taken her own photos. She now knew that Kiernan was not lying. She was so very sorry and hoped that Kiernan could forgive her. The message then ended.

At first, Kiernan decided to ignore it and leave the beautiful Ele Teal well alone. She was incensed that anyone would dare call her integrity into question and had spent the remainder of yesterday in a filthy mood. Even today at work, she'd not been giving the job her entire attention. Ele's accusations kept running, and rerunning in her head, like some horrid playback loop, interrupting her thoughts.

Kiernan had wanted to phone Tom Mitchell, an associate of many years who had become a friend, and let him know what had happened before he got Ele's inevitable call. The one thing that stopped her was that he was away for a few days on a compassionate matter; his brother had died unexpectedly. Tom was devastated, and Kiernan was damned if she was going to bother him at such a time. It would all have to wait until he was back in the office.

Yet now it seemed she might not need to talk to Tom, and here she was outside Ele's house again. Why was she bothering to come back here? Ele had apologized, but it was something any decent person *should* do after all that was said. What if Ele didn't want her back here? She would have to apologize again, and this time in person. It would all be very awkward and difficult. Maybe that was what Kiernan wanted, to give Ele a bit of how she had felt yesterday? But she knew it wasn't. It was something else. Something as yet, undefined.

She rang the bell and waited.

❖

Ele opened the door and was shocked to find Kiernan. She had apologized profusely on the phone this morning—a recorded message—but never expected to hear from her again, let alone see her. She was so sure Kiernan would want to put as much distance as possible between herself and some crazy loner living in a large country house. But here she was.

Caught short and unprepared, all Ele could think of was apologizing again. "I'm so sorry for my behavior yesterday. I was way out of line. I misread the entire situation and thought the very worst of you. I reacted without any decent thought—"

"Yes, I think I've got all that. You're sorry and you've made a mistake." Kiernan's tone was acidic. "Now it's my turn to talk and for you to listen." Her voice registered deep annoyance. There was a look of no-nonsense on her face, and Ele shut up faster than a Venus flytrap.

"You need to understand something. I'm not a person used to being called a charlatan, nor do I enjoy having my moral integrity called into question. Just so you know, and to save you time having to work it out, I come from a good and stable background where I was taught, and learned to be, an honest human being. I've worked very hard for everything I've ever achieved in life, and the mere intimation that I'd do something dishonest across you or anyone else is, quite frankly, insulting."

Blood felt as if it plummeted from Ele's face as her body temperature rose. She could do nothing but stand still and listen, hear the hurt behind the words. She was uncomfortable and recognized it as her penance.

"Ele, I was shocked when you accused me of trickery, and to say I left here angry is an understatement. Don't you *ever* treat me like that again. If you have a question about anything I say or do, you ask me. Give me the grace to defend myself rather than you put two and two together and make seven. Is that understood?"

"Yes, it is." Her throat felt tight.

"Good. Therefore, you have apologized and I accept that. You have now heard what I have to say regarding this, and you have implied you understand. I hope you do because I have no intention of repeating this. I think the matter is now at an end." She hesitated. "I'm just overwhelmingly grateful that you didn't phone Tom Mitchell."

Ele felt the atmosphere lift and welcomed the return of Kiernan's customary tendency to humor. She half expected Kiernan to turn and leave now she'd said her piece, but she didn't. Instead, her face turned soft, as though her venting removed a heavy weight from her shoulders.

"Isn't it nice that two adults can sort out a misunderstanding so decently?" A small smile formed on Kiernan's lips and her voice returned to its normal, melodic lilt.

Ele wanted to smile too, but wasn't sure it was appropriate, so she didn't. The thought that they had both "sorted out a misunderstanding" amused her. That implied mutual action, some unity. She was pretty sure she hadn't noticed any. She'd been in receiving mode as the admonishment had rightfully been delivered.

"I will say this," Kiernan continued, her posture relaxing. "In fairness to you, I started thinking of how I'd react to those photographs. I mean, the subject matter isn't something you come across every day, is it?"

"Not really." Ele's answer was limp. She was still unsure of Kiernan's reactions.

"And it isn't something I've experienced before. While I don't think I would have reacted the way you did, part of me understands."

Ele noted how the color of her eyes changed, an indicator of her mood. She found herself admiring Kiernan's response. She was brave enough to come and face her. Without being over dramatic or rude, she simply put her own case forward and reprimanded Ele for hers. It reassured Ele that she hadn't lost her ability to judge character. Kiernan Foyle *was* someone special, a woman with depth and maturity, and thankfully, one with a huge capacity for kindness as now witnessed by her ability to forgive. Ele considered that these traits were things anyone decent aspired to, and yet what many people lacked. She felt penitent and wished yesterday had never happened.

"So, everything is okay, right?"

It took Ele several seconds to register that she was staring at Kiernan who now regarded her curiously. She blushed and felt uncomfortable. Covering her embarrassment, she realized she was keeping Kiernan on the doorstep and that she looked chilled to the bone. Although it was only mid afternoon, it was cold and there was about an hour of light left. She ushered her into the hallway and closed the door.

"Everything is fine, Kiernan. Please tell me you'll come in and have a drink. You look frozen." She added, "And I think I need the opportunity to show you I'm not always a complete idiot who should know better, if you'll give me the chance."

"I'm willing to give you a second chance." The nuance suggested amiable teasing, and forgiveness, but there was nothing dismissive in Kiernan's features. She looked serious. A few beats of time passed before she added, "I think you might have a problem outside."

Ele heard the edginess in her own voice as she admitted, "I think my home is haunted."

# CHAPTER SIX

Keirnan allowed herself to be pushed into the sitting room as Ele then disappeared into the kitchen. She was glad they had managed to sort things out and that she wasn't now regarded as a member of some criminal fraternity. She was happy they were back on good terms. Losing Ele's trust was something she never wanted to do, although she wasn't sure why.

She relaxed on a large, soft, three-seat burgundy sofa, the type that swallowed you as you sank into it. It wrapped itself around her like a lover's arm as she stretched out her legs toward the warm fire that crackled away in front of her. She felt its warmth on her feet and realized how cold she'd been.

Kiernan waited for Ele to return with coffee and enjoyed the smell of wood burning. She'd spent all day outside taking photos of an historical building undergoing major restoration. The National Trust wanted to record the changes. There was nothing challenging to the work, but she'd been on her feet all day, and she was exhausted. It also hadn't helped that her mental state had been off-kilter. She hadn't realized how annoyed she was with Ele until she'd arrived on her doorstep and found herself reading the woman the riot act. But now everything was off her chest and the air cleared, she felt a thousand times better. Her current problem was that, as she loosened up, she was in danger of falling asleep in front of Ele's fire. She forced her mind into an attentive state.

Glancing around, she liked what she saw. Long, sumptuous drapes that shimmered, hung on tall period windows. The room was carpeted, and there were several large rich colored rugs in a traditional design in keeping with the elegance of the room. Four large table lamps were already on even though there was still some light outside. They cast dancing shadows across the room invitingly, courtesy of the firelight.

On a tapestry footstool opposite her sat an attractive long haired black cat, and she reached forward to stroke it. It hissed at her, and she was caught in the action of retreating against an unassailable and hostile force when Ele walked in with two steaming hot mugs of coffee.

"I see you've met Featherstone."

"I don't think your cat likes me," Kiernan said.

"Don't worry about Feathers. He's just contrary and takes his time getting to know people. He wouldn't hurt you; he's adorable."

Adorable was not a word that Kiernan associated with this cat. Ever since she'd walked into the room, he had followed her, watching every move she made. Even now, while he cleaned a paw meticulously, his large golden eyes, like an owl's, scrutinized her.

She sipped her drink, its welcoming liquid heat seeping into her. "Featherstone is a strange name for a cat."

"It was the name on the box," Ele said. "I was out for dinner one night with friends. As I walked back to the car park, I heard a noise like a squeak. It came from an old cardboard box up against a wall. When I looked inside, there was this kitten, very tiny, thin, and scared. It was no older than five or six weeks."

Ele reached over and stroked him. Featherstone lifted his head toward her, a look of pure ecstasy slapped across his feline face.

"It was raining," she continued, "and the poor mite was wet. I looked around hoping to see where he came from, who he belonged to, but there was nothing. I think someone dumped him. My conscience wouldn't let me walk away so I wrapped him in my scarf and brought him home. We've been great friends ever since, haven't we, Feathers?"

Featherstone looked at Kiernan, his eyes slanted and challenging, like a possessive lover. No, it wasn't an *adorable* look.

She changed the subject. "You know, for someone who has a ghost, you seem rather relaxed."

Ele sat adjacent to her in a matching armchair, and firelight played across her face. When she answered the door, Kiernan didn't expect to see her dressed so casually in a pair of ripped cargo pants and an oversized T-shirt with a motif so faded it could no longer be read. The fact she wasn't dressed up for the camera did nothing to diminish how attractive she was. She thought of some of the women she had dated and their finicky obsession with dress and makeup. Ungraciously, she thought how different some of them looked once the fine clothes and makeup were removed. They could have been other people entirely. True beauty held firm regardless of how it was presented.

Ele was answering her question, her eyes focused in some contemplative state, watching her own fingers trace around the rim of her mug. Her eyes were bright, and yet there was no customary smile Kiernan was growing to expect.

"Not relaxed," Ele said seriously. "I find this all rather frightening, but…" She swept a hand slowly, dramatically, in front of her, left to right. "I think this all explains a lot, and actually, I feel just a little relieved."

"Relieved?" *You have a spirit traipsing around your property, and you feel relieved?*

"I've had these funny feelings of being watched, and I was beginning to wonder if I was being stalked." Ele grew more thoughtful as she placed her mug down and bent forward, her arms now folded in her lap. She looked as if she were trying to contain herself. "Do you have to be anywhere?" Ele asked.

"No," Kiernan answered. She had nowhere to be, no one waiting at home for her. Not anymore. Not so long ago, she had loved. She had shared her dreams, and everything that mattered in life, with her lover. She had been loved back. She still clung to that, praying it was true, for if the love hadn't been there, then how deceitful and cruel life could be. But now it was all over, and the love was gone. She knew there was no place she wanted to be more than here at this moment. Her body turned toward Ele, almost without thought, the non-spoken message inviting her to continue.

"Things have been happening lately," Ele said. "I feel as if someone is observing me. I never see or hear anything, but it's when you just know something is wrong, when the hairs on the back of your neck—"

"You thought you were being stalked?"

"Yes. I had some work done outside, earlier this year. There used to be an old building opposite the kitchen and across the courtyard. It was a stable block divided into three separate areas. One was the stable, and another, the tack room. The third was additional storage. Anyway, I had a builder come in and knock the three into one and convert it all into my studio."

Kiernan had taken a few shots of Ele in her studio, a large bright room painted white and with a glass roof that flooded the room with natural light. It was where she had "captured" Ele's elegant hands.

"There was a young bricklayer working for Roger, the builder. I think he had a crush on me. It seemed everywhere I was, so was this young man. Whenever I arrived home, or went outside, he was always there, looking at me. Over time, it began to needle me, but I thought he was harmless and that once the work was finished, he'd be gone. However, I've been having feelings of being watched ever since."

"Like the ones at the gazebo when I was taking photos."

"Oh yes, and much more. I know he's a local lad, and he could easily walk up from Pegmire. I thought maybe it was him, but now these photos. They explain a lot."

*They explain nothing.* "How long have you lived here?"

"We bought it about thirteen years ago."

There was that *we* again, and Kiernan's thoughts returned to the photo on the piano. There were other photos in the room, many with the same affectionate looking woman. She saw none of any man. "And you've never had these feelings before?"

"Never." Ele rose. "Can I show you what work was done, while we still have daylight?"

They moved across the hallway and into a modern, contemporary kitchen. From there they walked out the back door and into a newly laid courtyard. Kiernan looked at a covered walkway about six yards long that stretched between the kitchen and the converted studio. A trellised frame ran along its length, where evidence suggested Ele was trying to train plants.

"Roses?" Kiernan asked.

"Wisteria," she said. "I did buy some roses to put in the borders, but I don't know whether I bought a dud lot or just left them in their pots too long before planting them out. They're all dead." She indicated a small garden refuse area to the far side of the studio where half a dozen roses, still in their plastic pots, were discarded.

"I think the Wisteria will look nice once it becomes established," Ele said. "I want to put some softness back into the area. I had Roger take out some of the old garden over there." She pointed to the right and farther down from the studio. "It was a mess. Just a grassy area with a few old shrubs and seating that always looked unkempt. Now it's all been paved over, I can drive my car up here and wash it if I want. It's far more practical and less gardening."

The new area looked fit for the purpose, and Kiernan thought the rustic, cobbled brickwork attractive. It felt in keeping with the period of the house, and she considered the builder had done a sterling job. She watched as the cat, which had followed them out, sat in the middle of the courtyard.

"And these feelings all started about the time of the building works?" Kiernan asked.

Ele looked at her edgily. "Yes."

"The builder didn't find anything?"

"Oh, wait. He did say he'd found a pile of bones and a human skull with an arrow through it." She smiled at Kiernan.

Kiernan shrugged as she realized the stupidity of her question. She grinned sheepishly. "Point taken."

"Yes, but you do *have* a point," Ele said. "These strange happenings have only started since the work was done. It stands to reason that something has been disturbed."

"The question is what."

Ele stood and regarded what lay around her, as if seeing it all for the first time with new eyes. Kiernan saw a change of emotions cross her face and an uneasiness fall on her as she spoke.

"What if someone is buried here and we've disturbed him? And if that's so, who is he and why is he here? Has he been murdered? I mean, you don't bury people in your garden, by a stable, do you?"

"No, you don't, but I think you're allowing your thoughts to run wild." There was a disturbing anxiousness building in Ele that Kiernan wanted to dispel, except she couldn't because she was having the exact same thoughts, and none of them were very pleasant. If this were happening at her property, she'd be hiding her head under her pillows.

"You can bury ashes," Kiernan said pathetically. It wasn't a frequent occurrence, but the bereaved sometimes buried or scattered the ashes of their loved ones in the garden. It was legal. Maybe this is what had happened, and the builders had disturbed someone's last resting place. Kiernan didn't rate this. Who would bury someone next to a stable unless it was their dying wish to be buried with their cherished, departed horse? Somehow the man in the photos didn't look like the horsey type. She added, "And this may have nothing to do with this area. He's in photos all over the garden, not just here."

But she didn't believe that either. Ele was telling her that the only recent changes to the place were by the studio. She caught herself thinking of her last few days and what started out as a simple photo shoot for a county magazine. Now it took a sinister turn. What was she going to send to Tom? She couldn't send him external photos. She'd have to send him internal ones and hope they'd suffice.

"What if he is watching us now?" Ele broke Kiernan's chain of thought.

They stared at each other, knowing it was likely. An inner voice whispered to Kiernan, what if he is watching Ele now? The ghost seemed interested in just her. A protective surge swept over her, and without voicing her worries, she placed a hand on Ele's back as she gently, but firmly pushed her into the kitchen and closed the door behind them.

Ele stopped halfway in the room and faced her. "I'm not a weak woman, Kiernan, and I don't frighten easily, but this is something beyond my scope of understanding. What should I do?"

The question was a good one. Unfortunately, Kiernan had no idea. It wasn't her problem, but she didn't feel obliged to walk away from it either. Although she was trying, Ele was having difficulty hiding her fear. It served to reinforce a decision Kiernan made earlier. "I don't want to impose or anything, but I'd like to help you, if I can."

Ele's hand reached for hers and Kiernan felt a tingle rush down her spine.

"Oh, thank you. I don't know where to start. A person can deal with a stalker. There's a well established process to follow, but this? My home is haunted and I don't know how to stop it."

Kiernan squeezed her hand with fake reassurance as she recalled her own fright from last night as she had studied the photos. She had needed to stop looking at the horrifying and intense piercing eyes of the unknown man. Her concern for Ele was genuine. If this was escalating, what might it escalate to? She also knew Ele's fear was greater than hers, for this was her home and she couldn't walk away. She was stuck with whatever was happening—or would happen in the future. Kiernan had believed that haunting and the uncanny were things you read in books or paid money to go to the movies and be scared witless. Ghosts did not exist. They were not real life. Not until now.

"I'm going to do whatever I can to help you. You're not alone in this." Gratitude flooded Ele's face. "It's getting late, and whatever is going on, we're not going to solve it tonight." She tried to formulate a plan on the hoof, to say anything reasonable that might give Ele hope. "I'm not working tomorrow. What if I come back in the morning and we fine-study those photos? See if we can find any clues, anything that pinpoints this man to a period of time. At least then we can narrow down our search."

Kiernan still held Ele's hand, not wanting to let it go. She tried not to dwell on why that was and forced herself to concentrate on the bigger issue. "I also have an idea, something I want to try. Something that's in the back of my mind, but I don't want to say anything now in case I'm wrong. Tomorrow would be better when we're both fresh." She was beginning to think about something she'd seen in the photos and how, tonight at home, she might run another computer program to test a theory.

Ele accepted, with resignation, that Kiernan spoke sense. "Thank you for offering to help. It seems a little incredible after all the insults I threw at you yesterday."

"Forget that." Kiernan meant it.

"There's no one I can turn to, at least no one I trust. That's the problem of living alone, I suppose."

She caught something in Ele's voice. The word "alone" echoed more than merely someone living in a house by herself. There was an ache behind it, and catching its resonance, Kiernan realized that while it answered one of her questions, it just begged more.

"I'll be back tomorrow." She tugged Ele's hand before letting it go. "I don't know how we're going to do this, but we will get to the bottom of it together."

As she drove home, the fettles of ghostly happenings dropped from her thoughts and a bombardment of other, more interesting ones crossed her mind. She could still feel her hand tingling, the one Ele had grasped. The one Kiernan hadn't wanted her to let go. Kiernan had been quick to volunteer her assistance and though genuine, her intentions weren't all about delivering good deeds and being concerned for someone's safety. Kiernan breathed out heavily as if she'd been holding her breath all the time she'd been with Ele.

She knew exactly what was going on. Her attractive "app" had switched back on and was focusing in on Ele. It had taken nearly two years for that to happen. "Damaged heart, lost love, and all that crap," Kiernan said to herself. "Just don't get too keen, Kiernan Foyle, Ele isn't interested in you, only your support, *and* do you really want to get hurt again so soon? You can sleep again now. How long has that taken?"

For less than fifteen seconds, she just concentrated on her driving. Then she said, "Yes, well, nothing ventured, nothing gained. False heart never won a lady's hand. I'm still a hot-blooded woman, and I can dream." Just don't do anything stupid, she thought as she turned the radio on to drown the irritating self-communing in her head.

## CHAPTER SEVEN

Ele was glad when Kiernan arrived early the next day. Although she could tell there was something on her mind and that she was itching to start taking photos again, she didn't do so immediately. Instead, she put her camera equipment down and concentrated on Ele.

"Now, how are you, Ele? Have you managed to get any sleep?" It felt far more than a passing "How are you," something everyone asks by rote, but very few genuinely want to know. Ele felt reassured. She still wasn't convinced that Kiernan forgave her recent rudeness. The fact that she was taking time to ask such questions, rather than forge ahead with ghost hunting, implied she had. Although the interlude was brief, it held such quality for Ele and brought her comfort. It was nice to know Kiernan was concerned for her. She really was beginning to like her.

Forty minutes later, they sat together in the kitchen. Ele watched Kiernan multitask as she consumed toast and coffee while loading the morning's shots onto her laptop. Whatever she was up to, she was excited and keen to reveal her discovery.

"Take a look at these three photos of the man," Kiernan said calmly, her focus intent on the screen. "Do you notice anything?"

Ele didn't, only that the photos were all taken the day before yesterday and in the same place, with the man staring at her. They were identical.

Kiernan looked disappointed and shook a finger. "They all look the same, but they're not. Look at his hands, specifically his one hand. It's moving. It's not moving much, but it is changing position."

"I don't see it." If there was movement, it was miniscule. She didn't understand what Kiernan was getting at, but she could sense she was on to something. Regrettably, it seemed Kiernan was an analytic type that talked around things before getting to the point. Ele was all action; show me the findings, then explain.

"This morning, I tried an experiment," Kiernan said. "I retook some photos of the places where the ghost appears, and guess what?"

"What?" Ele tried to hide her frustration.

Kiernan grinned, and Ele suspected she knew her slow deliberations aggravated her. It didn't encourage speed. "He didn't reappear in the photos, and do you know why?"

"No." Ele's answer was slow. Her eyes narrowed as her impatience grew.

"Because you weren't in them," Kiernan explained. "Now, this morning when I asked you to step into the sitting room and stand by your desk near the window while I took some shots...."

Ele sensed a fait accompli approaching.

"This happened." Kiernan turned her computer for Ele to see.

She was horrified. The ghost stood outside the window, about two feet away from the pane. His somber, unsmiling face with the haunting eyes stared at her. How many times had she sat at that desk working on her manuscript and thought she was being watched? Now it appeared her instincts were right.

"Our man reappears because *you* are there. It seems he only materializes when you are being photographed or when you take shots, and then only outside. Now, look at the photos I've taken this morning and where he's present."

Ele looked hard. "Sorry, Kiernan, I'm not seeing it." Her annoyance was self-focused. Why couldn't she see what Kiernan could and so clearly? "They just look like lots of shots of the same picture with him in them." She looked at Kiernan hard. "For heaven's sake, explain this to me, please."

Kiernan raised her hands. "Okay. This morning I used my motor drive on the camera. It takes multiple frames per second. Now look at those same photos when I show you them all, one after the other, but at speed. Watch his hands, Ele."

Ele nearly choked. Looking at each photo in isolation revealed nothing, but when they were speed sequenced, it reminded her of a book she once had as a child. As she flicked through each page, a little man "walked" along the top corner. It was a visual illusion, of course, but as she watched the ghost, he moved too, but this was real. His hand slowly rose from his side to rest at a right angle. There was no doubt he was pointing to something.

"He's trying to tell you something, Ele. *You*," Kiernan stressed.

"Oh, great. I'm being stalked by a ghost!"

It was a fascinating discovery, but it did nothing to eradicate Ele's fears. She was scared. It was a disturbing sensation to know a ghost had a personal fixation on her. "Why isn't he interested in you? You're the one with the camera, the one who might unlock this. Why is he so intent on focusing on me, and where is he pointing?"

Kiernan had no answers and said so. "I want to take some more shots of you outside using the motor drive. Maybe if we get different shots all around the house, we might be able to triangulate this and identify where he's pointing."

They took their shots, and it came as little surprise to discover that the pointing finger lead them to one general spot—where the building works had been.

❖

Later that day, they sat in Ele's sitting room, hunched close on the sofa, poring over photos with investigative absorption. They were seeking clues that might reveal who the man was and when he lived.

Ele was exhausted, and she felt like she was on an emotional pendulum. Last night, alone in the house, she had been petrified. She had closed every curtain, frightened to death that she might glimpse a ghost staring in at her. She even closed the curtains in her bedroom, something she never did. Her imagination wild, she conjured up thoughts of this strange man levitating from the ground and staring in at her as she lay in bed. Nothing happened, but the absence hadn't stopped her having a sleepless night, aware of every creak in the house and every shadow in her bedroom. It brought her little comfort that Feathers had slept undisturbed on the bottom of her bed, or that Kiernan believed the spirit only "functioned" outside.

Daylight brought a welcome calm; she always worried more at night and let her thoughts and emotions run rampant. Kiernan's presence helped too. Her quiet composure and control soaked into her bones, and she turned more rational and charged. Ele was determined to discover who this man was and why he now appeared. She had to stand up to this unique predicament. If she didn't, what was her alternative? To move? No way. This had been her home for too long and it held such precious memories. No ghost was going to rob her of those.

She nudged close to Kiernan and studied the man's face. At first glance, his eyes were all consuming and startling, with an edge of animosity lodged deep. It was not difficult to imagine he meant her ill will. But the more she forced herself to look, as the shock of this spectral discovery diminished, her opinion changed. It surprised her when Kiernan voiced the same view. Sometimes, she felt they were on the same wavelength.

"The more I look at him," Kiernan said, "the less I see him as willful or dangerous. His eyes *are* terrifying, but I sense sadness and loss there too, don't you?"

For a second, Ele wondered if Kiernan was making this up in a kind attempt to lighten the horror and to tone down its spine-chilling magnitude. Yet when she looked at her, she knew she wasn't. She studied the man's face again and knew it was true. His eyes begged, yearned for something, and there was desperation there.

"Yes, I see it, too."

They reexamined his attire and the way he groomed himself—the slim moustache, the slicked back hairstyle with its short back and sides. It was reminiscent of the 1920s, perhaps earlier, when personal grooming was at a high and appearance leaned to the immaculate.

"So what now?" Ele glanced at her, seeking comfort in serious eyes. She was grateful for her presence and to know she did not face this alone. She wondered if she would trust anyone else so quickly the way she did Kiernan. What if it had been another photographer from the magazine? Would she have felt so comfortable with them? It occurred to her, that their meeting was such luck. She might never have met her but for the article.

"Do you have any idea who has lived here before you?" Ele listened to Kiernan's rich voice. She loved the way it resonated.

"No. The house was empty for some years. The man I bought it from inherited it and never lived here. I can find out though by drawing the deeds from the safe custody box at my bank. Older deeds often record the names of past owners, and I seem to remember mine are quite detailed."

Kiernan liked the idea. "I also wonder if, given the history of this area, there might be a local historical society. If there is, they might be able to help."

Ele crossed to her desk and picked up a copy of the local Yellow Pages. She scanned through it. "Nothing." Then she riffled through a pile of paperwork before surfacing with a small pamphlet. "The village produces this twice a year. All the local businesses and social groups tend to advertise in it. I don't look at it much, but you never know." She flicked through its pages. "Aha! There's a local historical society that functions through Chestleton Library, and there's a number here. Shall I call?"

"Worth a shot."

A recorded message from a man with a heavy nasal accent and overly pronounced words informed her that someone from the society was present in the local town library mid week between ten and two o'clock. If she required any information, she was invited to drop in to the library between those times.

Kiernan had been about to leave when she said, "I'll come with you to the library if you like. Two heads are better than one."

Ele was delighted. She hadn't wanted to ask her in case she was being pushy. Kiernan was already doing so much, giving up her free time to help. When Kiernan volunteered, Ele couldn't believe it. It was as if she had read her mind. It was just another thing that made Ele realize how singular Kiernan was, and that her initial impression of her was right. Not for the first time, she thanked the magazine for wanting to do an article on her.

## CHAPTER EIGHT

On an unexpected sunny mid-week morning, Kiernan bounced into Chestleton Library. She was in a good mood and looking forward to seeing Ele. She hadn't felt this happy in a long time and knew it was Ele who evoked her elation. Though she reminded herself that they were simply becoming friends through *interesting times*, she couldn't help feeling the spring in her step. God, when was the last time she'd felt that?

They had agreed to meet at the library, but despite being a few minutes late, she arrived first. For a while, she hung around in the entrance waiting for Ele, but after the librarian at the desk stared at her for a third time, she decided to go ahead and seek out the representative of the historical society. She found him in a little room toward the back of the library, past the children's corner full of bright, mega-colorful books and huge hanging cardboard cutouts of big yellow sunflowers and bright green ducks.

Hugh Latimer's persona did not match the brightness and glow of the sunflowers or ducks. Instead, Kiernan found a balding, bespectacled middle-aged man in a sleeveless cardigan who looked like he'd just received a final notice from the taxman. He could not have been more disinterested in Kiernan's inquiries if he'd trained for it.

"The historical society is primarily interested in material of historical value," his monotone nasal voice declared in dismissive tone. "We seek to record, *and preserve*, those matters of historical past, be they people or buildings, that add to the rich narrative and import of this area." He glanced at her over the top of his glasses, and in an almost disapproving manner, added, "What we do not keep, nor have interest in, is an A to Z of every person who has lived in every domicile residence within the area of historic value, unless of course"—Latimer raised a single skinny finger in emphasis—"they are of historical interest and can add to the colorful account, figuratively speaking, of our boundaries."

It took Kiernan a few seconds to realize Latimer had finished talking and was now looking at her, total indifference registered on his face. He was hoping to dismiss her and get on with whatever he had been doing before her interruption.

Did people like this really exist? Latimer was like a modern day caricature of some slimy Charles Dickens secondary character whose task it was to hamper the hero or heroine's objective, and cause them nothing but distress. Her imagination ran riot, and she was mentally enjoying pulling what little hair he had left on his head out, root by root, when Ele walked in behind her. The change in Hugh Latimer's demeanor was nothing short of spectacular.

"Oh, Miss Teal…" he spluttered.

Kiernan watched as he rose from his chair and came from behind the desk, wringing his hands in delight and with a smile capable of lighting up Oxford Street's Christmas illuminations. *He's got more teeth than a tiger shark.*

She heard Ele's concise diction as she introduced herself and explained she also sought the information Kiernan did, that they were working together. Though she tried, Kiernan could not stop her eyebrows from rising high up her forehead. She stood dumbfounded as Latimer began imparting helpful information.

"I deeply regret that we hold no record of persons who have resided at that domicile since its demise as a vicarage, but all is not lost." He raised his index finger as he smiled at Ele. Kiernan ungraciously viewed a dirty fingernail. "However, there is an elderly gentleman, Mr. Edmond Riser, living in Pegmire who has proved most useful in previous inquiries. Although he is in his nineties, he is still quite sagacious and alert, and because he has lived and worked in the village all his life, he might be able to shed light on previous occupants." Latimer wrung his hands again, so overcome and delighted to be of assistance to Eleanor Teal.

Kiernan shook her head as she watched Latimer open up to Ele like orange segments. What was it with some men who were so shallow they could only react to beautiful women, and seemed dismissive of the remaining ninety percent of the population? Latimer was no Adonis, and she meanly concluded he had gone through life having difficulty finding a mate. Wasn't it in his interest to play nice with everyone? She rolled her eyes and continued to stand back and watch the ongoing performance. Latimer had to have been one of those adoring fans who had once fantasized over Ele when she was on morning television.

Several minutes later, it seemed Ele had all the information she wanted from Latimer. She patted Kiernan on a shoulder to indicate they were leaving.

"Well, that went really well," Ele said as they walked out of the library and toward the town car park. "Don't you think so?" She glanced over to Kiernan who stared back at her in total amusement. "What?"

They halted at a pedestrian crossing.

Kiernan drew herself into a hunched position and wrung her hands before her. She impersonated Hugh Latimer's pinched looks and nasal voice. "Oh, Miss Teal, how can I assist you? Whatever you want, please let me fall over myself to deliver it." She bared her teeth.

"I thought he was delightful and most helpful," Ele replied, poker-faced.

Kiernan straightened and sighed. "He was to you. He treated me like an imbecile. I couldn't get anything out of him. What a puffed-up pigeon of a man."

"Oh." Ele reached out and patted Kiernan on the shoulder in an exhibition of simulated sympathy, and in her most caring voice said, "You poor thing, he dented your ego."

"He didn't dent it," Kiernan said with mock defensiveness. "He crushed it."

"Oh, you're crushed." Ele was playing with her and Kiernan loved it.

She couldn't stop grinning and felt almost excited when Ele beamed back at her, her eyes sparkling and her face laced with fun. She allowed herself a laugh and as she did, emotional shackles fell from her, and she was *lighter* again—like she had been before Chrissie. Before Chrissie had hurt her so much, and she had feared she could never heal the wounds. She was drawn to Ele, like a compass point to true North. And it felt wonderful.

Ele reached out and wrapped an arm around her shoulder. "Why don't I make you feel better? Come home and have lunch with me."

Kiernan hadn't thought the moment could improve, but it just had. Ele's physical contact only added to her happiness, and though she reminded herself this was just the building of a firm friendship, a minute part inside her whispered, "Could it be more?" Was it possible that, in her dreams, Ele might also be attracted to her? The aperture of a memory opened and reminded her of a photo on a piano—that of Ele and another woman. It tempered her elation before she accepted the invitation without hesitation. She could think of no better way to finish an already perfect day.

Lunch over, she was even more content. Though it was cold outside, the sunshine poured into Ele's sitting room as they sat at a small round oak table that rested by a window overlooking the front of the house. Remains of lunch lay scattered before them.

Kiernan felt sated and leaned back in the chair. She looked out at the light reflecting through autumn leaves that still clung to branches despite recent high winds. November was such a destructive month.

Eyeing her car in the driveway, she joked, "Do I get my own parking space if I keep coming here?" Her light banter was rewarded with another rich smile as Ele sat opposite her finishing her coffee.

Quiet moments passed, and Kiernan allowed the comfort of silence to wash over her. It was something she cherished in life, the ability to sit with another—someone nice—and neither feel a need to fill silence with words. It was a behavior that spoke of contentment and well-being, of peace with the world. Well, at least it did to her. And she was at peace now. Usually, she was on the go and hated idle hands. She'd always been a busy person, the type who liked to put thirty hours into a day, but her hive of activity had increased lately. A deliberate action. Work stopped her thinking about Chrissie and curbed her pendulum of emotions.

Her last relationship had failed at the final hurdle, and the aftereffects had been colossal. It left her wary of trusting another too soon, fearing they too might let her down. She had given her heart to Chrissie, but it had been rejected. But time was ever the great healer, and she felt it was doing its job, for here she was contemplating the possibility—though slim—of another expedition into matters of the heart.

Ele invigorated her, and when she had put her arm around her after they had left the library, Kiernan had felt desire. She reminded herself to be sensible and not read what she wanted into otherwise innocent actions. The arm around her shoulder was simple friendship, a gesture to thank her for her support, nothing more. She doubted Ele was looking for love. Someone important was or had been in her life. Though the person appeared absent, she still wore a ring, and there were numerous reasons why that might be. Whatever they were, Kiernan was certain Ele was not in the market for romance. She found it disappointing.

Her attention was refocused as she heard the cat growling at her feet. It was a strange noise, and she wondered whether it was the animal's way of letting her know she wasn't welcome here.

He knew how to make his intentions clear. All through lunch, he'd eyeballed her from a distance.

"God, not another hairball, Feathers." Ele stood and moved to the front door to let the cat out. He followed swiftly. Kiernan felt relieved.

When Ele returned and sat down, she apologized. "I'm sorry for being late this morning. I went to my bank to get the house deeds, but they took a while to find them. Said they were filed in the wrong place." She raised her eyes. "You would think a bank would have a functioning filing system, wouldn't you? Hopefully, they'll tell us past owners. We might get lucky. I suppose I also ought to try to—"

Ele didn't finish her sentence. Kiernan saw the color drain from her face as she looked beyond her, and outside. Her smile disappeared and was replaced with a frozen look of horror.

"Look at Feathers," Ele whispered, her voice quiet as if she didn't want to disturb something.

Kiernan turned a few degrees to look over her shoulder. At first, all she could see was the cat outside on the gravel, but as she watched, she saw what Ele did, and what scared her.

Featherstone walked around in a small tight circle before standing up on his hind legs as if to brush against something, or someone, rubbing his face against an object unseen. He kept looking up, and when he resumed walking, it was as if he was weaving in and out of something.

Kiernan had seen him do this with Ele when they arrived back this morning; a welcoming behavior. He was now repeating this to nothing but the air. She saw him defy the law of physics as he stood once more on his back legs with his front paws resting in mid air for too many seconds.

Kiernan glanced at Ele and wondered if her heart pounded like hers did. Neither of them spoke as they continued to watch.

They could see Feathers meowing as he looked up again. Then he sat down, but his eyes seemed to move slowly toward them, as if he were following some movement, of something coming their way.

What happened next made Ele and Kiernan bolt away from the table and stumble back into the room, their eyes still fixed on the window. As they sat there, a sudden mist appeared on the glass before them. It stayed there for mere seconds before fading from the edges and disappearing into the middle.

Kiernan stared at Ele, who could only stare back at her. They had witnessed someone's warm breath materializing on a cold pane.

It was Ele who broke the silence of the terrifying moment. "We have to find Edmond Riser."

Ele did not want to spend the night in her house alone. It felt strange and alien to her. After Kiernan left, she considered booking into a hotel, but realized it wasn't practical. She had Featherstone to think about, and one night away wasn't going to solve anything. In time, she'd have to come home. But what happened at lunchtime filled her with dread, and she had been in a high state of anxiousness ever since.

She huddled up against the warmth of her sitting room fire, seated on the rug in front of it. All the lights were on and the curtains drawn, and she knew she should go to bed, but the thought of having to leave this room and move upstairs? What if something else happened? She was alone. Even Feathers, who was curled up beside her fast asleep, made her nervous tonight. What if he started acting strange again?

Ele ran her fingers through her hair. A shower would feel great, but forget that. A room full of mist and a closed shower curtain? The last thing she needed was an unwelcome scene from *Psycho*. She contemplated staying in her sitting room tonight and not moving upstairs.

It wasn't as if the haunting was her only problem. Today, which had started out so well, had turned from bad to worse. When she phoned Edmond Riser, there had been no reply nor a way to leave a message. At about that time, her phone started making strange clicking sounds that continued through the evening. If she picked it up to see if anyone was trying to ring her, all she heard was static. It added to her fright.

She looked down at the broken photograph she held in her hands, the one of her and Beth. When she scrambled back from the window earlier, she had knocked it off the piano and broken the glass inside the silver frame. Kiernan had picked it up and handed it to her, but not before long scrutiny. Ele had felt an instant distance between them. Ignoring it, she had asked Kiernan to stay on and have dinner, declaring—with frank honesty—that she was scared, but the invitation was declined. Kiernan left shortly afterward, obviously having put two and two together. She had recognized that the woman in the photo was Ele's lover, her partner. Ele had sensed Kiernan's disapproval.

She glanced at Beth again and was assuaged by conflicting emotions. She'd loved being around Kiernan today. She'd responded to her company as if they'd been lifelong friends; the lighthearted joking and gentle bantering. But something kept seeping into her thoughts, something that suggested she might want more than friendship—if that were possible. She didn't really know if Kiernan was into women or not, and her behavior over the broken photo suggested she wasn't. But regardless, Ele felt the tinge of guilt. She shouldn't even be thinking these thoughts. Wasn't Beth her one and only love? She was dishonoring what they'd had. Maybe the broken photo was a sign. And yet was it so wrong to have enjoyed Kiernan's company so much?

Featherstone stood and stretched, pushing his furry stomach low and down into the rug. When he arose, he meowed at Ele. It was the meow he used when he wanted to go outside. Ele wondered if she'd made the right decision to not put in a cat flap. At the time, her choice had seemed so simple. Keep things as they were or allow Feathers instant access in and out, plus the unwanted remains of half eaten mice on her carpets in the morning. Ele girded herself and bravely went to the front door. It surprised her to find it was already open, and she watched Featherstone run out. She frowned. Had she left the door off the latch? It was a careless thing to do, for anyone could have walked in. She admonished herself and pushed the door shut. Feathers would meow on the windowsill when he wanted to come in.

She returned to the sitting room and made the conscious decision to sleep there for the night. It was warm, and she didn't want to leave its sanctuary. She pulled an armchair up closer to the fire and settled into it, but just minutes later, the sitting room door creaked open and she felt a cold chill sweep around her. She stood to investigate the source of the cold. Her front door was wide open again, valuable heat seeping out. She slammed it shut this time, convincing herself that the lock might need repair. Nerves wouldn't quite let her trust her reasoning. As the door closed, she heard its familiar click.

Back in the sitting room, she warmed herself by the fire and grew calmer. Less than five minutes later, she heard Feathers howling on the sill. She tutted. When he was in, he wanted to be out. When he was out, he wanted to be in. One thing was sure, she would never put weight on while she owned him. She was always at his beck and call and up and down like a bungee jumper.

As she moved toward the sitting room door, Feathers walked in, and she saw the front door wide open. Cold fear and adrenaline rushed through her as she forced herself not to panic. She closed it again. This time she bolted it and put the strong night chain across. She had shut the door properly the last time. Now she was scared.

# CHAPTER NINE

It was no good, Kiernan thought, as she ran down the stairs of her flat and out into the frosty night toward her car. How could she have left Ele alone in that house after what had happened at lunchtime? She had behaved like a rat, scampering out as fast as possible, and why?

She hated to admit it, but it hadn't been the ghost that had made her bolt. Well, not entirely. It had been the photograph, the one of Ele and the woman at her side. The picture had been so sensual, so intimate. How could she not have seen that the two were lovers?

Holding that broken frame, she had looked into Ele's eyes and caught the loss and sorrow behind them. Kiernan had seen that look before. Her mother had worn it when her father died. She had seen it in her own eyes as each of her parents passed. That awful unique look revealed you had lost someone irreplaceable; someone so loved.

The answers to many of her questions hit her like a boxer's southpaw, and Kiernan now understood who the *we* had been and why there was no longer a *we*. The woman had died. That look of intense love and adoration in the photo hadn't been one that had dwindled and turned barren over time. Now she understood why Ele lived alone.

When the photo frame fell and broke, Ele had looked so devastated, and Kiernan had wanted to throw her arms around her, hold her tight, and tell her it was only a frame that could be replaced. But she hadn't. Instead, she had selfishly left the house as soon as she could. The revelation of the photo had shocked Kiernan. That, together with the mixture of fear from what had happened earlier, she knew her emotions were out of control. Kiernan hadn't trusted herself to stay. She had wanted to kiss Ele, but that might have ruined anything they had now. Kiernan had no idea when or how Ele's lover had died, all she knew was the pain of loss that she was still suffering. It was a loss that might not welcome a romantic introduction. Leaving had seemed the better option, though now it didn't.

When she left Ele, they had parted on good terms, but not the right terms. Kiernan had seen the confusion in her face—something she had put there. It was another memory Kiernan was unable to shake all night. She thought of Ele, alone in her house, and knew she couldn't leave her there by herself, not after what had happened. Kiernan was still scared witless. What must Ele be feeling?

It was almost ten at night as she jumped into her MG BGT, a sports car old enough to be a veteran. She turned the key. Nothing. The engine didn't even turn over.

"Not now," she rasped as she laid her head on the steering wheel. Her relationship with this car was never going to be easy. They shared a love/hate affair. She turned the ignition again, praying that this time it would start, but still nothing.

She hopped out, lifted the hood, and began pressing leads down on the engine casing, hoping it was just a loose connection. "You worthless piece of—" She stopped herself mid flow. It was no good insulting the vehicle. That behavior never worked in her favor, and she did love this car. She closed the hood and casually, slowly, moved back into the vehicle. Once inside, she closed the door and began to speak in a quiet, intimate tone.

"I'm sorry. I know I ask too much of you sometimes and that it might seem I take you for granted, but I do care." She leaned in tight against the steering wheel. "What if I promise to clean and polish you at the weekend? Put some black on your tires? I'll also book you in for a full service and an oil change." She ran her fingers seductively across the dashboard. "You know how much you like that."

Kiernan eased back in the seat, took a breath. "I need you."

She turned the key. The car erupted with life.

It took under thirty-five minutes to get to Ele's. The roads were empty at this time of night, and thankfully, the recent pea-soup fog of the last few weeks hadn't reappeared. The night was crisp and clear.

As she drove up the unlit driveway, Kiernan could see Ele's sitting room lights still on behind drawn curtains. She wondered momentarily if anything else frightening had happened since she left. During the short drive over, the closer to Ele's she drew, the more her own state of alarm rose. She was scared. It didn't help that as she slowed to park, she realized she was at almost the exact spot where Feathers had acted up that afternoon.

Swinging the car around, its lights swept across the front of the greenhouse set back in the garden to the far left. Light reflected back off the panes of glass in normal fashion, but Kiernan saw something else that made her slam the brakes on and freeze the blood in her veins.

From inside the greenhouse, she saw the shadowed shape of a man watching her, his eyes reflected back. She wasn't imagining it. She saw his strong, clear shape before the car lights moved off the building. This was bad. The ghost was now manifesting itself in physical form, beyond photographs. This alteration was sinister and unwelcome. Her fear extended to Ele's safety.

Desperately trying to draw in breath, she slammed her hand on the car horn and let its intrusive sound slice into the quiet of the night. Then she dashed from the vehicle and ran as fast as she could toward the front door that, thank heavens, was opening. She could see Ele's perplexed face.

Kiernan threw herself past her and slammed the door shut. She tried to speak but couldn't. All she could hear was her breath wheezing away like bellows in a foundry as she reached out and clung to Ele.

An asthma sufferer, Kiernan's breathing was always worse in the winter when the damp air arrived, and it took only some minor exertion to bring it on. People said it gave her a sexy, husky voice. Right now, she had neither of those attributes. Her chest hurt as she struggled to suck in air, and her heart beat furiously. She knew there was a pained expression on her face because she saw the escalating fear registering on Ele as she drew back to try to talk.

"Oh God." Her words spluttered. "Something's out there... the greenhouse..." Kiernan let go of Ele and forced herself to straighten and breathe. Her hands were on her chest.

"What is it? What's out there?" Ele's voice trembled as she reached out to hold Kiernan's shaking hands. Kiernan's panic was contagious. Ele was petrified.

"I saw him...saw the ghost." She gulped breath. "He was watching me...from inside the greenhouse."

"You saw him?"

Kiernan nodded, staring into Ele's horrified eyes. She felt terrible. She had come here to give support, something she should have done earlier. Instead, she was frightening her to death. "I could see his shape inside. His shadow, and his eyes, his horrible eyes glowing bright and orangey yellow."

Did Kiernan imagine it, or did Ele's demeanor change? She seemed more relaxed and less disturbed? She was frowning. Surely she believes me, Kiernan thought.

"Where was he standing?" Ele probed.

"In the greenhouse," Kiernan repeated.

"To the left? The right? Central?"

Did a ghost's precise position matter? Kiernan was mystified. "He was standing over to the right, by a broken—"

"Pane of glass," Ele interrupted, nodding as if it all made sense. Ele walked over and picked up a flashlight off a very fine three-legged mahogany side table.

"Yes," she said, before watching in horror as Ele pragmatically opened the front door. "You're not going out there?" Ele shone the light over to the greenhouse and then she looked back at Kiernan, her face transcending from no-nonsense to total relief. Ele beckoned her to the door. *You have to be kidding!*

"Please, Kiernan, it's okay. Come and look." Her voice was laden with compassion as she held an arm out to entice Kiernan to be brave.

She edged forward and tried to control her nerves as she peeped beyond the door over toward the greenhouse, to the spot where Ele focused the light. There she saw again the man's shape and his terrible glowing eyes. Her heart was in danger of exploding.

Ele shouted an order across the driveway. "Feathers! Come on, come inside now!" She gave a sharp whistle.

Suddenly, the illuminated eyes disappeared, and Kiernan watched as the cat slipped through the broken pane and ran across the gravel toward them. The shadow of the man was no longer present. Kiernan's ghost was Featherstone. She looked at Ele, and they began to laugh hysterically as he darted in the door and straight into the kitchen.

"He's been in and out all evening."

"Dear Lord, Ele. I didn't mean to scare you. How could I make such a stupid mistake?" It was the afternoon that had left her so skittish. Was Ele feeling this bad? "I hope nothing else has happened since...earlier?" she stammered.

"Since you mention it"—Ele grabbed her arm—"something has, and is. Watch this." She closed the front door. "Did you hear the latch click?"

"Yes."

"Good. Would you like to test it, make sure it's shut properly?"

"Not really," she said. Ele threw her a look that implied it was the wrong answer. She corrected herself. "I'd be delighted."

There was something in Ele's voice, something Kiernan didn't like, and it made her more nervous. She pulled the door. It was shut. What a curious thing to ask her to do. It was even more curious when they remained standing, looking at the door for a few minutes. This is exciting, she thought dryly. "Am I missing something?"

"The door is shut, right?" Ele sought confirmation.

"It is," Kiernan said as Ele then guided her into the sitting room. They stood and waited ten seconds before moving back to the front door—which was now wide open.

"What? How did that happen?"

"New party trick," Ele said. "It's been happening all evening. The only way I can keep it shut is to put the bolts across." A mixture of resignation and forced calm rested on Ele's face.

"I don't like this." Kiernan coughed.

"I'm not thrilled skinny, either," Ele said. "Do you have an inhaler?"

Her impressive wheezing was concerning Ele. "In the car dash," she answered guiltily. Ele took a deep breath, sprinted to Kiernan's car where she retrieved the small device, and dashed back inside, throwing the bolts and chain on the door.

❖

They adjourned to the welcome warmth and sanctuary of the sitting room. All the time, Feathers, who was now seated in front of the fire, watched Kiernan as he methodically cleaned each sharp-looking nail on a paw. She swore he had a smug, satisfied look on his face. Damn cat. He had succeeded in frightening her half to death. Perhaps that was what he wanted, to be left alone with his owner. Kiernan glanced at Ele who warmed her hands by the fire, and found she couldn't blame the cat. Ele was a catch, and for her to be living alone didn't seem right to Kiernan. She eyeballed the cat back with contempt. He needed to know he would not get the better of her and that she was the alpha.

Kiernan wasn't sure what felt better, the deep breaths she took on her inhaler or the single malt whiskey Ele thrust into her hand without asking. But now, with her breathing returning to normal, it was time for apologies and explanations.

"The way I left this afternoon, Ele, it was wrong. I should have stayed with you after what happened and not left you here alone, but I was scared shitless. I've been petrified ever since, and I can't imagine how you feel." Kiernan lied. There was only so much she could tell her.

Ele, still crouched on one knee in front of the fire, swiveled to face her, and Kiernan found herself catching her breath. It wasn't the asthma. "Unfortunately, I haven't helped ease your agitation tonight, have I?" she said. "Anyway, my intention was to drive over and see if you wanted company tonight, or to let you come back to my place. I did try to phone you, but couldn't get through."

Ele stood and walked over to her. For a moment, Kiernan wasn't sure what Ele was going to do. Kiss her? There was a look on her face that suggested intimacy, the look a lover gives you before sealing their lips with yours. But Ele bent down to grasp Kiernan's hands. Briefly squeezing them, she said, "Thank you for coming." She squeezed them one last time and then returned to the fire.

Her face was a picture of relief as she said, "My phone's been acting up." She mentioned the strange clicking and white noise, before adding more seriously, "I did wonder…"

Ele hesitated, and Kiernan sensed something important coming. "That photograph you picked up, the one of Beth and me…my partner, my lover…"

Kiernan had been right.

"I did wonder, when I saw the way you looked at our photo, I thought—"

"I know what you thought, but you thought wrong." She wanted to chase the pained look on Ele's face away. It grieved her to think she put that there. She started to smile as she sensed a way. "My last affair of the heart"—she theatrically placed two hands on her chest—"was a female. And the one before that, and the one before that." She cocked her head. "I think you get the picture." She didn't need a response. It pleased her beyond words that Ele's eyes, eyes that had earlier registered misunderstanding, were now crinkled with warmth and clarity.

"Oh, I'm so pleased," Ele purred. "I didn't want to lose you to bigotry."

*Lose me to bigotry?* Was that what Ele had thought and what had fueled the look of anguish on her face as Kiernan had left earlier?

"No chance," Kiernan whispered. She was finding this evening emotional on many levels.

Ele saw the honesty in Kiernan's face and not for the first time this evening, felt relief. This afternoon, after Kiernan departed, she thought she had lost her. She realized how quickly she had come to count on her, not merely as support as she struggled to explain the haunting. Kiernan had become special. A thrill had run through her as Kiernan declared she was a lesbian, too. Yet, at the same time—inexplicably—she experienced panic. They were getting on so well, so fast. Might Kiernan, if single, want something more? Ele was on edge. Why should that worry her? Hadn't she dated other women since Beth? It had never posed an issue then. Why now? Ele didn't know the answer.

"Can I ask what happened to Beth?" Kiernan's direct question forced Ele's self-reverie back to the present. Kiernan's forthright approach didn't surprise her, not given what had happened over the photo. And she found no objection in it. Sometimes an upfront question was best. It was kinder than some continual skirting around an issue, trying to piece together the bits like a jigsaw.

Ele wondered where to begin. She wasn't used to answering this question. When Beth had died, the pain had been so intense she hadn't been able to talk about it. Eventually, people stopped asking, which pleased her. But now she could talk, and she wanted to tell Kiernan.

She moved into the comfort of an armchair and focused on a photo of Beth on the wall. Suddenly, Beth was alive again, and she could see her short, thick brown mass of hair, and the way she always wore her black framed reading glasses on the tip of her nose. Ele could smell her perfume again, always the same one. Beth had been a creature of habit and would never wear anything else, like the sloppy clothes she favored at home. If her academic colleagues had known what a slob she looked like away from work, compared to her neat, fashionable, almost meticulous appearance at university, they would have been amazed. Beth had also been a creature of opposites; the hard, no nonsense lecturer who demanded perfection from her students, yet the softie who cried at romantic movies and who jumped a mile at garden spiders.

"We were having a new bathroom put in, and Roger was here, the local builder," Ele reminded Kiernan.

"He had just brought down the old bath, and it was outside at the front of the house. I don't know why, but I was looking at it, all the stains and chips on the white enamel, its history." She smiled. "I remember I was kneeling by it when Beth came out. She'd been in the kitchen preparing lunch—she loved to cook—she held a small cutting knife in her right hand." Ele studied her own empty right hand.

"She was talking to me, but all the time her head was making this strange bobbing action, and at first I thought Beth was messing around. She had a warped sense of humor, but then I realized she wasn't, and that she didn't even seem to know she was doing it. I asked her if she was all right, and she looked down at me peculiarly and said she was fine. But I stood up and went over to her, put my arm around her shoulder, and asked again. This time she looked at me and said no. I remember seeing the shock in her eyes, like a frightened little girl who didn't understand something huge, something alarming. One minute she was standing and the next, leaning into me, and I felt her weight." A stab of pain shot through Ele as the memory grew in strength, becoming more vivid. She drew breath and closed her eyes for a second.

"I managed to get her to the bath, to let her sit on the side of it. She kept asking me not to let her fall backward, and although I had her by her arms and was looking into her face, I couldn't reassure her."

Ele looked at Kiernan who sat fixated, listening to her every word, empathy etched deep on her face.

"I became aware that what she was saying wasn't coming out right, that she was slurring, and that her face, her beautiful face, seemed distorted." Ele ran her hand slowly down the side of her own face. "Then Roger was there and he was phoning for an ambulance. It was all so quick." Ele's words dried and she fell silent. The memory was stuck in her mind, and she was there again, with Beth and Roger.

"Are you okay?" Kiernan had moved across and now had an arm around her.

"I'm sorry," Ele said. "I don't know where all that came from. I've never told anyone about this before…about how the stroke came on. Poor you."

"No, not poor me," Kiernan said quietly as she pulled Ele closer to her, wrapping her in her arms. "I feel rich in the knowing that you trust me enough to share something so personal, so private. Thank you."

"Trust you?" Ele contemplated Kiernan's few words. She hadn't said much and yet those words were right. Being held in her arms also felt right. She knew it shouldn't. She pulled back a little from the embrace. "Yes, I do trust you, you know." She did. She remembered how much she had trusted Beth, too.

But Ele sought the comfort of Kiernan's arms again. It had been so long. "It was why I stopped working. Beth seemed to recover. It was a mild stroke. A lucky warning, they said. And for a while, she took time off work and stayed here to recuperate. I looked after her, but eventually, she grew bored and wanted to go back to work. She taught physics at Oxford University. Although I told her it was too soon, the fool wouldn't listen." Ele drew back again and looked into Kiernan's face. "Oh, Kiernan, I thought because she was on medication, and all the myriad of tests she was having, I thought they were sorting her out and that she'd be okay. But she wasn't." Ele fought the emotions that bubbled up. She didn't want to cry again. She had done too much of that over the years. "A few months later, she had a massive stroke."

Ele shook her head, fighting the tears. "She lasted a few days, but never regained consciousness and I lost the glue in my life, the person that gave it meaning. Everything I did, all my plans, they were all for her, and hers for me. We were childhood sweethearts who had known each other all the way through school. When she died, my whole life imploded, and I fell to bits. I suppose grief is the price we pay for love."

Ele could no longer talk. Everything had been said that needed to. She was grateful that Kiernan allowed her the time, and silence, to pull herself back together. It didn't take long, and Ele squeezed Kiernan's arm as she disengaged herself. She walked over to the mantelpiece. "Now you know. I miss her so much, even now, after all the years."

Ele watched as Kiernan returned to where she'd previously been seated. She took a deep breath. She needed to *lighten* the conversation. She would talk of ghost hunting.

"I've found some detail in the house deeds that I think is interesting."

Kiernan appeared to accept the mood change with ease. "I'm listening."

Ele leaned on the mantelpiece and tapped its top with her fingers. "As I thought, the deeds hold names and some information about past owners. There are two that stand out and might be associated with the time period we're interested in. They are J. Stafford, Esquire, who lived here from nineteen twelve until nineteen twenty-one. The other is an E. W. Winterman from nineteen twenty-one until nineteen thirty-five. Beyond that, there's not much else to go on. I'm hoping Edmond Riser might know more."

"I think we should ring him," Kiernan said. "But we'll have to wait until the morning. It's too late now." Ele agreed. "Do you want to stay here tonight or come back to my place? I don't have a ghost."

Ele heard the dry, understated wit as she looked at Kiernan's contagious smile.

"Whatever you decide, I'm with you tonight, Ele."

Ele nodded her thanks. "Call me chicken, but I don't fancy leaving this room tonight. When was the last time you slept in a chair?"

Kiernan didn't answer. She shrugged as she stretched herself out on a sofa.

"Thank you again, Kiernan."

"No problem. Just make sure that damn door is bolted well."

Kiernan was joking, but Ele's shiver was real.

Exhausted, they spent the remainder of the night sleeping in the sitting room.

## CHAPTER TEN

K iernan woke first and could not believe the aches and pains she felt. She glanced over at Ele who was beginning to rise, and who looked worse than she did.

Ele bent to put her shoes on. "Ouch." She placed a hand on her back.

"One cannot underestimate the value of a good bed," Kiernan said as she followed Ele without energy into the kitchen. It was still dark. She prayed that coffee would ease the crick in her neck, and stiffness of her back. She dropped onto a stool and lay across the breakfast bar.

"Tell me about it," Ele said as she switched the kettle on. "We're idiots. There are perfectly decent beds upstairs. We should have slept on them."

"Now you tell me," Kiernan bantered back. She had no idea what position she slept in last night, but it hadn't been a good one. Her body felt as if she'd been hung, drawn, and quartered. "I'm only thankful I haven't got an assignment today. I'm not sure I could lift the camera."

Kiernan saw Ele cringe with guilt. "Hey, forget I said that. There was no way I was letting you spend the night here alone. Any problems I have with this body"—Kiernan dramatically swept her hands from shoulder to waist—"are all my own doing. Frankly, after my last romantic venture, and what I was forced to suffer in that, this is a picnic."

There was an unexpected surge of energy from what, seconds ago, had been a sluggish Ele. Kiernan swore she felt a swift movement of air as Ele moved faster than a vortex to sit opposite her.

"Oh, intrigue. I love it. Elaborate."

Kiernan eyeballed Ele who sat like a praying mantis, hungry for detail. Kiernan sighed and must have shown that she didn't really want to discuss this topic right now, not while she felt like a contortionist. She didn't think she *ever* wanted to talk about Chrissie to anyone again, regardless of her body distortion. Period. But she could see she'd opened Pandora's box, and Ele wasn't going to let her put the lid back on.

"I know nothing about you," Ele said. "You now know far more about me. We need to balance."

"Balance, is it?" Ele leaned forward and placed her elbows on the table as she supported her face in her hands. Kiernan recognized there was no deflecting Ele's curiosity, and it occurred to her that the latter might be fueled by a real interest in her. That nugget of revelation pleased her. A lot.

"Chrissie, my last, loved camping. She had this unnatural desire to commune with nature, and how better to do that than to mix with the wild, and sleep under canvas. Now you have to realize that she was a few years younger than me, and was a closeted Olympian athlete dying to emerge. Her idea of getting away for a break involved going to mountainous parts of this country, picking the steepest hill possible, and then climbing to its peak as fast as she could—with me gasping for air behind."

Kiernan thought it was to Ele's credit that she cringed in all the right places. She had the distinct impression that Ele was not of Chrissie's *vim and vigor* desires. Another brownie point, she thought.

"The type of tent you could stand up in was not for her. She said it stank of modernity and ruined the real sense of adventure. So *we* camped far too often, in all weathers and always the Bohemian way. She said it made her feel invigorated and alive. It made me feel exhausted and bad tempered. I hated every damp blade of grass we camped on, and you can stuff the dawn chorus of bird song at three in the morning. I've put up with moles coming up in the tent overnight, and have shared a sleeping bag with earwigs. I don't see that as an adventure. It did nothing for me, other than bring on early arthritis and hay fever."

"I take it you don't enjoy camping." Kiernan didn't miss the understated humor in Ele's dour tone.

"Be nice to me; you have a ghost," she said. "But you take it right. My idea of camping is in a four star hotel."

"Your Chrissie sounds an interesting woman. I'd love to hear more about her."

Kiernan wasn't an inexperienced teen, and recognized that Ele's interest was more than a passing conversation point. She began to hope. Maybe there was mutual emotional investment beginning here, and Ele's attention might hint at more. While she longed for the intimacy that could bring—the sharing of life's guarded and innermost experiences—did she want to dredge up how her relationship with Chrissie had gone wrong? No.

"I'd rather not talk about her if you don't mind. Chrissie is part of my past now, and that's where I'd like to keep her." She tried to sound as upbeat and normal as possible, but she failed because Ele reached out and put a soft hand over hers. It was an innocent gesture, but Kiernan felt her face warm.

"I understand."

She wondered if Ele really did. "Let's get cracking and find Edmond Riser."

❖

White-haired Edmond Riser was a dapper gentleman dressed in smart gray trousers, a fresh laundered check shirt, polished brown shoes, and a well worn tweed jacket. On the latter, Ele could see the leather patched elbows, sewn on to hide wear. She reasoned it was a much loved item, for everything around her spoke of a comfortable existence, and if Riser wanted a new jacket, she was sure he could afford it. But she did wonder, in a very non politically correct way, who sewed for him. He seemed to live alone, a widower. He was not a man she envisaged with a needle and thread. Maybe he had a caring daughter somewhere?

Although he was elderly, he possessed a youthful, lean face with sparkling brown eyes that held genuine delight and interest in his two unannounced visitors. She had a feeling that, though very much the gent, he loved the ladies and their company.

He recognized her, more as a local neighbor than some celebrity, and welcomed her and Kiernan into his small, cluttered cottage full of books and sports memorabilia. She noticed an aged cricket bat hanging on a wall and endorsed with many signatures. Her late father had a bat on a wall too, something her mother always moaned about, although she had secretly loved it. He and Riser would have had much to talk about.

"I tried to call you last night, and again this morning, but my phone is playing up," Ele said.

"No, no," he was quick to say, in his clipped 1940s voice. "All the lines are down at the moment. British Telecom has been working on the fault all morning. My landline has been clicking away like mad."

Ele and Kiernan exchanged a glance. So the ghost was not trying to communicate over a landline? It was a relief. It was a frightening prospect to think some spectral spirit was trying to find her dialing code. Phone calls and open doors made her tense, but thankfully, so far, he seemed content to remain an outside ghost.

Ele got straight to the point, telling him just enough detail that was healthy. "I've always been interested in history, Mr. Riser. I'm quite keen to find out whatever information I can of all the people who have lived in my house. There are some names on the house deeds, but that's all they are—names. Hugh Latimer at the historical society thought you might be able to fill in some details?"

"I know Hugh," Edmond said. "Strange sort of chap."

Ele thought he sounded dismissive of Latimer. She caught Kiernan's eyes. She looked smug.

"Anyway, the names I have are J. Stafford, Esquire, nineteen twelve to nineteen twenty-one. Also E. W. Winterman, nineteen twenty-one to nineteen thirty-five. Can you help?"

"I do remember the Wintermans. There were Mr. and Mrs. Ernest Winterman and their three children. He was an accountant. They were a nice family. Colin, their youngest, was my age, and while they lived here, he was my best friend, although we went to different schools. The family had an account with my father who owned the butcher's shop here before I took over. I ran the shop until I retired twenty years ago and sold the business."

Ele remembered the shop closing about seven years ago when a big supermarket moved into the area. The village fought to keep their butcher shop open, but failed.

"The Wintermans immigrated to Australia," Riser said, "just before the war."

"All of them?" Kiernan asked.

"Yes. Colin wrote to me for a while, but then stopped as these things do."

"Do you remember a J. Stafford, Esquire?" Ele asked.

"No. But the dates you've given, nineteen twelve to nineteen twenty-one, I wasn't born then. My father probably would have known him or his family. The locals all used his shop, but I don't have any records now so there's no way of knowing. It's a shame because I kept them all and the ledgers from the business, including Father's, until a few years ago. It seemed pointless hanging on to them so I destroyed the lot. They held the names of all his customers."

Ele knew her disappointment showed. After yesterday's fright, she was pinning her hopes on Riser, hoping he might know something, but it seemed he didn't. A gloomy feeling swept over her as her imagination bolted. Thoughts of an undiscovered body buried in her grounds, a spirit disturbed by the builders, rose up. Something had been awoken, and unless she could find out more, she had no idea how to put it back to sleep. She heard Kiernan talking.

"Pegmire's a beautiful village, Mr. Riser. You've lived here all your life? Never wanted to move?"

Riser shrugged. "I worked for my father and then inherited the business. The thought of leaving never crossed my mind, and I married Jeanne, a local girl who was more than happy to stay here. The only time I left home was during the war. World War II," he clarified. "I joined the Royal Air Force and served in Cyprus for a while. Frankly, I was glad to get back here."

Kiernan turned jocular. "I expect you could write a book about Pegmire and all its goings on."

Riser laughed. "That I could. It's amazing what a butcher knows. Who's living with who, who's left who, who is eating more meat than for just one person, if you get my meaning." He winked.

Kiernan responded to his subtle introduction of intrigue. "Anything exciting ever happened here? Any murders? Any ghosts?" Her laughter hinted at conspiracy.

"No, none of that. We did have an enemy plane come down a few miles away. It was heading for the Midlands to bomb the industrial areas, but our guns got it. The crew parachuted out and ended up prisoners of war in a camp near Oxford." Edmond Riser's mind was still focused on the war. He looked at them and smiled. "We could have done with a few murders round here, brightened things up a bit. Pegmire's always been a dozy place—apart from domestic goings on."

Ele started to thank him for his time and was rising to leave when he said, "Beatrice Lavish worked at the vicarage for years, and she'd know more."

Her heart expanded like heated metal at the chance of a lead.

"But of course she's dead now," he added.

Her heart sank.

"She had a daughter," he continued.

"Is she dead, too?" Kiernan asked blankly.

"No. Dorothy Harding is as fit as a fiddle, and she lives nearby in Chadlington, on the Chipping Norton road. I went to school with her and have her phone number here somewhere." He crossed to a bureau and seconds later announced, "Got it." He reached into a pocket and pulled out a cell phone, which he waved victoriously in the air. "My grandson got me this for Christmas. Who needs a landline? Shall I give her a call and see if she knows anything?"

Dorothy Harding answered the call immediately, and Edmond Riser chatted away to her like the old friends they obviously were. He told her of Ele's search, and it sounded as if his old school friend would see them. Ele felt awash with relief, and Edmond's kindness of an introduction removed the cold call that many elderly didn't trust these days.

He would glance at her while talking to Dorothy, repeating things that needed Ele's answer. Did they want to see her today about four o'clock, or wait for a week? Ele agreed to the afternoon meeting. Though it would be getting dark, she was desperate to find out more of her uninvited guest.

Would Dorothy Harding know anything? Ele hoped she would. She didn't like being alone at her home now and loathed the sense of dread that was quickly becoming her companion. Everywhere she went, inside or out, she was hyper-aware that something unearthly and non-corporeal was trying to communicate with her, and *her* alone. She felt a hand on her shoulder and a gentle, but firm tweak. Kiernan was looking at her, her eyes full of understanding and unspoken support. She smiled back, her spirits lifted.

As they left Riser's home, Ele apologized to Kiernan. "That was rude of me. I never asked what you wanted to do." She referred to the afternoon's arrangements. She was so preoccupied in her thoughts, she failed to consult Kiernan. But Kiernan seemed to understand her sense of urgency.

"I'll do whatever you need me to. I'm here for you."

*I'm here for you.* The words echoed in her head. They sounded personal, and she thought of the hand on her shoulder, and how it made her feel. She wasn't imagining it. There was a connection building between them. She sensed its potential. That strange sensation in her stomach rose again, and she found herself thinking of Beth. They had shared an incredible, "once in a lifetime" love. She experienced guilt, thinking these thoughts about Kiernan. She'd had something so singular with Beth. Was she degrading that? Was she betraying her by even thinking of moving on? She was confused and pulled—the past laying claim to the future. It also plagued her why it was around Kiernan that she felt like this. She had dated others since Beth's death. This had never been an issue before. Was it because none of the other women had mattered to her? That was it, she was sure. Kiernan was the first real contender since Beth.

"I've a suggestion," Kiernan said, interrupting Ele's thoughts. "Since Chadlington is a stone's throw from where I live in Enstone, why don't we drive to my place and have lunch and then go see Mrs. Harding?"

Ele agreed. Despite her personal censure, she was keen to learn more of Kiernan. This would be like food for her soul. She'd have an opportunity to see her home. Silly though it sounded, she thought you could learn a lot about a person from how they furnished a place. How they treated their sanctuary gave much away.

She heard herself volunteering to drive. "It's pointless taking two cars."

## CHAPTER ELEVEN

Kiernan's home was the top floor of a two-storied converted mill on the edge of Enstone village. It sat past the old post office on the main road and down a lengthy, narrow, twisting country lane. Its old red and brown brick appearance lent it to a time long gone, and Ele was reminded of something found comfortably in an old classic novel. The place had an air of money to it, and Ele wondered how a freelance photographer could afford a place like this.

As they entered a small lobby, the entrance to Kiernan's floor was up a wide, but impressive steep stone staircase. Ele gazed up at it, taken aback. Kiernan caught the look and gave a half grin. Ele gathered her surprise wasn't unique.

"If you're hoping there's an elevator, you're going to be disappointed. You soon get used to these, and they keep you fit."

She noted the almost perverse delight in Kiernan's statement. "If you say so," she said as she trailed Kiernan up them. The climb was worth it. As Ele followed her through a large rustic oak front door, she was met with bright, natural light.

Before her lay a huge open plan sitting room that ran the entire length of the building. Nestled next to it, almost like an afterthought, was a small galley kitchen immediately to the right. Kiernan's home was the complete antithesis of hers; everything was modern and vivid, from the whitewashed timber floorboards, to the creamy covered chairs, and the pale, painted surfaces of texture in a monochrome scheme.

What took her breath away was the stunning vista at the far end of the room. It was the wow factor of Kiernan's home, its fait accompli. Wall to wall, floor to ceiling glass revealed a panoramic view. She was looking over the top of the small village's modern and medieval roofing that pulled her eyes to the distance, to reveal a horizon of stunning Oxfordshire countryside.

"This is wonderful," she said, walking forward toward the glass. "What a stunning view."

"I had those windows put in. There were smaller ones when I moved here, and it seemed such a waste not to capture that scene in all its majesty. Cost me a tidy sum." She swept unruly hair off her face. "And it took ages to get the council to approve the planning, but it came, eventually."

Kiernan quirked an eyebrow and tilted her head to one side. It was something she often did and Ele found the habit attractive.

"I love the simplicity of white as a backdrop." Kiernan referred to the color of the walls. "The way it bounces light back into the room even on the dullest of days. Some of my friends say the place is too utilitarian and doesn't feel as if it's lived in. I suppose it is a bit sparse and could do with more color."

Ele saw the truth in that. Her place had the classic touch and was full of rich, warm colors and old furniture. She was a hoarder of knickknacks, all of which she and Beth had gathered over the years, and each with its own cherished memory. Kiernan's home was modern and functional and seemed bereft of any treasured belongings. It was minimalist. Yet, different though it was, it felt a home. It didn't stop Ele's traditional roots itching to throw vibrancy into it.

She looked around, this time concentrating on the decorative accessories; the brown-black wrought iron lighting fixtures, the plain gold trimmed mirrors, and the artwork on the walls. The latter were a mixture of black and white, with a scattering of large colored photographs of heavy metal album covers. She could see Severed Head, The Rum Mixers, Bad Behavior—all albums she had at home. So she and Kiernan had something else in common—they were closet rockers.

"We like the same music," she said as she stepped closer to The Rum Mixers photograph, realizing the photo was an original, not a copy. She started to frown as she realized *all* the photos were originals. Kiernan had a quiet fortune on her walls.

"They're all signed by the band members on the back," Kiernan said with pride as she walked up to the Severed Head cover and turned it over to reveal the signatures.

Ele stared in awe. "That's Billy Mantoff's signature! It'll be worth a ton." Mantoff had been Severed Head's lead singer until two years ago when he'd overdosed on drugs and died. She looked closer and could see Mantoff had written, "Foyle, Fab Phot." The penny dropped. "You took these?"

"I did." Ele noticed the way Kiernan fought to conceal her pride. She found the act attractive.

"Ye gods, I've most of these albums at home. I love the Rum Mixers, and I've always loved this album cover." Ele couldn't hide how impressed she was. Now she was beginning to understand how a freelance photographer could afford a home like this.

"This is my other life," Kiernan said. "You get in with one band and it leads to others. My first album cover was with Severed Head, and it turned out to be a bit successful. I won some awards. From then on, the Heads wanted me to do all their successive covers. Other groups seemed to like my work, and one thing led to another."

"Do you still do this?"

"I don't do so much now, mainly because I've moved out of London and turned mellower in my old age," she said wryly. "But I still keep my hand in. I've just done some work for a new group called Regurgitate."

"I don't know them," Ele said.

"I don't think anyone does yet, but they will do. They're good, and quality always shows through eventually. We'll see." Kiernan seemed done with talking about rock. She turned domestic. "Do you mind if I go and change? I feel as if I've slept in my clothes all night. I need a shower, and you're welcome to do the same if you want. I'll show you the guest en suite. Then I'll rustle up something to eat."

Ele followed Kiernan as she showed her to the guest room. She did need a shower. Still spooked, she hadn't ventured upstairs that morning.

"Just make yourself at home and use whatever you want. There are some spare T-shirts and sweaters in the drawer if you need them."

It crossed Ele's mind that Kiernan's petite size did not lend itself to her tall, lean frame. Any sweatshirt Kiernan owned wouldn't cover her midriff.

"I ought to mention I'm a lousy cook." Kiernan leaned through the room doorway, her face mock serious. "People have died of my cooking. The only safe food I can give you comes in packs you heat up in a microwave. Do you like chicken korma and rice?"

"One of my favorites," Ele lied as Kiernan disappeared.

She showered and found some clothes to fit her. They didn't belong to Kiernan—the T-shirt would have touched her toes. She wondered if they were the mysterious Chrissie's.

As she returned to the sitting room to wait for Kiernan, she surveyed her surroundings once more, hoping to discover other stunning revelations about her. She found something, but nothing as dazzling as the music covers. There were two quite specific and very different collections of CDs. On one side of the room was a large compilation of heavy rock music with a smattering of classical. On the other side were several piles of CDs that just didn't gel with the others. As she crouched down, she viewed them with suspicion. They were almost all a mixture of boy and girl band music. None appealed to Ele.

"Not mine," Kiernan said.

Ele turned to find Kiernan in fresh blue jeans and a crisp pink cotton blouse that showed off her trim, athletic figure. Her hair was still damp and sat close to her head, swept back off her face. A warmth grew inside her, but her feelings were mixed. In the same moment of physical awareness, something else competed for her attention—an inner voice—telling her this was wrong. She was betraying Beth. "Chrissie's?" she asked.

Kiernan grimaced. "They are. I've been meaning to get rid of them, but I haven't got around to it."

"Why haven't you?" she probed.

Ele watched Kiernan pause to think, as though for the first time. She watched as she puckered her lips before answering.

"My mother kept Dad's best suit for years after he died. It wasn't as if he was ever going to wear it again. But I suppose it was not wanting to let go of a memory, one that had been special."

"And is that what you feel?" Ele thought of Beth's hairbrush and perfume, still on the dressing table. She'd never been able to part with them even after all these years.

"I suppose it is. Chrissie and I were good together. It just fell apart because she wouldn't make the commitment."

"But it is over." It was something important Ele needed to know.

"Oh, yes. Nearly two years now. I should return her CDs, but it means contacting her and I don't want to do that. I don't think she really wants them anyway. She took many others, but left these."

Ele was learning about Kiernan. She had a hunger for any and all information. "I really would like to hear more about her, if you'd share it." She'd asked earlier and been fielded away. She received a similar response.

"Maybe later. But right now I think we should eat." Kiernan moved off toward the kitchen and Ele followed her, planting herself against the doorframe. She watched Kiernan read the cooking instructions on the package of the chicken korma. The scene was so pathetic, it was amusing. There was something rather nice about Kiernan's lack of culinary expertise.

"Here, let me." She took the package out of Kiernan's hands. "At least if I die of food poisoning, it'll be my fault." She brushed against Kiernan as they swapped places in the small space. The brief contact surprised her, and she felt her already sensitive body respond to the unintentional touch. It was a calling she had not felt for a long time. She pushed the lingering thought of Beth to one side and enjoyed savoring the unexpected reaction.

"I won't argue. I know my limitations."

"We'll cook this in the oven," Ele said. "It'll take longer, but we've time, and I always think it tastes better than microwaved."

Kiernan offered no resistance. "Whatever. You're the cook."

Ele placed the food in the oven and then carefully pushed past Kiernan with the intent of returning to the large window. She loved the view and wanted more of it, but her journey was cut short as she moved past a huge houseplant that robbed an already tight corner of too much space. It had grown to gigantic proportions. The tip of it was touching the high ceiling, and bending. She could stand beneath its warped thick branches.

"What do you think of my tree?" Kiernan asked as she stepped under to join her.

"Big leaves," Ele answered matter-of-factly. Kiernan grinned. "What is it?"

Kiernan fiddled with a leaf that was touching her face. "Damned if I know. I've never worked out whether it's an overgrown plant or an undeveloped tree. I had it at my last home. It started out very small, but as the years have passed, it's grown bigger. I tried to leave it when I sold my house, but the buyers didn't want it." Kiernan's disappointment showed.

"No kidding." Ele pursed her lips. It was an unattractive product of nature that didn't have much going for it. Its green leaves were like frying pans, and they were curled and brown at the ends. She thought it was the most hideous plant—tree—she'd ever seen.

"I know what you're thinking. It's an ugly brute, but it's my ugly brute, and we're an item now."

Ele heard a mother's defensive protection of a child as Kiernan caressed distorted branches and gently kissed a leaf. Kiernan then scrutinized that same leaf as if inspecting it for imperfection. "Everything deserves to be loved regardless of whether it's beautiful or not."

Ele leaned in closer to study what Kiernan was looking at with such attention. Kiernan turned unexpectedly, and as she did, their faces drew close, almost colliding. For a moment, neither moved, and Ele thought she recognized a flash of desire in Kiernan's eyes. She experienced a corresponding want and for a split second felt her body move forward, inviting a kiss. Something made her stop, and she deliberately walked out from under the plant. Flustered, she looked back to see if Kiernan had experienced what she had, or if the temptation of a kiss had been only in her mind. She could see that she was not alone. Kiernan looked confused.

Ele broke the awkward silence. "I think this is a plant that would like a move down by the window. There's more room, and it could spread itself. It would like it."

"You may be right." Kiernan joined her at the window. She stared at the panoramic view. Ele continued her forced conversation. "I like Edmond Riser. He reminds me a lot of Dad."

"How so?"

"All that cricket memorabilia. Dad used to have that stuff— signed bats on the wall and magazines all over the place. He was crazy about the sport. Poor Mum. She attended all his local matches. He used to say she was his lucky talisman. He never won." Ele knew she was talking total rubbish.

"It was rugby with mine, and he was a lousy player, too."

They looked at each other and smiled. Ele drew the chat back to the haunting. "It looks like the ghost isn't one of the Wintermans. I wonder if he is J. Stafford, Esquire? I do hope Dorothy Harding knows something."

The room grew dark, and Ele saw black clouds building, robbing the sky of its earlier patchy blue. Where had they come from so quickly? Over the roofs of the houses she saw a panoply of fields, trees, cattle, and sheep. She watched as a farmer cut across a field in a small tractor. The view was mesmerizing, and it affected her. She was still trying to understand what had happened under the leaves.

"It's going to rain," she whispered, more to herself than Kiernan who was now at her side. "Beth loved the countryside."

Ele didn't know why she said that. Maybe it was because Beth was on her mind, and because she had spoken of her to Kiernan. It seemed the lid was off the proverbial pot and things were bubbling to the top. Perhaps it was also the perceived sadness of the picture that lay before her. Here was a land about to close on the seasons of growth and nurture. It would yield and give itself over to a cold, relentless winter that would rob it of its color, its life, and its vibrant green. All would be barren and bare, like her heart had become when Beth died. There was a similarity. Except Beth would never return with the spring. She kicked herself. How morbid she had become.

"I'm sorry," she said, but Kiernan seemed to understand.

"Go on. Sometimes there's a time for things to be spoken. Maybe it's now."

Ele accepted the quiet permission and continued. "It was why we chose to live where I am now. Beth always said you needed a home where you could run out into the garden stark naked if you wanted, and no one would ever know." She glanced at Kiernan and saw the look of surprise on her face.

"Not that she—or I—ever did, but it was the privacy thing, especially as I became better known. Our time alone seemed in jeopardy. We both wanted to be able to retreat to our own little golden nest, just us. The house gave us that. I thought it was our forever home, that we would have more years together than we did."

"You've been lucky." Kiernan spoke quietly. "Terrible though it's been to lose someone like Beth, what you've had with her has been wonderful. Two people in love and so right—able to commit to each another."

Ele hadn't expected a response, and not this. Kiernan gazed down at her hands, very un-Kiernan like, and then rubbed them together, tracing the shapes of her fingers.

"What you had was perfect," Kiernan said. "I see it in your face when you speak of Beth. You and she found the holy grail of love, something we all search for, but very few of us find."

"I was lucky." Ele had always known this. She had won the lottery in love. "I met the right one at the beginning and didn't need to search further."

She looked again at Kiernan and saw such sadness. Whatever had happened between her and Chrissie, it had left an indelible mark. She had no right to ask again, but she *needed* to know what had happened. Something intuitive suggested Kiernan wanted to talk. She would ask a third time. Third time lucky?

"Tell me?"

For what seemed the longest few seconds, Kiernan stared at her. Then she smiled.

❖

Kiernan knew she didn't have to tell Ele anything. She had known her such a short time, and yet everything felt right. What was the song about an enchanted evening and seeing a stranger across a crowded room? She always thought that song fanciful, but now its lyrics rang true.

"It was around the time I found this place." Kiernan hooked her fingers into tight jean pockets and gazed out the window at the countryside beyond. "I was at a party in London. It was an art studio showcasing some untalented, pretentious artist's work—hideous color schemes and overlapping cubes. The place was packed. I don't know why they invited me, but I was happy to go. Free wine and small eats." She glanced at Ele. "A meal I didn't have to cook." Ele watched her, with wide open, hungry for detail eyes.

"This rather attractive woman stood in a corner. She had spilled wine down the front of her dress and was trying to clean it up with a tissue. I had a surge of chivalry and went over to her with a load of paper napkins I swiped off a table." Kiernan remembered how grateful Chrissie had been and how she'd instantly engaged her in conversation. Chrissie told her she'd been watching her, wondering who she was. The attraction had been mutual. Kiernan felt the old ache return. She still missed her despite what had happened. Resurrecting the memories always did this.

"We started to talk—really talk. Not about usual party stuff, but about who we were and what we did, and what had been happening in the news that day." Kiernan couldn't stop grinning. "She told me how she enjoyed traveling and going on camping walks along coastlines. That should have been my warning then!" Ele joined in her laughter.

"Chrissie's an architect, and was then a post grad studying at London South Bank Uni. We clicked straight away, and ended up leaving the party early, and going for dinner. She was fascinated in me, who I was and what I did. I was fascinated in her, too. Before I knew what hit me, we were going out. We never stopped laughing, and were always planning our time together. If we weren't working or studying, we were in each other's company, and very quickly, our different circle of friends accepted that. I was never so happy. I was totally in love and it felt wonderful. Maybe it was my age, but I started thinking of settling down, wanting to make Chrissie a permanent part of my life."

"And Chrissie?"

"She was in love with me. I still believe that. And I thought she wanted the same as me, maybe she thought she did. But in the end, she didn't."

"What went wrong?"

Kiernan looked at Ele, unsure at first, how to explain. She didn't rush the answer. She thought first. "When you're in love, you put your partner first. You think more of them and their needs than your own. That's how you know it's real. I knew Chrissie had a lot of qualifications to get, a lot of study to do. She was a born architect, loved her profession. She was constantly seeking to broaden her knowledge and experience. She was always studying for something or other—a diploma in this, then a professional practice course in that. But I always saw an end to all the study, where she would settle down into her own practice. It was something she wanted. She had talked about working in the city or maybe in Oxford, and both very commutable from here. We'd be able to continue doing what we do—but together."

"But that didn't happen?"

"It didn't. We'd been together several years, and she'd finished a particularly challenging course of study and was working for a London designer. I was looking forward to more stability—more us. She announced that she was going to do a one-year course at the University of Milan. I didn't like it, but I wasn't going to stand in her way. I wanted her to be happy. I wanted her to succeed in her profession. But while she was out there, she got an offer to work for some apparently well known and respected designer with his own studio—Alessandro Tagliatelli or something…" Kiernan hesitated. "That's a pasta, isn't it? Well, some Italian sounding name." She sighed. "It was the final straw, Ele. I knew then that Chrissie was never going to commit to a relationship with me. She loved me, but when it came down to it, she chose her career over us."

Ele put a hand on her shoulder. "I'm so sorry. That must have really hurt."

It hurt all right. Kiernan had loved Chrissie and she had wanted to settle down with her. She was ready to commit. "I realize now that I was always playing second fiddle to her career. It wasn't her fault, it was just our needs didn't dovetail, not in the end. Not where it was important. I should have seen the signs. They were there. The positive responses, but never enthusiastic. Always me suggesting how our future might look. She never did. Well, it's over and we all move on, don't we." She felt her eyes sting.

"I'm sorry, Kiernan. I can't begin to imagine how much this all hurts."

Kiernan could now make out Ele's reflection in the window. It was getting dark outside. "Just sad, Ele." She glanced at the sky and the dark clouds that had appeared from nowhere. "It's starting to snow."

Her dredging up of the past was over, and she was thankful that Ele recognized that and wasn't uttering platitudes of understanding and concern. Kiernan didn't want sympathy. She hated that. It had been her problem, and she was over it. Life moved on. Her disappointing relationship with Chrissie was nothing new. Hundreds of people went through the same issues every day. Tough.

The timer buzzed in the kitchen announcing lunch. Though Kiernan had not wanted sympathy, what she got was an arm gently taking hers. Ele leaned in close as she guided her toward the kitchen.

Kiernan considered the token act worth more than all the kind words in a dictionary.

## CHAPTER TWELVE

The drive from Enstone to meet Dorothy Harding, the daughter of Beatrice Lavish who had worked for the Staffords, wasn't bad even though the short snowstorm turned to rain. Dusk was beginning to fall. Ele maneuvered the small country lanes through the fields with extra caution as the temperature plummeted.

She had never been to Chadlington even though it was only three miles south of Chipping Norton where she sometimes shopped. Looking at the array of pretty Cotswold properties, she marveled at how newer homes were built in similar style to conserve the area's heritage. Sometimes she thought everything traditional was disappearing. It wasn't something she liked. She was old-fashioned and longed to keep many of the former ways. Her father had always said she was born for the wrong period.

Kiernan sat in the passenger seat next to her, chatting away as if she didn't have a care in the world. Maybe she hadn't, not anymore. Perhaps, as Kiernan was apt to keep telling her, she was over her relationship with Chrissie. But Ele sensed the scars, the small internal reminders that would always be there. She thought of how easily Kiernan had spoken to her of Chrissie, and how straight-forward her account had been. Very much that of someone who had come to terms with her loss. And yet, she had also heard Kiernan's voice tremble, and had seen her eyes water as she reconnected with the past. Ele knew the scars were there—scars you expected when deep, meaningful relationships went sour. But she suspected that, despite Kiernan's bravado, the scars weren't healed and still had power to hurt.

Ele reached across and placed a hand on Kiernan's leg, a show of unspoken support. Kiernan stopped talking and Ele sensed her eyes on her. A warm hand then covered hers before Kiernan carried on chatting. It suddenly felt wrong, and Ele wanted to take back her hand. It was only a show of friendship, she thought, but she knew it wasn't. She was reaching out in a most intimate way, trying to make a connection with someone who was becoming important to her, so fast. But it felt like she was committing a sin. Beth entered her thoughts. She waited for an acceptable time and then removed her hand, feigning its need for driving.

As they entered the small village of Chadlington, they passed an impressive ancient church set back in grounds surrounded by old gravestones.

"Look." Ele drew Kiernan's attention to the high walls of the church building. "Those are gargoyles." Ugly medieval stone creatures with tongues sticking out, sat high on the parapets, visible from the road.

"That's Saint Nicholas Church." Kiernan looked back over her shoulder as they sped past it. "It's Norman, and in the thirteenth century, they added the North and South aisles. The tower is fourteenth century, but the chancel wasn't added until the Victorian period so it's a bit of a work in progress."

Ele glanced at her before watching the road again. Kiernan didn't seem to have noticed.

"If you go around to the side of it, there's a stone carving of two green men," she added.

"What are you, a walking encyclopedia?" Ele's question wasn't answered, and she considered she was being deliberately ignored. Kiernan suffered from selective hearing.

"It's believed Chadlington was named after Saint Chad and…" Kiernan paused for effect. "Chadlington is actually mentioned in the *Domsday Book*, written in ten eighty-six." She grinned as she turned her head to look slyly at Ele. It reminded her of a look Feathers sometimes gave her—the one that spoke of omnipotence. Kiernan was playing with her. "Admit it. You're impressed, aren't you?"

Ele was impressed, but wasn't going to let on. "I'm not sure I know how to answer that in fear of discovering you're some closeted type of geek."

Kiernan laughed. "You're safe. I accessed Google before we left, so we could find Dorothy Harding's house."

Ele sighed. "I'm mildly reassured. I'm not sure I can handle geeks."

"Again, you're safe. But just to keep your suspicions alive, every summer, Chadlington has a music festival for three or four days, mostly classical. Last June, they held a beautiful candlelit twilight recital in the chapel here. I attended, and it was wonderful. We ought to come next year, if you're up for it." Her easygoing manner became urgent. "Hey, turn left up here and then stop as soon as you can on the right."

Ele hardly had time to register the subtle invitation. It was said and gone in a blink. She was now forced to concentrate on parking her larger than normal vehicle in a narrower than normal side lane where other cars were parked, leaving little room. With grim determination, she managed the task.

As they hopped out of the car, she said under her breath, "I do hope Dorothy Harding still has all her marbles, and that she'll know something."

Kiernan led the way to the door and then watched as Ele rang its bell. She was still watching as Ele rang it for a fourth time. She could see the disappointment building on Ele's face. Ele clearly thought as she did. The owner of the property was either deaf or out. Perhaps someone of Mrs. Harding's age had forgotten their appointment?

Ele looked miserable. "What if she isn't in?"

Kiernan faked confidence. "She will be. Ring a fifth time. Five's a lucky number."

A petite, elderly, but very sprightly woman appeared from around the back of the house. Dressed in an old pair of dark green corduroys, muddy boots, and a heavy brown jacket, she was carrying an armload of rotting vegetation. She stopped in her tracks and smiled at them.

"I expect you've been ringing that for ages. I can't hear it when I'm up the garden. Never mind. Doesn't matter." She spoke quickly and in an indomitable manner. "You must be the ladies Eddie rang about. You want to know about some of the folk who used to live at Pegmire Vicarage?" She didn't wait for an answer. "Well, you'd better come in, but come around the back. It's easier."

As she moved back the way she came, she threw her cargo into a large brown bin. She dusted soil off her arms and hands, and announced, "I've been clearing the vegetable patch, getting rid of all the old growth so it's ready to plant for next year. I grow all my own stuff."

Kiernan glanced up the garden, which was about half an acre. There was a small cultivated area of lawn and flowerbeds in the forefront, with a larger vegetable plot to the rear. All was immaculate. The white-haired woman caught her looking.

"I do all my own gardening. It keeps me fit. I'm not like some of these others, you know, spend their lives sitting in front of a television, wasting away. I'm Dorothy Harding, by the way." She thrust her hand to shake theirs. "You can call me Dot."

Kiernan eyeballed Ele, unable to contain a grin. It seemed Dorothy Harding was an eccentric, and not likely to be missing a single marble.

Inside, her home was like her garden—colorful, and a feast for the eyes. Though her sitting room was large, it was full to the brim with furniture and belongings. There were two huge floral designed sofas covered in a multitude of comfortable cushions that didn't match in size or color. Every flat surface seemed to have fresh flowers in large vases on it, and if it didn't, there were trinkets of every shape and size to fill the gaps.

One wall was an entire bookcase stuffed full of books and magazines, but in no neat order, and any space left on the walls was festooned with mismatched paintings and photographs. Everything in the room seemed a cherished belonging, a memory.

Dot Harding was a natural host and insisted on making them a warm drink before any discussion began. They waited as she finished pouring them tea from a large brown crockery teapot.

Kiernan took to Dot in an instant. Her mother had owned a teapot, and had loathed the modern progress of throwing a tea bag into a mug. Harding still favored the old ways, and graced the small lace-covered table they all sat around with pretty bone china cups and saucers, none of which matched.

"Do I recall J. Stafford?" Dot repeated Ele's initial question. Her face brightened. "Oh yes, John and Harriett Stafford. They were my mother's favorites. Of course, I never knew them. They were gone before I was born, but Mother worked for them all the time they lived at the vicarage."

"Did they move on then?" Kiernan couldn't help interrupting. They might as well know now, like the Wintermans.

"No. They both died."

Kiernan tried to catch Ele's attention, but her concentration was on Dot. She saw an intensity in her that reminded her of the younger Ele, when she had been interviewing someone with tenacity on morning television, and looking to unlock the locked.

"Can you tell me what you know about them, Dot?" Ele asked.

Dot placed her cup back in its saucer and scrutinized them both before eyeballing Ele. "Can you tell me why you're so interested? They've been gone a long time, and since none of us here knew them personally, I'm intrigued."

How would Ele tackle the question? She and Ele had already talked about this, as they had expected Edmond Riser to ask them why they were interested in past owners, but he hadn't. The problem was telling someone the truth, that you had a ghost. It wasn't wise. They would either consider you some crackpot, or worse, given Ele's celebrity background, they might leak the story to the press. The tabloids would have a field day. The latter would do their research, and Kiernan could only imagine what would follow. *"Eleanor Teal, lonely lesbian loony."* Sometime after that, the ghost hunters would appear in her garden.

"If I said I was just interested in researching the previous history of my home and its past occupants, would that suffice?" Ele said. It had worked with Riser.

"I wouldn't believe it, my dear."

"I didn't think you would." Ele leaned forward, her breasts pressed against the table, her hands beneath it. Kiernan saw the slight twist of a smile on her lips.

"I heard you in the background when Eddie phoned," Dot said. "I sensed some desperation, some rather urgent need to see me as soon as possible. And you don't seem too interested in any other occupant of the house except the Staffords."

Not a single marble out of place, Kiernan thought again as she watched two intelligent minds negotiating the way forward.

"You're right, Dot," Ele said, and Kiernan watched her considering what she wanted to admit.

Dot interrupted her struggle. "I do recognize you, you know. You used to be on the television and in the press." She drummed an arthritic, knobbled finger on the table. "My mother loved the Staffords, and I wouldn't want to be part of anything that did her or them any disservice."

Ele smiled. "I understand completely." She glanced at Kiernan before looking at Dot again. "Dot, if I told you something…do you know how to keep a secret?"

Kiernan knew Ele was about to take a leap of faith with Dorothy Harding. But she felt that trust was in safe hands. There was a quality about Dot that told you she wouldn't let you down.

Her own comment about wanting to safeguard the integrity of the Staffords said as much.

"If the secret doesn't concern illegal or criminal activity, you have a deal."

Ele spoke with her usual determined and clear diction. "I've lived at the old vicarage for many years and been perfectly happy, but recently, some strange things have been happening there. They are things that are not quite...*natural*, things that are a little *unnatural*." Ele raised her brow and emphasized words to ensure Dot comprehended the gravitas of the situation.

Kiernan studied Dot's face for ridicule, but found none. Dot sat expressionless, listening intently.

"Dot, I don't want to go into too much detail, but I think what's happening has something to do with the Staffords." Ele breathed out. "I can only promise you that I have no intention of doing anything with this information other than finding out what is going on. It really is a personal matter."

Dot studied Ele like she might an oil painting by a Master looking for signs of forgery. "Are you alone in your feelings?"

"No, she isn't," Kiernan said quickly. "I've witnessed...some things."

Dot's eagle eyes rested on her for an uncomfortable minute before she eased back in her chair and crossed her hands in her lap. "Well, if I was intrigued before, now I'm very curious. Okay, I can understand why someone of your background, Ele, might not want this information to fall into the wrong hands. The media would love this."

*My thoughts exactly!* Kiernan liked Dot more and more.

"Very well. What would you like to know?" It seemed they had passed Dot's assessment.

Ele shot a huge smile at Kiernan before asking, "Tell me anything you know about the Staffords?"

Dot began.

"My mother was born in eighteen ninety-three, and as soon as she could, she started work in service. In nineteen twelve, John and Harriett Stafford moved into your house, and my mother, Beatrice Lavish, went there as a housemaid. Soon after, the current housekeeper left the area, and my mother took that position. She was young for the role, but she had a steady head on her shoulders and got on very well with Mrs. Stafford, who was only a few years older than my mother.

"John Stafford was something to do with banking, and I think he had been promoted and moved to this area. As I recall, Mother thought they had been married but a short while when they took up residence there. That was another similarity Mother had with Harriett. She had just married my father, Thomas…Tom. She and Mrs. Stafford became quite close despite their differing status. Although my father worked on the railways, he would sometimes go over to the house if any odd jobs needed doing. It was extra income, you understand."

Ele interrupted. "I don't suppose you have an idea of what John Stafford looked like? Did your mother ever describe him?"

"I can do better than that," Dot said, rising. "I take it his appearance is of interest to you." The statement sought no answer, and Kiernan surmised that Dot was already piecing together a large chunk of the missing element that neither she nor Ele spoke of.

"Come and look at this," Dot beckoned them over to an old photo on a far wall. "Tom, my father, was an amateur photographer. One of the first villagers to get a Kodak box Brownie camera. He was always taking photographs. Mother used to moan about the cost."

She pointed at the photo. "He took this of my mother and the Staffords one summer in the vicarage gardens, just before the war." Dorothy's finger moved across people in the shot. "That's Harriett, that's Mother, and that, of course, is John Stafford."

Kiernan felt the breath catch in her chest. John Stafford was their ghost.

Ele saw Kiernan stagger back and knew she was ill. She steadied her as she guided her straight to the nearest chair. She felt her own heartbeat increase and her breathing quicken. For a moment, everything around her seemed to slow and go dull. She was afraid Kiernan was going to pass out. She didn't, but Ele still sat on a chair arm and wrapped an arm around Kiernan's shoulder in support. She found herself fighting to keep her own alarm in check.

Kiernan was white. "Sorry."

"It's okay, Kier. Don't talk." Ele's heart still pounded. She was frightened.

Dot moved forward. "Are you all right, my dear? You've gone very pale." Dot looked down at Kiernan who was slumped in an armchair panting for breath.

Ele tried to reassure Dot that all was okay. She wasn't sure herself. "Kier gets asthma, and I think the winter air gets to her," she lied. Frightening though it was to hear someone gasp for breath, she knew what had brought on the attack. "It's probably because we came in from the damp air and into the warmth."

Dot didn't believe her. "It's probably because she—and you—saw something in that photo." She was no one's fool.

"I'm okay," Kiernan wheezed, shaking an index finger in the air, and looking at Dot apologetically. "This is embarrassing."

"Do you have any medication?" Dot asked.

Kiernan looked up at Ele. "Wrong car," she wheezed.

Ele saw her frustration and rubbed her back as she thought of the inhaler's location—in Kiernan's car, parked back at her place. She explained this to Dot who disappeared into the kitchen, talking about paper bags.

Dot's absence gave Ele the opportunity to confide in Kiernan. "Stafford is the ghost," she whispered.

"I know," Kiernan spluttered. "You called me Kier..."

Ele nodded. "Yes." Was she treading on sacred ground?

"No one calls me Kier. Only my mother did that."

"Oh, I'm sorry." Ele could almost hear the blessed terrain crunching beneath her big feet.

"It's okay. I like it."

"Oh." Ele couldn't hide the satisfaction in her voice, but her sudden *joie de vivre* didn't last long. Kiernan was coughing, and her wheezing grew louder. She could hear her continued fight for breath. Her fear for Kiernan's wellbeing returned, as did her anxiety. It annoyed her that she never had her medication on her at the right time. "You really should carry your inhaler in your pocket. Keep it on you at all times, especially when you know this can happen."

"I know," Kiernan said, resignation on her face.

"Well, it's no good saying that when you don't do anything about it."

"I know."

Ele wasn't finished. "When we get home, I'm going to tie the bloody thing around your neck." She caught the surprise on Kier's face as she looked up at her. Could Kiernan see how worried she was—because she was. She fought to regain her control. "Well, someone's got to look after you." Her discomfort was stemmed when Dot walked back in with a plain brown paper bag, which she thrust toward Kiernan.

"Breathe in and out of that," Dot ordered her. "Not really high-tech, but I'm told it helps. It's probably an old wives' tale that won't work. If you die, we'll know the answer," she said wryly.

"That's not reassuring, Dot." Kiernan lifted her head from the bag.

With one commanding movement, Dot shoved her head back in the bag. "Shut up and keep breathing."

Ele bit her lip. The scene was classic. "What did you do before you retired, Dot?" *A Royal Marine Commando?*

"I was a civil servant and ran a department in Westminster full of bureaucratic idiots who didn't listen. They spent money like water, and now the country wonders why we're in a recession." She bent toward Kiernan. "You should keep your inhaler on you."

"I *know*," Kiernan's muffled, aggravated voice spoke into the bag.

"It's quite stupid when you know you're prone to attacks," Dot continued.

"I know," Kiernan repeated.

"Only an idiot would leave it in their car."

Kiernan lifted her head from the bag and looked at Dot. "I know!"

Dot weakened. "Never mind, my dear. This time I think you're going to live." She took the bag off Kiernan, rumpled it up, and threw it into a wicker waste paper basket. Turning to Ele, she said, "You know, you don't have to tell me anything you don't want to with regard to the Staffords, but…" She smiled conspiratorially. "If later, when you think you can trust me, I would like to hear the full story. I'm old, and so little excitement surrounds me these days. Whatever is happening at the vicarage must be very interesting."

Ele wasn't sure *interesting* was the word.

Minutes later, Dot resumed her story of the Staffords.

"When the war came, John Stafford joined the army and went off to fight. I believe he was in the trenches at Flanders and also the Somme. The last year of the war, nineteen eighteen, Mrs. Stafford received a telegram that her husband was missing in action, presumed killed. You can imagine it was quite a blow for such a young woman. Mother stayed with her a few nights until Harriett's family came down to join her. They wanted her to go home with them. To Northampton I believe, but she refused. She was convinced her husband was still alive and wanted to be at the house when he returned home." She hesitated. "Mother always said it was a shame she hadn't gone back with her family because of what happened next."

Ele's attention was split. She was trying to take in everything that Dot was saying while focusing on Kiernan, needing to know she was okay. She glanced down at her and was relieved to see she seemed better. Her breathing was less labored. Ele's concentration returned to the story, and she wondered what disaster was about to further befall the Staffords, and whether anything they heard might tell them why the vicarage grounds were now haunted.

"During the summer of nineteen eighteen, a great influenza hit Europe and this country. It's said that more people died of the flu at that time than those who had perished in the Great War. The influenza hit this part of England particularly hard, and Harriett Stafford contracted it. She became very ill, and her family came down again to look after her. When her condition seemed to lighten, they insisted she go home with them so she could be better cared for. But the flu often struck a person with a second wave. Just as they thought she was recovering, her condition worsened, and she died in Northampton.

"Several months later, after the war had ended, Captain Stafford came home. He had been injured during the Somme, and for whatever reason, no word of his survival had made it home." Dot smiled sadly. "Harriett had been right all along. He was still alive, but arrived home too late, after she died."

Dot ran her hand along the top of the table. "Mr. Stafford was devastated to learn of his wife's death. They had been so very close and had such a wonderful marriage filled with love. Mother always said she wished such a marriage for all of her three children. She continued to be the housekeeper until Mr. Stafford died at the vicarage early nineteen nineteen. Everyone said he died of complications of his injuries, but Mother always said he died of a broken heart."

"You know a lot." Ele wondered how Dot could know so much about someone she had never known.

Dot nodded. "My granddaughter has been researching the family tree and interviewing us all for the record. I'm on DVD you know," she said proudly. "I'm the last one who remembers my parents. I find the more I'm asked to think about them, the more I remember. But Mother was always talking to me about the Staffords, what they were like, and how much they loved each other. I was the only girl you see, and she never spoke to the boys about this. It was a very traumatic time in her life; she lost two people she regarded very highly. I know she always liked Mr. Stafford and thought him the most handsome gentleman she ever met. She never told my father that." Dot laughed.

"Where are they buried?" Ele asked.

Dot hesitated before answering. "I don't know. I assume John Stafford is buried in Pegmire churchyard. His wife is probably buried with family up in Northampton. I doubt they would have brought her back down here, thinking her husband was dead, his body lost on some battlefield." She leaned back in her chair. "All a sad tale, isn't it?"

She and Kiernan said yes at the same time.

"I don't think there's much more I can tell you." Again, Dot rapped her fingers on the table. "Has any of this been of use to you?" She looked at Ele.

"You've told us so much, Dot, and it's been very helpful." Ele smiled at Dot and received the warmest one back.

"Yes, but has it answered any of your questions?" Dot probed, and Ele sensed she understood more than she was letting on.

"I think you've answered some of them." Ele hoped her answer didn't give away her disappointment. The ghost now had a name, but his reason for haunting remained a mystery.

"But there are more?" Dot sensed her frustration.

"Maybe, Dot. I'm just not sure what they are yet."

"Such intrigue for an old woman." Dot smiled before turning efficient. "I'm off to Bewdley tomorrow, to stay with my daughter for a week. If I remember anything else about the Staffords, I'll let you know. And if you have any other questions, you just contact me and I'll do my best to answer them."

As she and Kiernan stood to leave, Dot reached out for her hand and held it tight. "I mean it, Ele. Don't hesitate to come to me again for help."

Ele thought how strange it was. You could meet some people and in the blink of a second, form a bond. As she looked at Dot, she realized this is what had happened. The old lady liked her. The feeling was mutual.

As they drove back to the vicarage, Kiernan thought how sad the story of the Staffords had been. Such tragedy. She was grateful that Dot had known so much and also had a photo of the ghost. Seeing his picture had shocked her, enough to bring on an attack. She was feeling much better now, but she still couldn't seem to get a full breath, and she longed to get to her inhaler. She glanced over at Ele driving and who seemed deep in thought. She saw a frown on her face, and wondered if she was trying to process all of Dot's information, of how it would help solve the haunting.

Kiernan was suddenly aware that the heat in the car was robbing her of valuable oxygen. She needed to get some decent air in her lungs.

"Can you pull over, Ele? I need to get some fresh air."

Maybe it was the way she said it, but she saw the alarm on Ele's face as she pulled off the road onto a verge at first opportunity.

"You're okay?" There was panic in Ele's voice.

"I'm fine." But Kiernan hopped out of the car quickly, and immediately took the best intake of oxygen she'd had all afternoon. As she felt the satisfaction of the invisible elixir of life fill her lungs, she closed her eyes. When she opened them, Ele was stood close at her side, frantic concern etched on her face.

"I'm okay, Ele. Really." Kiernan tried to reassure her. "Look." She made a point of taking a deep breath and smiling.

Ele grabbed her, pulling her into a tight hug. "You scared me, Kier."

"I didn't mean to. I'm okay," she repeated.

"I thought I was going to lose you."

Kiernan pulled back. "Hey, it's only an asthma attack. They sound worse than they are."

"You went so pale."

Kiernan tugged her back into the hug and massaged her back, like she had done for her at Dot's. She realized how much Ele must care for her. It felt good. She felt her body respond to Ele's, and wondered if Ele felt the same. She must have, because Ele leaned back just enough to look into her face before kissing her. It was a deep kiss, not something done in haste, a mere meeting of lips. Kiernan felt heat explode between her legs. Too soon for Kiernan, Ele broke the kiss, and stepped back from her.

"You're sure you're okay?"

"Yes," Kier said. She noted how Ele avoided eye contact. Not the usual behavior after a meaningful kiss.

"You feel better?"

"I feel better." Dazed, Kiernan watched as Ele returned to the driver's side of the car and got back into it. As she climbed into the vehicle, she thought she'd never felt so much better in her life. Not the usual way she was after an asthma attack.

## CHAPTER THIRTEEN

It was late when Ele and Kiernan returned to the old vicarage. "Well, it helped," Ele said as she locked her car door and they moved toward the house. "We now know who our ghost is, but we're none the wiser for why he's haunting the place."

Kiernan was also none the wiser, but not regarding the ghost. Ele had made no reference to what had happened earlier, when they had stopped the car—when she had grabbed Kiernan and kissed her. It was as if it had never happened, and it left Kiernan bewildered.

For the remainder of the car journey, Ele had deliberately spoken about everything and anything, avoiding discussion of her sudden show of affection. Kiernan, on the other hand, had obsessed over nothing but that. She now *knew* there was a connection between them and that it served reciprocated, deeper, feelings. You don't kiss someone *like that* that you don't like, she thought. It's a kiss that moves things on—and yet it didn't appear to, and Kiernan wondered why? Her own feelings were clear. She was drawn—attracted to Ele and now, she wanted more. She just couldn't fathom Ele's behavior. Daring to kiss and now distant. Why?

"Do you think he's buried here?" Kiernan wheezed as she followed Ele into the hallway and was glad when the door closed.

The house felt safe and secure. "His ashes might have been scattered or buried here. Maybe that's what's been disturbed."

"Maybe." Ele seemed pensive. She dropped her car keys into a small dish on a hall table. "The way Dot described the two of them, they doted on each other. Do you think it's because they're not resting together, if his wife is buried somewhere else?"

Kiernan scratched her head. "I've thought of that but, if it was you, wouldn't you have started haunting a lot earlier? Why wait till now to let the world know you're not crazy with burial arrangements?"

Ele gazed emotionless at Kiernan. "Yeah, I suppose so." She fingered the car keys, moving them around mindlessly in the dish.

Kiernan wondered if Ele's odd behavior wasn't staring her in the face. Had today been too much for her? She hadn't been sleeping well of late, and who could blame her with a ruddy ghost clomping around outside? Today's revelations had been exhausting—discovering the ghost's identity. Her asthma attack hadn't helped. And then that kiss? Kiernan knew Ele must be thinking of Beth. How could she not? Ele had spoken with such heartache of how she'd loved Beth, and how she still missed her so much, even after all these years. Maybe Ele was feeling remorse? Kiernan thought that natural. But hadn't Ele dated others? She wasn't the first.

"You do realize we're sitting on a goldmine here," Ele said.

"How so?"

"Everything that's happening. All these photographs with a ghost in them and one we can now name. They'll be worth a fortune. To have actually captured something like this, and all the evidence."

Only once, for a trillionth of a second had Kiernan ever thought of the material value of what was happening. For her, this was never going to be about money, about making a sale and a profit. Even before she knew who the ghost was, something had reverberated deep within her. "For anyone to haunt, to be trapped in the wrong time, great suffering must be involved. Knowing who the ghost is, and all the tragedy surrounding him, this is so private and personal. I could never betray his trust, Ele."

For the first time since the kiss, Ele smiled at her. "I can't betray him either. It's a tragedy. It makes you wonder if other *real* ghosts exist," she said. "I've never seen a photograph of a ghost I believed in…until now. I wonder if there are others like us out there who have also kept the secret. Maybe we're surrounded by ghosts and decent people."

"I wish," Kiernan said. "Not many people are too honorable these days. They'll do, or sell, anything to make a buck."

"But not us."

"Not us." The way Ele spoke *us* sounded close and private, hinting of connection. It gave Kiernan hope. Hope that something *was* growing between them and that she just needed to be patient and move at Ele's speed. A small voice reminded her that she'd done precisely that with Chrissie, and look where that had led her.

She blotted the thought from her mind. It had been a long day, and Kiernan was tired. She could see Ele was too. Her face was drawn and paler than usual. She still had a ghost to contend with and no real idea of how to send him back to wherever. Though Kiernan longed to talk to Ele about certain aspects of the day—the personal ones—she now just wanted to get into her car, grab her inhaler, drive home, and sleep. She had a huge day tomorrow at work.

"If you want, you could stay the night. I've a spare room, and the bed is made up. Maybe you shouldn't be alone tonight given your attack?"

Kiernan believed the invitation was genuine, but she caught the importance of the spare room. Ele wasn't looking for a bedmate. Not tonight, anyway. Again, she put this down to Ele not wanting to rush things. In truth, she was also a little thankful. She needed to remember to go slowly. Chrissie had made her wary of jumping into another relationship too soon. Steady as she goes, she thought. Make sure this is what you want. But she already knew that answer. She wanted Ele. She was falling in love with her.

"I'll stay if you're worried about Stafford, but I'm okay, and I've a photo shoot tomorrow in Cambridge. It'll be an early start, and all my equipment's at home." She had a sudden thought. "You could come with me, if you like?"

Ele shook her head. "No. But thank you. I feel stronger now I know who my ghost is. I can't think there's an ounce of harm in John Stafford, just a huge sadness." She opened the door for Kiernan. "Can you imagine living through the hell of those trenches, getting injured, but making it home only to find the woman you adored had died of flu?" She didn't wait for an answer. "I could sleep through an air raid tonight."

Kiernan didn't know how to say good-bye. Should she hug Ele, or kiss her, or simply walk out with a farewell. She decided on the latter and nothing Ele did suggested she'd got it wrong.

"What are your plans?" she asked as she walked through the door, and out onto the gravel.

"I'm going to go to the churchyard and see if John Stafford is buried there."

"Shall I phone you when I get back?"

"You'd better," Ele said. "I need you."

❖

Ele stared at her reflection in the bedroom mirror. "Oh God, what have I done?" Her hands rose to her face. "I kissed her. *I* kissed her. What was I thinking?" She was trembling. Everything *right* had led her to that kiss. Why then did it feel so wrong, and why was she having a panic attack? It's because you're tired and emotional, she thought. You'll think clearer after a decent night's sleep. *What would Beth think?*

Not a day went by where she didn't miss Beth, and she could still hear her voice after all these years. She could feel her touch and the way her breath had felt when she nuzzled up to her in bed. Her heart ached; she missed Beth so much.

It had been a long time since Beth died, and the aftereffects had been traumatic. When she had fallen ill, Ele had taken leave of absence from the morning show in order to look after her. Even when Beth returned to work, Ele had insisted she drive her in to the university and back daily. Beth had no longer been able to drive, and Ele had not trusted placing her beloved cargo into the havoc that was public transport.

When she died, Ele had been so shocked she couldn't face going back in front of the cameras and had, to everyone's regret, terminated her media contract.

In the years since, she had learned to cope with her loss, or thought she had. Attempting to reconnect with life, she did the occasional research job for TV documentaries and a small amount of broadcasting for local radio and the BBC. She had taken her bird-loving hobby and artistic abilities and turned them into an illustrated book.

Ele had been brave with dating too. She had met several women through social links, and although they had been nice people, there had been no electricity, no connection. The relationships had withered before they had even begun. She sometimes wondered whether Beth had ruined her for anyone else, that no one would ever come close. But that was before Kiernan had appeared.

"Do I want Kiernan, or am I leading her on? Am I replacing Beth, putting everything that was between us, on a shelf?"

Her agitation and confusion grew. Everything had been so comfortable until Kiernan arrived. She had her home, her albeit solitary existence, her writing, her cat. She was happy, she reasoned. But she was also lonely. She realized that today when she'd looked into Kiernan's face under the hideous plant with the ugly leaves. And then the kiss. Her body alarm had gone off like a siren. How she longed for physical comfort. If she entered into a relationship with Kiernan—highly possible after today—would it last? Could it ever be anything like she'd shared with Beth? She might not even like Kiernan after she really got to know her. Her heart sank as she remembered. "I kissed her," she repeated. "Oh, Beth, what am I going to do?"

She was in a flat spin. Featherstone broke her angst by meowing at her feet. Ele bent down and stroked him. *Stop thinking, Ele. Shut up. Feed the cat, and get some sleep!*

## CHAPTER FOURTEEN

Pegmire churchyard was not a place to be on a morning like this. It was freezing, and a cutting north wind blew around Ele as she walked with haste around gravestones looking for John Stafford. She was disappointed. Not only did she not find his grave, many of the stones seemed to have disappeared, and there was a large expanse of bare churchyard where no gravestones remained. It was as if the land had been cleared.

A sharp gust of wind blew across and buffeted into her. Ele reached out to a gravestone for support. She considered that if she stayed out here any longer she might end up a permanent resident. She thought of Kier in Cambridge and hoped she wasn't working outside. The TV weatherman had said the conditions were freezing over that side of the country today.

Looking toward the church, she could see inviting lights behind the stained glass windows, and every now and then, on the turn of the wind, she thought she could hear music. Seeking sanctuary, she hurried to the church porch and entered.

There were young children inside rehearsing for a nativity concert. Milling around them were proud parents and stressed teachers trying to bring order to chaos. Ele watched as a little boy, no older than six, ran past her.

"James, where are you going?" a man shouted.

The boy stopped and looked back, his face scrunched up. "I want the toilet."

"Wrong way. It's back here." The same man now pointed to an area behind him. James raced back toward the man.

Ele sat in one of the many rows of pews and felt the comfort of the bench and its back support. Now she was out of the wind, her body turned warm, and she undid the scarf from around her neck. Again, she thought of Kier. Ele hadn't asked her what her photo project was today, and Kier hadn't mentioned it. *Stay warm, Kier.*

She listened to the silvery voices of the children as they started singing traditional carols. Their voices were enchanting, and the choirmaster had introduced a gentle descant from several boys who sang as if angels. Five minutes later, the angels disappeared and chaos returned as the children rushed by and out of the church. James walked past her, his gloves dangling from where they were attached to his coat sleeves. He smiled at her—a cheeky smile—and she smiled back.

Ele loved children, but she didn't miss not having her own. Instead, she lavished affection on her brother's children on the rare occasion she saw them. Richard was an industrial engineer and now lived and worked in Italy. He was her only sibling, and despite loving him and his family to bits, she was always glad when any visit finished, and he and his wife went home—with their children.

The church became eerily quiet, and Ele was about to leave when she saw the vicar moving and stacking chairs at the front where the choir had practiced. She went down to him and introduced herself.

The vicar was the Reverend Miles Green, a man in his early forties and with a boyish countenance. He possessed a smile that lit his entire face and, with his ruffled sandy-colored hair, she could see why villagers thought of him as a huge teddy bear of a man. He was very popular with the congregation, and more so, the children.

Rev. Green recognized her. "You live up in the old vicarage." He placed a chair down and came forward to greet her.

They spoke for a while of trivial, polite things before she turned the conversation to the matter of John Stafford, and that she was researching former occupants of her house.

"If he is buried here, you'll be lucky to find his gravestone," Rev. Green said. "That period of time, most of the burials were in the north facing side of the churchyard. It's the side that catches the worst of the weather, and a lot of the stones are deteriorating badly. Those that are still standing, many of them you can't read who's buried there." He sat in a pew with her. "Because of health and safety, we've had to clear a lot of them. We've started placing any of the stones that are still legible and in good condition, around the outer church walls, but the rest, I'm afraid, are beyond repair.

"This is happening in a lot of old churchyards all over the country. There's also the problem of space. The land fills up, but the new occupants keep coming." He smiled respectfully. "If we can, we clear the very oldest parts of the churchyard and then reuse the ground. It's either that or turning to cremation. Not something everyone wants."

Ele understood. "Are there any records I can access to try to establish if John Stafford is buried here?"

"Oh, yes," the vicar said. "Every church has them. It's where we record christenings, marriages, and burials. Of course, most of them are kept, like ours, in county records offices. That way they can be maintained and preserved in a humidity-controlled environment. I can give you the contact details of where ours are kept."

She thanked him and was about to leave when he asked, "What year did you think Stafford died, when he might have been buried here?"

"I think either late nineteen eighteen or in the first few months of the following year. I don't have precise dates." Ele wasn't sure how accurate Dot Harding was. All she knew was the house was sold in 1921 to the Wintermans.

Rev. Green rubbed his hands together with glee. "You might be in luck. Follow me."

Ele tagged behind him into the vestry. It was a small room at the back of the church and was used for keeping vestments, vessels, and the robes of the clergy and choir.

He caught her looking at the choral clothing. "Do you sing?" he asked hopefully.

"Like a chain saw," Ele replied dryly.

"Pity. We're always looking for new voices."

"Not mine, you're not. Sorry."

He gave a huge belly laugh.

He leaned his hands on a central table. "The vestry is where we used to keep the church records. Occasionally, we get some of the records back—they're still our property—to do some research." He looked down at an old wooden table, which was covered in aged leather books. "I get requests almost daily from people tracing family trees. I don't have time to help them all, and I put them on to the county records office. But occasionally, we get requests and we like to be more helpful. I don't get involved, but there are a few interested parishioners who look into these things."

He pointed to a letter. "We've had a request from a Canadian family who once had roots in Pegmire. They're coming over here this summer and have asked if we can help them. Mary Marsh, a parishioner, has taken up the challenge. Now the interesting thing"—the vicar stabbed a finger at the same letter—"is that their time period is the same as yours. That means, here on this desk somewhere are the burial records of the church nineteen seventeen to nineteen twenty-three. If you've time and don't mind wading through them, you're very welcome to look."

As he excused himself to return to his previous task of clearing chairs away, he added, "Try not to move things around too much. It may not look like it, but Mary does have an ordered system in there somewhere." Again, he grinned with boyish charm. "If you're here long enough, you might meet her. She's also been trying to work out who is buried, and where, so we can draw up a few plans for any future requests such as yours."

He disappeared, and Ele sat and started going through the record of burials. Instinct told her to start with January, 1919, but she found nothing. It was when she got to Tuesday, 18 February, 1919, that she found a simple entry for Captain John Charles Stafford, late of Richmond, born 10 July 1890, died 3 January, 1919. The address given was hers. She found nothing else and no mention of his wife, but now she knew more. John Stafford was not buried, nor had his ashes been scattered, at the house. His remains lay here, in Pegmire Churchyard. She continued to search the entire book for burials in 1918, hoping to find some mention of Harriett Stafford, but she was disappointed.

As she was leaving, she thanked the vicar. In passing comment, he said he would mention Ele's search to Mary who might be able to shine light on the actual spot where John Stafford was buried.

Though her search had been successful, the fruit of her day left her depressed. She couldn't stop thinking how terrible it all was, that the loving couple had been robbed of life at so young an age, and then to be robbed of resting in peace together.

As she crossed the road to where her car was parked, she wandered over to look at the large stone World War I Remembrance Cross that dominated the village square. Its large base held the names of villagers who had given their lives during the Great War. How many times had she walked passed this memorial? This was the first time she had stopped to look at the names.

She hadn't expected to find Stafford on it since he had not, technically, died in the war. But his name was there for everyone to see, and it filled Ele with an unusual feeling of pride, as if he were a friend or someone related to her.

As she arrived at her car, someone called her name, and she saw Roger, the builder, waving a walking stick and limping her way.

"Roger, what have you done?" she exclaimed walking up and putting her arms around him. He was more than a builder to her. He had been such a tower of support when Beth had fallen ill.

"Broke my ruddy foot! I kicked something heavy in the garden, nothing on my feet. Serves me right."

They exchanged pleasant conversation, catching up on what they'd each been doing for the last few months. He was delighted to learn that Ele's illustrated book on woodpeckers was about to be published and mentioned how much his wife, Joan, was looking forward to purchasing it. "She loves birds and has even more bird feeders in the garden now."

"Don't let her buy the book, Roger. I'd love to give you a copy for her. I'll write something nice inside it."

"That would be kind of you." He hesitated, his face more serious before continuing. "I don't suppose you'd like to bring it over and hand it to her personally? She'd love that, and it might give her a lift."

Ele could tell something was wrong and asked Roger directly.

Roger was not the type of man who shared his problems easily, but perhaps that barrier had been erased when Beth had died. Roger and Joan had been true friends and a great support to Ele during those black days. He had driven her to get the death certificate and also helped her to make funeral arrangements. Joan had sent him over to the house with more than a few prepared meals she just had to heat up. In those days following the death, Ele had not wanted to eat, let alone cook. She lost count of the number of meals she had with him and Joan. Even when her own, and Beth's, family had been there at the Oxford funeral and where she was buried, Roger had stood by her side in the church and held her hand. That something was wrong with Roger and his family, Ele wanted to be there for him, to repay all his kindness.

"The wife's not too well," he confided. "She just can't sleep. It's been going on for months. At first, I thought it was because Sarah had left for uni—the last kid to flee the nest—but it's not that. She's been to the doctor's and he's given her a full checkup. He can't find anything wrong. But she still can't sleep, and it's dragging her down and making her very depressed, and very bad tempered. I tell you, sometimes, Ele, I dread going home."

"Maybe you should see another doctor," Ele said.

"My brother says that. I suppose I'm a bit frightened in case it's something more serious, maybe mental issues."

"How do you mean?"

"Funny things, Ele. She loves the garden, but won't go in it anymore. Says being outside scares her." He laughed self-consciously. "The doctor thinks she's agoraphobic. Can you believe that? You know how much she loves her garden and her birds. She won't even top up the birdseed in the feeders now. On the rare occasions she manages to sleep, she has nightmares. Bloody awful. She wakes up in a sweat and then refuses to try to go back to sleep." He shrugged and looked every bit uncomfortable. "This foot hasn't helped. I've been at home more than usual, and we just snipe at each other. Frankly, I'm at my wit's end."

Roger bit his lip, forcing back emotions. She placed her hand on his arm. "I'm expecting some of my books to arrive imminently. I get them before the publishing date. As soon as they do, I'll pop round with one."

"You won't say anything, will you? You won't let on what I've said?" He couldn't hide his concern. "She'd kill me."

Ele promised she wouldn't say anything and watched as Roger hobbled off down the road.

Her day was turning into a hodgepodge of emotions.

Later, Ele decided to work on some illustrations. If her book on woodpeckers did well, she thought of doing one on kingfishers and other river birds. Even if her book didn't do well, she'd still end up in her studio painting. She loved this space. It never mattered what the weather was like outside; this room, with its whitewashed walls that looked like fresh laundered sheets, was always bright. The skylight windows above her kept it flooded with natural light regardless of what was going on outside, which was just as well; today was another of the meanest of days, weather-wise. How she pined for spring.

As she sat hunched over an unfinished watercolor of a small common kingfisher, a sable artist's brush in her hand, she listened to the raw, abrasive sound of the wind gusting outside. There was still no snow, but this weather was heralding its imminent arrival.

She loved the contrast of the situation. She was inside a warm studio where everything was calm and controlled, but outside, it was cold and wild, cruel and hard.

Ele dabbed small spots of lighter blue on the dark blue wings of her subject matter. It was such a beautiful bird that if you were patient and knew where to look, you could often see them hovering over water at a riverside or as a flash of blue as their long, dark beaks grabbed a small fish.

Kingfishers were amazing creatures that needed to consume their own bodyweight in food each day. Winters always worried her because it made the little birds so vulnerable; they were small and found it difficult to keep warm. Severe winters could often kill off over fifty percent of them. Ele thought it a shame that she couldn't protect them, build somewhere for them to stay during the cold. But they would never come. They needed the rivers. Besides, if they did come, there would be other threats. She glanced over at Featherstone who was curled up asleep on an old wicker chair with a large pink cushion on it. Oh, he would love the little blue birds.

As Ele washed her brush in readiness to paint a tawny color on the bird's chest, she was disturbed by Featherstone. He sat bolt straight in the chair, his attention concentrated on something outside the window. At first, Ele thought he heard the wind and told him to settle down again, but when he arched his back and his fur stood on end, she grew nervous.

Her thoughts turned to that time before, when he had behaved strangely at the front of the house, and when the mist had appeared on the sitting room window. Coldness ran down her spine and she felt sick. It did not help when Feathers spat a low hiss and backed as far as he could into the rear of the chair, his eyes wild and alert.

At first, she didn't move. She was afraid, and some inner primeval instinct told her that if she kept still, whatever was out there might not know she was present. She sat motionless for a full minute, watching the glass, praying she would not see it mist up. She was just about to move again, when she heard something. It was a noise in the wind, a sound that did not belong to its natural symphony.

If someone asked her to describe what she heard, she couldn't. It was indefinable. She only knew that it was unnatural and didn't belong in the wind. The sound had a cadence to it that altered as the wind gusted. It was a wailing sound, barely audible but just there, and then it would turn and sound like muffled voices. But the voices were gone almost before she heard them. There was nothing for her reality to grasp on to. She wondered if someone real, someone corporeal, was stumbling around on her property and seeking help.

She stood as quietly as she could and advanced to the window to look out. She saw nothing, just dust and dried leaves being churned up in the newly laid courtyard.

A strange impulse overcame her, and she opened the studio door and went outside. Nothing looked unusual or out of place as she scanned the area around her. She watched as the wind took leaves and blew them all around. She had almost convinced herself that her imagination was on overtime, when something froze her to the spot. The wind suddenly grabbed leaves and forced them to dance in a tight circle that reminded her of a mini tornado. She saw it move to the center of the courtyard, almost outside her kitchen window, where it hovered and failed to move on. Reason told her it was not natural.

Ele shivered, not from the cold, but from something deeper within her. A feeling came over her, and she felt compelled to walk toward the circle of wind. As she did, her hair blew in all directions. Her actions were stupid. She should get out of the wind, but still she was drawn, as if her mind was no longer hers.

When she got to the point where the leaves orbited for too long in their bizarre way, they stopped their whirling dervish behavior and fell away, scattering in many directions.

And then it happened. She saw a shape pass so quickly in front of her she could barely make out what she saw. It was like a tight knot of circular air with a darkened composition that moved at head height. She would have reasoned that it was one of those strange anomalies of nature, but for the fact the object turned, and against the direction of the wind, returned back to pass again in front of her. Frozen in fear, Ele thought she was going mad. Could she see, in the speed and the blurriness of the shape, the distorted outline and features of a face?

The wind dropped before raging and buffeting again. Ele found power in her body and ran back to the studio to get Feathers, but he was gone. Habit made her turn the light out and bang the door shut before she sprinted back into the kitchen and slammed the door behind her.

## CHAPTER FIFTEEN

K iernan drew up in front of her home, turned off the car engine, and bent her head in exhaustion against the steering wheel. She should have stayed the night in Cambridge and driven home the next morning, but the thought of a second night away wasn't something she could stand. She was missing Ele.

It was almost midnight, pitch-black, and very windy as she grabbed her equipment out of the car and struggled up the stairs toward her front door. She should have made two journeys with the equipment, but instead she was burdened down like a donkey carrying camping gear on some archaeological expedition. She'd pay for this in the morning when her shoulders and neck ached. Still, she didn't care. All she wanted was a hot shower and her bed.

She also wanted to phone Ele. Despite her manic photo schedule, she had spoken to her yesterday, but it hadn't been enough. Today, she'd done nothing but think of her. She wanted to hear her voice again, to connect. Yesterday, Ele had told her of the bitter wind in Pegmire, and how it had put her off going to the church to do research. But she had planned to go today. Kiernan had tried to phone Ele this afternoon to see if she'd discovered anything, but despite leaving a message, Ele hadn't phoned her back. She hated not hearing from her, but figured she must have been at the church, or following up on another lead. Eager though Kiernan was to hear Ele's voice again, and to learn what she'd found, she recognized that the hour was too late to phone. Ele had been so weary when she'd left her last. She didn't want to disturb her. She needed her sleep. Kiernan would ring her tomorrow morning, first thing.

When Kiernan's head finally hit her pillow, she found she couldn't sleep straight away. Her thoughts were still dominated by Ele. She could see her laughing face, feel her touch, smell her perfume—experience that kiss. How she wanted to be with her tonight. She knew she was being silly, but not hearing from Ele unsettled her. Ele didn't seem the type to not return a call. If she'd been to the church this afternoon, she could still have phoned her this evening? A small part of Kiernan worried that everything might not be all right. Ele had seemed okay with her when they'd last spoken, and although the kiss hadn't been mentioned, the friendship had still been there. Had something else happened? Something ghostly? She shook herself. Ele was probably busy and waiting till tomorrow to ring *her*. It would be interesting to see who rang who first. Sleep finally claimed her.

It felt like minutes asleep before the sound of a buzzer rang in her ears, its sound unpleasant. She awoke with a start.

"Hold your horses, hold your horses!" Kiernan growled as she flung herself out of bed and then cursed when she stubbed a toe on a nearby chair. She had been in such a glorious and welcome deep sleep. Whoever woke her now had better have a damn good reason or they weren't going to celebrate Christmas.

The door buzzer continued its relentless noise, sounding louder in the night silence. Its persistence was irritating.

"Yes, yes, I hear you. I'm coming, I'm coming." Logic told Kiernan that her visitor couldn't hear her, but she said it anyway.

She squinted at the bedside clock and registered two thirty in the morning. Growling again as she wrapped her dressing gown around her, she shoved her feet into a pair of mules and then struggled in the semi darkness toward the door.

"Yes?" she mumbled into the intercom. A voice she knew well echoed back with urgency.

"It's me…Ele."

*Ele?* Kiernan didn't wait for an explanation. She hit the entry key and opened her front door. The electronic lock clanked as the main door below opened and Ele bounded up the steep stairs. She ran fingers through her hair, simultaneously realizing it was a waste of time. Only water and a hairdryer could improve her appearance after sleep.

As she flicked a table lamp on, Ele swept through the door looking like a witch's apprentice. Her hair was wild and unkempt, her makeup smudged. Under an unfastened jacket, she wore a heavy, navy blue cardigan with the buttons done up unevenly—as though at speed—hanging over a loose fitting pair of blue jeans with more holes in them than a cheese grater. Even her white sneaker laces were undone.

Kiernan closed the door before turning back to face Ele who was now leaning against a wall looking sheepish, realizing what an entrance she had made.

"Hi," Ele said between steepled fingers. "Bet you weren't expecting me."

Kiernan's earlier anger evaporated immediately to be replaced with concern. Whatever brought Ele here at such an hour, it had to be of the utmost importance, and seeing how flustered Ele was, she had a damn good idea what that might be. Kiernan knew better than to rush the explanation. Ele looked startled, like a horse that had just bolted and needed a reassuring hand to calm her. "Well, now you mention it," she said.

"You're thinking this is all a bit odd…" Ele stuttered.

"Understatement." Tenderly, Kiernan took one of Ele's cold trembling hands and led her over to a couch and planted her there. "But always a pleasure to see you," she added with light theatrical aplomb.

A few more table lamps later, and Kiernan could see how pale Ele was, the vision of someone in shock. She was certainly behaving that way. She seemed incapable of stringing two words together. Her entire body was shaking. She looked frozen and plunged her hands between her thighs for warmth.

Concerned, Kiernan grabbed a wool blanket she kept on a chair for cold evenings, and flung it around Ele. Ele took its ends and wrapped herself in it.

"I'm going to make a cup of hot chocolate and then you can tell me what's happened, okay?"

Ele nodded. Kiernan could see her fighting for composure. She was desperate to find out what was wrong, but knew a hot drink was needed first.

A few minutes later, Kiernan thrust the drink into welcome hands and sat beside her waiting patiently while Ele drank greedily. Ele gulped the drink, and Kiernan hoped she wouldn't scald herself. She watched Ele's unbrushed, messy hair fall toward the cup. Kiernan couldn't stop herself from sweeping it out of her face. Ele didn't even notice.

All the time, Kiernan waited patiently for Ele to calm down and be able to tell her what had happened. Her own mind was running riot. She knew this had to do with the haunting. What could make Ele this scared, this vulnerable? It had to be something worse than what had happened to the two of them that lunch. This was far more than ghostly breath on a windowpane. A chill ran down her spine as she at last saw Ele place the empty cup on the side table and turn to her.

"Oh, Kiernan." Ele sounded petrified. Her voice still shook.

"Take your time."

"This afternoon…" Ele pulled the blanket tighter around her. "I was in the studio, painting." She began to recount the whole saga of what had occurred outside her workspace. Kiernan saw the fear in her eyes. "I didn't imagine any of it. It happened. It was terrifying."

Kiernan's mouth went dry. This was the sort of stuff you read about in ghost stories, not the type of thing that happened for real. If she were honest, Kiernan had never believed in spirits, but she damn well did now. What was happening at Ele's was petrifying and nightmarish. Things were escalating. This latest turn had made Ele bolt in panic from her own home.

"Where have you been since this afternoon?"

"I ran into the house and hid in the sitting room. I crouched down by the side of the big armchair by the fire so I couldn't be seen from the windows. I couldn't move, Kier. All I could hear was the wind gusting outside. I was frightened to move out of the house in case whatever was there was waiting for me."

Kiernan heard the raw edge of fear.

"I've been there for hours, not daring to move," Ele continued. "It was only when the wind dropped tonight that I bolted for the car keys and drove over here to you." Ele seemed to be calming, and her breathing was less labored. "I arrived here just after ten but could see you weren't in. I've been driving around since. I didn't know what to do or where to go. I couldn't book into a hotel; my purse is still in the house."

She glanced up at Kiernan with such wanting. "You've no idea how wonderful it was to see your car here when I drove past again a few minutes ago."

They were close, and Kiernan could feel Ele's breath. It would have been so easy, so right, to lean in and kiss her. They had kissed before. Would it have been so wrong? But Kiernan held back. Ele was upset, and the last thing she needed was her crawling all over her. Kiernan still remembered the way Ele had behaved after their kiss. She had acted as if it hadn't happened. Kiernan wondered if she regretted it, or if she'd just been tired? She held back. These were questions to be answered later. Right now, Ele needed support.

"Whatever was there, Kier, it was using the wind. It was *in* the wind."

"It's okay. You're here now and safe." Kiernan put her arm around Ele and pulled her close. She could feel her trembling beneath the blanket. "Why didn't you phone me?" she asked.

"My cell phone is still in the studio and the landline—"

"—is over by the window," Kiernan finished. It was the same window where Stafford's breath had materialized. She wouldn't have wanted to go anywhere near it either.

"Oh, God, Kier. I'm so scared. Whatever it was, I swear it drew me out of the studio. It got into my mind and pulled me outside. I still don't know what I saw, but I know it was a face. I could see the shape—"

"Was it Stafford?" Kiernan interrupted. Her own sense of alarm was building inside, but she pushed it down for Ele's sake.

"I don't know. I could hear voices, but I couldn't tell you how many or whether they were a man's, or a woman's, or both. I've never been so petrified in all my life." Ele looked at her. "I can't go back there, Kier. I need to stay somewhere tonight."

Kiernan worried as she wrapped her arms tighter around Ele. Things were escalating at the old vicarage, and there seemed no way to stop it.

"You'll stay here as long as you have to until we get to the bottom of this." She hoped they *could* get to the bottom of it. This haunting was turning into a complex and alarming problem that held—for the moment—no solutions.

"Where's the cat?" Kiernan asked.

"Still there. I haven't seen him since he bolted out of the studio. He must be outside somewhere."

"Poor Feathers," Kiernan said.

"I thought you didn't like him?"

"I never said that."

Ele drew back and looked at her, frowning. "You don't have to. I can see it in your face."

"You're biased. That cat doesn't like *me*. I'm just reacting to that."

Kiernan feigned shock. The moment was presenting an opportunity for levity. Something desperately needed.

"He's a darling."

Kiernan shook her head as she listened to Ele defend the bloody thing.

"Why can't you two just be friends?"

Because he knows I like you, and he feels threatened, Kiernan thought. "He'll have to make the first move." She playacted defensive, and Ele rewarded her with a small smile. For the first time that night, her shaking had stopped.

"Have I said how thankful I am that you are here helping? I'm not sure I can cope with this."

"I'm not sure anyone can cope with this on their own." Kiernan tilted her head and cocked an eyebrow as she stated the obvious. "And yes, you've thanked me before, and it really is okay. I'm determined to sort this out, as much as you are."

"What are we going to do?"

*We.* That one word gave Kiernan such immense joy. She couldn't help smiling. But then she looked at Ele and realized how tired she was. There were dark circles under her eyes. A protective instinct swept over her. "You need to sleep, Ele. I think a hot shower and then bed. In the morning when we're rested, we'll think what to do next, but until then, try to put this out of your mind."

Ele looked at her as if she were insane. Kiernan raised her chin to the air. "Well, try anyway." She pulled Ele off the couch and led her to the guest bedroom. It wasn't where she wanted to leave her tonight. Kiernan wanted her in bed with her. She wanted to hold her close and let her know she was safe. But these things couldn't be rushed, and again, she reminded herself that now wasn't the right time. She thrust towels into Ele's arms. "Everything you need should be in the bathroom, but just holler if you want anything else."

When Kiernan finished locking up and putting all the sitting room lights out, she popped her head around Ele's bedroom door. She was already in bed and fast asleep with exhaustion. Kiernan crept up to the bed, whispered, "Good night," and switched the side light off.

When she'd climbed into bed earlier, it had welcomed her with its warmth, and she had eventually fallen into a happy state of oblivion. Now the bed felt cold and lonely, and she struggled to find sleep. Kiernan's mind was wide-awake and alert. She couldn't stop thinking of everything that had happened to Ele this afternoon. Now she understood why her calls had gone unanswered.

She mentally kicked herself. Intuition had told her something was wrong. If only she had driven past Ele's—dropped in on her way home to make sure all was okay. It would have been a detour, but not a huge one. Ele could have been *rescued* hours ago. But Kiernan had been exhausted, and desperate for sleep. Now her guilt gave way to other thoughts. They reminded her that Ele was in the room next to hers. So close, and yet so far. She longed to just hold her.

Kiernan pulled the covers over her head and told herself to shut up and go to sleep. But it felt good feeling this way about another human being. It had been too long.

## Chapter Sixteen

Ele arose late, and as she walked into the sitting room, she heard Kiernan moving around in the galley kitchen. "Good morning," she said as she peeped around the door and was welcomed by a genuine smile. "You look very industrious."

"Tea and some breakfast?" Kiernan asked, holding up a cup.

Ele dipped her head. She hadn't eaten since yesterday lunchtime and was starving. She couldn't hide the joy on her face when Kier planted a load of toast on the table in front of her as "something to be going on with." She thought briefly of grace and good manners and not appearing greedy, but she ignored the lot and ate ravenously. Never had tea and toast tasted so good.

"How do you feel? Did you sleep okay?"

Ele loved Kiernan's show of concern. "I slept well. I wasn't sure I would. Yesterday was horrible. But I feel better now." She looked across at Kiernan. "Thank you for all of this." She wasn't referring to breakfast. It was her kindness, her support—the way she made her feel again. Kier shrugged.

Sharing breakfast together, Kier then listened as she recounted what she had learned at the church earlier.

"John Stafford is buried there, but not his wife. I couldn't find any record of her. Given that her family took her home when she was ill, I suppose she's buried somewhere there. I now have no idea what it is the builders have disturbed or what to do next, Kier. We're lost."

"No. We're just not found," Kier said.

"You're so positive."

"You're too negative."

Kier smiled. "You'd be too after yesterday."

Kier nodded. "Could they have had a child?"

Ele gave it a quick thought and then dismissed it. "Dot would have said. That wouldn't have been hidden from her mother, would it," she added, not as a question.

"I know one thing, Ele, and you're not going to like it. We have to go back to the house today to find Feathers. If he's outside, he's going to be frozen."

Ele shivered. Featherstone was very much on her mind, and she was worried. She was sure he had not been in the house when she ran out, which meant he was still outside. He was not a night cat and he didn't do hunting in extreme conditions. He liked luxury and warmth. He wouldn't understand what was going on. Neither did she. However, as much as she loved him, the thought of returning home filled her with dread. At least Kier would be with her, and the wind had died down. She agreed, and resumed eating lethargically, her initial *joie de vivre* dampened.

"What's this?" she asked, holding yellow stuff on her fork.

"It's an omelet," Kiernan answered as she sipped tea from a bone china cup with pretty flowers on it.

"No, it isn't." Ele was dismissive. She had eaten many omelets in her life, and this was not of that family.

Kier placed her cup in its matching saucer and glanced at her, a mild look of desperation in her eyes. "Is it edible?"

"Well, yes…" Ele had already eaten half of the mystery substance. She felt guilty for mentioning it. "I just wondered if it was something wonderfully Irish that I've not been introduced to before."

"Hmm, did I mention I'm not gifted in the kitchen?" Kiernan looked at Ele apologetically. "Why don't you just go ahead and pretend that's what it is, an Irish omelet? I can promise you that everything in, whatever it is, is fresh." There was a wonderful lilt of gentle humor in Kiernan's voice, something Ele adored.

"The toast is marvelous," she said enthusiastically.

Kiernan gave a crooked grin and then studied the food in question on her own plate. She asked, "Are you sure this isn't an omelet?"

Ele shook her head, unable to hide her own amusement.

"I wonder what I've been eating all these years, Ele."

Soon after breakfast, they left for Ele's home.

Kiernan drove up to the front of the house, and already there was a light dusting of snow on the ground. It was always the same year after year; the snow seemed to sneak in during the quiet of the night, often unexpected.

As she parked the car close to Ele's front door, she heard Ele sigh.

"Oh, God." Ele had grown reticent as they'd driven closer to her house.

Kiernan wanted to chase her fears away, but wasn't sure how to. "Be brave. It'll be okay, and I'm here with you."

"And what will you do if Stafford materializes?" Ele said. Kiernan could see Ele didn't have the right amount of faith in her.

"I'll shout 'Boo.' That'll do it." She leaned toward Ele. "I can sort this all out if you want. You can just sit in the car."

Ele was already reaching for the door handle. "No. I need to get some overnight things and a change of clothing, and I must find Feathers. I know all the little places where he sleeps or hides. I just hope he's inside." She was worried, and it showed. "What if he's run off, Kier?"

Kiernan put her hand on Ele's and tweaked it. "We'll find him. He won't have gone far, and besides, I seem to remember he likes the ghost."

"Not after yesterday, he won't." Ele's face was ashen.

Kiernan didn't argue. She wanted to allay Ele's fears, but it wasn't working. Ele slowly, warily, climbed out of the car, but not before having a good look around her. Kiernan caught her anxiety like a contagion. She didn't like what Ele told her of yesterday, and for the first time, she sensed danger. Whether they could be in danger from a ghost remained to be seen. Theoretically, a ghost might not be a physical threat, but it could do a lot of damage to a person's mental composure. Kiernan was not keen to test theories.

She heard Ele calling Feathers inside the house, a continuous activity that led her to believe he was nowhere therein. Kiernan hopped out of the car and started calling too. Not that he was likely to come to her, but she would try. She looked toward the large greenhouse. In daylight, she could now understand how she mistook several old wooden seed boxes, a bag of opened compost, and a pile of terracotta pots with a cat perched on top for a shadowed man with frightening eyes. She scoffed at her foolishness. Ele must think her an idiot.

Stuffing her hands inside her jacket pocket, she shivered from the cold as she walked past the greenhouse. Beyond, she could see a small garden shed. The freshly fallen snow was virgin and nothing had walked across it in several hours. Regardless, she called out to Feathers and was about to return to the front of the house when she heard a small noise. She stopped and looked toward the shed; she called again, but the noise did not repeat.

Nothing ventured, nothing gained, she approached the shed with caution and pulled the thin wooden door open, hearing it creak as she peered into the darkness. It smelled musty and damp. She called Feathers again and heard a muffled meow, but she saw no movement. Now she bent and this time called his name attempting to put affection behind it. The ploy worked, and an empty potato sack moved as the cat appeared from beneath it.

He looked cold and vulnerable, his fur all puffed out, as he crept toward her. This was not a cat used to staying out all night. He couldn't understand why Ele wasn't there. Kiernan suffered a compassionate attack. She didn't think twice as she reached out and scooped him into her arms. He pushed himself close to her and began purring. She felt his cold fur against her face and the iciness of his front paws, now supported in her one hand.

"Poor Feathers," she said with surprised genuine affection. Could they be friends? "So, you're delighted to see me, eh?" The purr increased. "Never mind, my new friend. I'm delighted, too. I was worried about you." She walked back around the front and into the house. As she did so, she caught Ele coming down the stairs.

"Oh, Feathers..." Ele gushed, reaching out to be reunited with him.

Kiernan thought how lucky the cat was to be adored so much. "I'm impressed," she said.

"Don't be too overwhelmed," Ele said as she rubbed Feather's head. "This is only because I am the bringer of food, the Goddess of the Tin Opener. I am but the provider of love, affection, and fish."

It might have been true, but Kiernan noticed how Featherstone banished thoughts of food in favor of a hug. She was glad she had reunited them. "Should we bring him back with us?" Since Ele was going to stay at her place at least another night, it only seemed polite to ask.

"Hell, no." Ele put him down and moved into the kitchen to feed him. "He'll be happier here—inside—and as long as I..." She looked at Kiernan with eyes that said *we*. "...come over and feed him, he'll be okay."

Controlled relief surged through Kiernan. The unusual, temporary peace pact between Feathers and her was one thing. Welcoming him into her home was another. "I bet now you wished you had a cat flap."

Ele looked at Kiernan deadpan. "Absolutely not," she replied indignantly. "When I was growing up, we had one. You'd wake in the middle of the night to a crunching sound, and in the morning, you'd stand on something that had been disemboweled. I can't begin to tell you how disgusting that is."

"Any messages?" Kiernan changed the subject.

"Only yours. No others." Ele looked uncomfortable. "I think we should leave now."

Something has to change, Kiernan thought. Ele shouldn't be frightened out of her own home, and certainly not by a ghost who was old enough to know better.

CHAPTER SEVENTEEN

Ele sat on the floor in Kier's sitting room with her back against a cream covered couch, a glass of red wine in her hand while she listened to a rock band called Regurgitation. Music hammered her eardrums, and she could feel its vibration in the furniture around her. Somewhere to her right, she could hear glass tinkling with the sound waves. She was thankful that Kier's neighbors below were holidaying in South Africa. Kier was introducing her to this new band as a way to help her forget her frightening experience back home. Forget? After this album, she might never have another cogent thought again.

Seated beside her, Kier was oblivious to everything, her head tilted back and supported on the couch seat, eyes shut listening to every inharmonious cord. Every now and then, Kier moved a hand in the air as if she was conducting the music and she hummed out of tune. Ele laughed, not that Kier could hear her. Weren't the Irish all supposed to be natural musicians? It seemed nature had overlooked Kier.

She was facing the floor to ceiling glass pane, and everything inside the room was reflected back with clarity against the night darkness. Kier shared that it was one of her favorite places and that she had put a couch here so she could relax and watch the hamlet light up at night. Kier said it was peaceful, and Ele could only agree. She felt a sense of total serenity regardless of what Regurgitation was doing to her hearing system.

She loved music, and a memory reminded her that after Beth had died, she'd been unable to listen to it. That had been a loss, too. But music evoked emotion, and passion. She'd been unable to cope with it. Her grief, too raw.

She jolted as the music came to an abrupt halt and everything went tomb quiet. "Wow," she breathed out, breaking the stillness. Her ears fizzed. "I can't hear anything, and I think my brain's exploded."

"Yeah, great, isn't it?" Kier's rich, deep tones laced with infectious excitement pushed the silence away. She had opened her eyes and was looking at Ele in the reflection.

"Yeah." Ele felt young again, like a kid staying overnight at a best school friend's house. How many times had she done this in her teen years? Countless, she thought. They remained quiet for a minute before Ele added, "I should play this music at home. It might persuade John to stop haunting."

Kier sat up and leaned in close toward her. "You know, we could try that." Ele saw the playful twinkle in her eyes and felt her breath on her cheek. She caught herself looking at Kier's lips. Kier had such an effect on her.

She held her breath and wasn't sure if she was relieved or saddened when Kier resumed her previous position. Ele wondered if her face was red. She felt hot, but her reflection in the window gave nothing away. If it was, she hoped Kier would think it was the wine.

"I like being with you, Ele."

The words shocked her. Maybe she hadn't got away with it. Ele sensed the moment turning intimate, private. It was the way Kier spoke, the softness in her voice. "I like being with you, too," she answered. It was the truth. That day, before Stafford had tried to send her to an early grave, she'd done nothing but think of Kier, her thoughts fixated. She'd never felt so conflicted. To think such things in the house that she and Beth had shared.

"Ele, about that kiss."

Now she *knew* she hadn't got away with it. Kiernan must have seen her react. She heard the tension in Kier's voice, brought about by that nervous edging forward, in a new relationship, to see if the other feels the same way.

Ele's previous state of euphoria slid away fast and was replaced by nerves, and an unusual position of defensiveness. She wasn't prepared for this. Why did Kier have to ruin an otherwise perfect evening? "Yes, I know. I'm sorry. I shouldn't have done that." Sometimes she wished she hadn't. Other times, she was glad she had.

"I liked that you did." Yes. Ele could hear the intimacy in Kier's voice.

*Oh?* Her panic escalated. She had started a chain reaction with that kiss, and now she wanted it to stop. She floundered, not knowing what to say. She couldn't look at Kier.

"Did you like it?" Kier sounded patient. Caring. Gentle.

"Yes, I did." Her response was out before she could stop it.

"I wish you didn't look so disappointed when you said that." Kier spoke lightheartedly, but Ele could see her reflection. She looked disheartened.

"I don't mean to." She needed to explain. "I was so worried about you. I didn't think."

"You acted on impulse."

Ele hated hearing the doubt in Kier's voice. Now she looked at her. "Yes, I did." It sounded a terrible answer, but she didn't want to lead Kier on. She didn't want to make her think she was ready for any relationship when she herself didn't know. She was confused. If only she had more time. "But I liked it too," she repeated.

"But something's wrong." Kier wasn't asking, she was stating the obvious. Ele couldn't answer.

"Are we friends, Ele?"

Ele turned to Kier and looked her straight in the face. At last, something she did know the answer to. "Of course we are! How could you ever doubt that, Kier? I've only known you a short while, but you've become so dear to me, so valuable. Don't ever doubt that."

"I don't." Kier spoke with heartfelt meaning. "But you must know how I feel about you. It's taken me by surprise too. I only know that I want something more with you." Kier reached for Ele's hands. "The question is, do you want more?"

Kier's eyes searched hers. She knew they were looking for answers, but the longer she took to reply, the more she saw her disillusion build. It looked like a weight was bearing down on Kier, as if something fragile might break. Ele longed to chase that shadow away. She didn't want to hurt Kier. Maybe if she was honest, if she tried to explain the battle that was going on inside her?

"It's difficult for me, Kier. I know it's been a long time since Beth died, but I feel so divided. My emotions are all over the place. Beth was unique; we shared such a deep love. We were so right for each other, from the start." Ele thought back to how they had met at school when they were only eleven. The friendship had been instant. The love had grown later. "I'm just not sure I can do this, and I don't want to hurt you—lead you on—if I can't. Maybe Beth has spoilt me for anyone else."

"I understand, Ele. I do. That kind of deep love can't be swept aside as if it never happened. But I know this. You need to move on, whether with me, or someone else. The guilt and the fear of that step is natural, even after all these years, but you mustn't live your life in memories. You're too beautiful, too wonderful for that. You deserve all that life can give you. I think Beth would want that." Kier let her hands go. Ele hated it.

"I'm not rushing you, Ele. I just wanted you to know how I feel—that I like you very much—that I would like something more."

It was comparable to a physical blow for Ele when Kier raised herself off the ground and chose to sit on the couch, leaving her alone on the floor. The distance felt huge and she wondered what damage she had just caused. Kier looked crestfallen. Ele blamed herself. She was acting badly. She knew she had hurt Kier. It was a while before the silence broke.

"You know, it's just occurred to me why John Stafford is so intent on haunting *you*."

Ele took time to accommodate the shift in topic. "I assume it's because I live in the house, and because of something I've done, something I've altered," she said as she too, now rose and sat on the couch, allowing a graceful distance between them.

"No, it's way deeper than that." Kiernan rubbed her chin as she looked at her. "John Stafford has always been consistent. He's always been trying to communicate with you. He appears only in photos with you, or when you take them. You have always been the link, and that's what's been puzzling me all this time."

"Puzzling?"

"Think about it. If you were the ghost, and something needed changing or putting back, wouldn't you try to communicate with anyone likely to listen? He never appears in any photos I've taken without you around. *You* are the link."

"Why me, then?"

"It's because you have something in common with him. Something very important."

"Go on," Ele whispered.

"You have both loved very deeply. Both suffered. You have both lost the most important person in your life under incredible circumstances. He feels your loss. It's what draws him to you. The pain and sadness he would have suffered in that house, so have you. He knows you understand."

"And yet I can't help him." Ele felt hopeless. There was far too much hopelessness in the room this evening.

Kiernan drew her feet up under her on the couch. "Here is a man who had to leave the woman he loved, to fight in the Great War, and to experience the horror of the trenches. He is then injured and can't get home, and worse, comes to realize his wife probably thinks he's dead, but he can't do anything about that. When he does get home, he discovers that she has died of the influenza."

Ele saw how much Kier was affected.

"There's real tragedy in that. Oh yes, Ele, he talks to you because you are the one who understands his pain. You are the one who can resolve whatever it is that needs resolution."

"And he's getting angry and frustrated, Kier, and I don't know what to do about it."

*You are the one who can resolve whatever it is that needs resolution.* Kier's declaration was meant for the ghost, but it felt closer to home for Ele. There was so much she didn't understand, and much of it had nothing to do with John Stafford. All these memories and feelings about Beth that were resurfacing after all this time, and only since Kier's arrival. What did it all mean?

❖

That night, Kiernan could not sleep. She shifted and twisted in bed. Her mind kept replaying the entire evening over and over. She tried to analyze what was going through her head, rubbing her temples with her fingers.

She was falling in love with Ele. Perhaps she had been from day one? Sometimes love hit you in the face when you weren't expecting it. It was a love that was instant and powerful.

Chrissie had broken her heart and left her with the constant cross-examinations that kept her awake at night demanding if she had done anything wrong; if she could have changed the outcome. She knew now that nothing would have altered Chrissie leaving. She just hadn't been ready for commitment. Simple. True. But now Kiernan's heart was alive again, and it sang when she was with Ele. It sang when she wasn't. Yes, she was in love.

The evening had been magical and she'd been so happy. But then she had dared to speak of matters of the heart. She wished she hadn't. She wished she'd been more patient, but she longed to tell Ele how she felt. To see if Ele returned those feelings.

Kier *knew* that Ele did. All the signs were there; the touches, the stolen glances, that kiss. Ele had said the latter was an impulse. Maybe it was, but Kiernan reasoned that there was much more emotion behind it. How could Kiernan flesh out those feelings from Ele?

She'd told Ele that she was a friend, but told her too that she wanted more, and asked Ele if she did. She hadn't got the response she longed for. Instead, Ele had declared, with brutal honesty, that maybe "Beth had spoilt her for anyone else." That had stung. She remembered how Ele emotionally retreated after the kiss. Kiernan found herself wiping tears from her face.

She was up against a memory of infinite size. One that, over time, had taken on immense proportions, and evolved into idolatry and gilded existence. Beth was untouchable. How could she compete with her? Ele had placed her lost lover on a pedestal and was possessive of her memory. Yes, but Kiernan deduced, Ele had shared those memories with her and her alone. Was that cause for hope?

Kiernan understood the emotional hurdles Ele had to clear. How could she show Ele that the risk of love was worth it? She chastised herself. Was she being selfish, thinking that she was "the one?" But the risk was worth taking. She just couldn't show Ele that. That, if ever, would need to come from within her. After tonight, Kiernan felt the possibility slipping away.

Despite all her bravado, her own willingness to enter another relationship after Chrissie, she was still wary, still cautious. Kiernan knew she mustn't make the same mistake again—see what she wanted to see. The signs had been there with Chrissie, but she'd ignored them. Those commitment concerns were here now with Ele. She ignored them at her peril.

Maybe there was no future with Ele. Maybe it was all dead before it had even started.

In time, sleep claimed her, and when she awoke the next morning, the light snow had disappeared. She felt more stoic and managed to put away all emotional thoughts circling in her head. She would make no decisions yet, but she would tread carefully and not repeat past mistakes.

## CHAPTER EIGHTEEN

The next morning, she and Ele returned to the vicarage to feed Featherstone. There was no mention of the previous evening's revelations. It seemed to Kiernan that they were both in "containment mode." Perhaps because they were unsure what to do next? She knew there would be other conversations.

They found a note inside the door from Mary Marsh. She had found something that would interest Ele, and she could be contacted at the church most weekdays after one o'clock. They decided to waste no time and meet Mary later that day at Pegmire Church.

Kiernan found the woman fascinating. She guessed she was in her mid sixties and was a precise sort of person whose appearance was meticulously crafted. She imagined that Mary would inspect herself in a mirror every day before leaving an immaculate home. She would check every cardigan button was done up, and that the small handkerchief just visible from a pocket was neatly folded. Mary wore her glasses around her neck, and they hung on a shiny, delicate gold chain. Her hair, still brown and without any visible gray, was tied in a perfect bun.

"As soon as I heard the name, I recognized it," Mary said amiably as the three of them stood in the vestry. She raised a small pocketbook to consult notes that were written in very minute, precise handwriting. Kiernan smiled.

"The records show that Captain Stafford's wife, Harriett, died of influenza in August nineteen eighteen, and that she was buried at St. James Parish Church in King's Cliffe, Northamptonshire." Mary licked a finger and flicked over a page. "Her family lived in Thrapston, her father a practicing attorney. That sort of money would explain it."

"Explain what?" Ele asked.

"How they managed to get the body exhumed and moved down here."

Kiernan couldn't hold her excitement. "You mean Harriett and John Stafford are buried together?"

"Yes." Mary seemed pleased with herself and her findings. "The body was exhumed by the family sometime during nineteen nineteen, and her body was brought down here so that her final resting place could be with her husband. Of course, exhumations weren't regular happenings, but they weren't totally unheard of. I suppose hearts and regulations were a little more giving at that time because of the war. So many people lost their loved ones. Those who didn't fight or who survived wanted to see things were done decently, as it were."

Mary kept putting her glasses on and off her face, and Kiernan wondered if the very particular woman wasn't just a little vain. Mary bent over the wooden table and picked up some papers, and then put the glasses back on.

"All of the documentation referring to the exhumation still exists. It wasn't something that had occurred here before, so as a unique event, it's probably why the paperwork has survived. I don't think it's ever happened here since. Anyway, I have a photocopy of the main record, which shows Harriett Anne Stafford was buried here in October nineteen nineteen." She passed the photocopy to Ele. "I hope this has helped."

"It has." Kiernan genuinely believed it had, if only to clarify that the haunting had nothing to do with the Staffords' final resting place. "I have to say you're very good at this. Have you done it for a while?"

Mary seemed to enjoy the compliment. "I've always been in research. I was a university librarian until I retired four years ago. I'm used to analytical investigation and empirical evidence in the formulation of study. I was immensely pleased when the vicar said he needed me, well, not exactly *me,* but my skills. He's overwhelmed with people requesting ancestral information or historical detail about Pegmire and the church. He asked for volunteers to help. I was glad to step in. Retirement has bored me rigid."

Kiernan couldn't stop grinning. Now she understood where Mary's methodical, precise nature came from.

"Of course, the task is immense," Mary said in a hushed voice, as if sharing a secret. "Previous ecclesiastical members may have been touched by divine inspiration, but their abilities to keep records are nothing short of appalling. It isn't that the information isn't here, it's just discovering where 'here' is." She laughed at her joke. "But I enjoy the challenge and procuring data."

Mary patted the table in front of them. "Ah, I almost forgot. If you're interested, I can show you roughly where the two of them are buried. The gravestone has gone I'm afraid, but I can point out their resting place within a few yards."

"We'd love that." Kiernan took the lead. Ele's disappointment was written all over her face, and her mind was elsewhere searching for other *haunting* possibilities.

They followed Mary outside, and she stopped at the north side of the church where much of the land was cleared and no gravestones remained. She pointed to the general vicinity.

"They rest close to here." Her hand hovered over a small area, and she turned thoughtful. "Wonderful to know they are buried together, that the family cared enough to reunite them in death." She faced them. "Do you know the outbreak of that virus killed over seventy million people, three percent of the world's population, more than died in the Great War itself?"

Kiernan shook her head. "I know John Stafford died on the third of January nineteen nineteen, and yet, he wasn't buried until the eighteenth of February. What would the reason be for that?" Ever since Ele had told her this information, she had wondered why it had taken so long to bury the man. Had there been suspicious circumstances surrounding his death that required an inquest or autopsy?

"That's an easy one," Mary said confidently. "The winter of nineteen eighteen has gone down in the records as a particularly bitter one. There was very heavy snow, and the ground froze like cement. Unlike today when we have mechanical diggers, then we relied on two good men with shovels to dig the graves. Most of the good 'young' men were still overseas, either deceased or waiting to sail home. Gravediggers during the war tended to be men well past their best. In nineteen eighteen and into early nineteen nineteen, the church had to wait for a sufficient thaw before anyone could be buried. Many others researching their family around that period have asked the same question."

"So, no other reason for the delay?" Kiernan continued her line of inquiry.

"None. The records and death certificate are quite clear that Captain Stafford died of complications brought about by his war injuries."

Mary Marsh was thorough in her research, and they both thanked her as they left the church and walked back to the car.

"I can feel your depression," Kiernan said once they left the church grounds.

Despite the cold, Ele stopped walking and faced Kiernan. She shrugged. "What now? John Stafford's ghost isn't going away."

It wasn't, and Kiernan tried to lift Ele's glumness. "What do we know?" She started to summarize in no particular order. "We know the haunting started when the building works commenced and that Stafford is always looking or pointing toward the general area outside the kitchen, by your studio, where the builders were.

We know the ghost *is* John Stafford and that he and his wife are buried together in the church. We know they had no children." She caught Ele looking at her unimpressed.

She felt helpless. "Are we sure the builders found nothing unusual while they were working there?" It was a feeble question, but she was clutching at straws.

"Roger would have told me. Besides, I was around most of the time, and I'm sure I'd have noticed."

"But you were trying to avoid the young builder who was lusting after you." Kiernan imagined how the youngster would have tried to impress Ele and have dreamed of starting a relationship with her. The poor besotted fool.

"True." Ele seemed despondent.

"Is it worth talking to Roger again? Double-checking?"

Ele said she would ask, but Kiernan knew she wouldn't. She was just being polite, but she did mention that she needed to contact him anyway with regard to seeing his wife, Joan.

Ele's face creased with worry when she spoke of Roger's wife, and Kiernan wanted to ask more, but the weather was raw and they were both cold. It was another conversation for later.

## CHAPTER NINETEEN

E le stayed at Kiernan's a few days more, but after four nights away, she knew it was time to go home and face whatever waited for her. She also felt guilty about Feathers. He was becoming a "home alone" victim, and she could see the normally cool and aloof cat, who faked a joy for independence, was disturbed by her absence. This wasn't fair on him.

She was dealing too with a gnawing feeling that she was overstaying her welcome. Kier had not said or done anything, and Ele considered this absence of output was indicative of the problem. Since their sharing of matters of the heart a few nights ago where she had revealed she wasn't sure she could move forward beyond Beth, Kier had become less open, and more reticent. She wasn't any less friendly, any less capable of holding warm conversations into the early hours of the morning. Kier just wasn't quite the same—as if she held back. And as the days marched forward, Ele sensed an important distance growing between them—something deeply personal. Kier was not her old self.

Ele wondered if she was imagining all this. Was she thinking too much? Maybe this was all in her head and wrong. As the days had progressed, she'd felt the time drawing closer when she would have to go home and face whatever waited for her. Nothing had happened each day as she and Kier had returned there to feed Feathers. But she didn't think Stafford would have disappeared, and she dreaded what he might do next. She and Kier were still laughing and co-existing well. They were sharing other "neutral" less emotional parts of themselves. But she realized it was more the discovery of friendship, not the already hinted blossoming of something better. Something quiet inside her missed that.

She cursed herself. She had been heavy handed that night and blurted things that had the power to hurt. She could have just asked Kier to slow down—to give her time. That would have given her the space she needed to work out what she really wanted. She still wasn't sure, but she felt she had hinted too much that there was no hope. That wasn't true. At least she didn't think it was.

She cursed again. Ten years! You've had ten years to sort this out. How much more time do you need?

She packed her belongings and walked into the sitting room where Kier was reading a photography magazine. As she looked at her, a wave of emotion rose, and she realized how much she was going to miss the closeness of Kier's company. These past few days had spoilt her. "I owe you so much, Kier."

Kier looked up and smiled. "No, you don't. You'd be doing the same for me if I had a ghost, which mercifully, I don't." The way Kier's eyes feigned thankfulness raised a laugh from her. Laughter always came easily now when she was around Kier. Something desperate inside her worried that she wouldn't see enough of her anymore. A plan sprang into her head.

"Kier, I want to take you out for a meal to say thank you for putting up with me."

She watched Kier shrug. "That's not necessary. I haven't done all this to get a free meal, regardless of how bad my cooking is." It was a reply laced with humor, but Ele noted that the levity didn't rise to Kier's eyes.

Ele would not take no for an answer. "I insist. I know this fantastic country pub outside Alcester. They do great food and are renowned for their fish and chips. I've been looking for an excuse to go back there, and you're it. Just say yes, Kier!"

Thankfully, Kier folded. "Since you put it like that, I accept." Kier put the magazine down and rose. "Why don't you let me follow you home and make sure everything is all right?"

All morning, Ele had been adamant that she return alone even though Kier kept volunteering. Ele won the argument, but Kier's insistency pleased her. It gave her hope that maybe she hadn't ruined everything.

"Shall we do dinner the day after tomorrow, Thursday evening? Is that all right with you?"

"It is." Kier appeared happy.

"Great. In that case, why don't I drive here and pick you up? I almost pass your door, and it seems daft to take two cars."

Kier shifted awkwardly, and after a moment's hesitation, she said, "No, Ele. I'll drive there myself. I've an appointment with a potential client over that way so I'll meet you there, say about seven o'clock?"

Ele's nugget of hope faded. She knew something wasn't right. Yesterday, Kier had said she didn't have any other commitments this side of Christmas. Ele had the strongest sense that she was being evasive. She mentally thumped herself. She was thinking like a pubescent youth with all her insecure emotional doubts. Kier had either forgotten to mention the business arrangement or was looking for some space. Ele *had* been leaning on her a lot. Maybe she was hypersensitive about returning home.

They agreed on a time and parted with a hug. Kier made her promise that if anything unpleasant happened at the house, she was to ring straight away. Kier would drive over. When Ele climbed into her car, she forced the negative thoughts from her mind. She had something important to do when she got home.

Despite the house being empty for most of the week, as Ele opened the front door, she felt her home's warm embrace and welcome. It was like the house knew she was coming home for real this time, not a fleeting visit, and that it missed her. Feathers certainly had and ran down the stairs meowing. She was wanted.

She walked into the kitchen and deposited a few groceries she had bought on the way home, before feeding Feathers and letting him out. Then she wrapped herself up warmly and put on a thick pair of gloves and a wool hat before walking outside to her studio—the area where she had been when she had seen the manifestation.

Everything was quiet as she looked around her. It was so different now from the last time she had stood here. She walked over to the area where the leaves had drawn her. There she waited, expecting something to happen, but nothing did. She took a deep breath and began to talk.

"John Stafford?" she called out. "John Stafford!" she said with more urgency. "I know you're here." Still nothing happened. All she could hear was the dullness of her own voice reverberating off the brick buildings surrounding her.

"I want you to listen to me." She was amazed at the sound of her voice. It sounded authoritative and calm, not like she felt inside. "I know who you are, and I know you lost Harriett under terrible circumstances. I know where you and your wife are buried together, and I know that you are here for a reason that I, as yet, do not understand. But you have to stop frightening me like you did the other day. It isn't helping, and it will only make me run. Whatever it is you need, I am looking, and I am trying to understand."

Ele bit her lip as she stopped and listened. Still, she heard nothing. It occurred to her that if anyone was secretly watching her, besides the ghost, they would think she was barking mad, standing in the cold, talking to herself.

"I'm open to gentle clues, John, and I do mean gentle." She found herself exhaling heavily, nervously. "I am determined to find out what's wrong, but you have to be patient, and you have to trust me."

Had she been expecting something miraculous to happen? Had she expected to hear someone unseen whispering the missing clues in her ear? Nothing awful or eerie occurred, and in the end, she walked back into the kitchen and shut the door. She just hoped John Stafford was listening.

As she closed the door, Ele glanced back in time to see Feathers outside, playfully running round in circles near the spot where the leaves once danced.

The next day, Ele walked the mile and a half stretch down into the village of Pegmire and beyond to the small hamlet where Roger and his wife, Joan, lived.

Ele was in awe at the wonder of nature and how it could take her breath away. She was in a fairyland scene of white. It was not snow, but a sparkling layer of ice crystals on everything. Every treetop, every twig, the gates and gateposts, the blades of grass— everything was glistening silvery white.

Hoarfrosts were rare, but when they came, you reached for the camera. This picturesque vista was the scene of many a beautiful Christmas card, but it came at a price. Though pretty, a hoarfrost was dangerous and lethal for motorists and pedestrians. When they arrived, they were usually accompanied by freezing fog and black ice. Under normal circumstances, Ele would not have ventured out, but she had a promise to keep.

Her complimentary copies of her book on British woodpeckers had arrived from the publisher. After running her hands proudly over its cover and feeling fit to burst at the fruits of her labor, she knew she wanted to take a copy to Joan today. She penned a few heartfelt words inside the cover, and after wrapping up warm, walked into the village to see her instead of driving. Though the foot journey would take her a good hour, she thought it safer than the car, and cherished the benefit of exercise.

It was also a way to keep her mind from doing overtime. She had not heard from Kier in the last twenty-four hours, and although there was no reason why she should, she had hoped to get a phone call. She couldn't stop the little niggling sense that all was not well between them.

The ground was frozen, and she heard it crunching beneath her feet. The air was so cold, it made her cough as she breathed, and she was forced to wrap her scarf around her face. But it was beautiful and Ele didn't care.

As she walked up the short pathway that led to Joan's semidetached house, she looked at the crystallized spider webs linking a couple of small bushes. Every minute web of lace could be seen clearly, and she thought how clever the spiders were, how intricate their labor.

Joan opened the door and welcomed her inside. Although still plump, she had lost weight and her clothes seemed too large. She looked tired and haggard.

That morning, when Ele phoned Roger to see if a call today would be convenient, he told her that things were still no better, and if anything, Joan's condition was getting worse. The nightmares were increasing, her sleep diminishing, and her agoraphobic behavior was worsening. She would not go outside, and now believed she was being watched by someone.

It was one of the first things that Ele noticed as she entered Joan's lounge. The curtains to the back window that highlighted the pretty garden with all the bird feeders, were pulled close. Joan must have caught Ele looking.

"I don't open them. It keeps the heat in."

Ele knew this wasn't true. She lost count of the times Joan and Roger invited her to the house after Beth died. The couple had pulled her into the center of their family until she was able to stand on her feet again. It had taken some time. Ele knew that the view outside and into the garden was the most precious of things to Joan whose objectives in life were homemaker, cook, and bird watcher. When she wasn't doing the first two, you would always find her in the garden or at this window watching the different species of birds that visited the myriad of feeders she had hanging all over.

Ele smiled and nodded. She said nothing, for there was nothing to be said. Furtively, she noted the dust on the mantle above the fire and the thin coating on other furniture. The carpet, though clean enough, needed a vacuum. At face value, none of what she saw meant much, and yet it did. Joan's home was normally like a show house. She and Roger did not have much, as they had chosen to spend what little they had in providing their children with the best education, and that meant university. Seeing Joan like this hurt Ele. This was not the Joan she knew and loved.

"I've brought you a present." Ele sat and pulled a wrapped package from her handbag. Joan sat opposite her, and when the small gift was thrust into her hands, Ele watched the dawning recognition fall on Joan's wan features before she started removing the paper eagerly.

"Is this what I think it is? Oh, my word." Joan's surprise and joy was genuine. "Your book. I told Roger I was going to buy it as soon as it became available."

"Well, now you don't have to, Joan. I wanted you to have a copy before anyone else because I know how much you love birds."

Joan was overwhelmed and grasped the book to her chest, occasionally looking at the cover.

"I've written something inside it for you," Ele added and watched the interest on Joan's face as she flicked through the first few pages.

Joan must have read Ele's inscription several times because it took her a while before she spoke again. Eventually, she looked at her with tearful eyes. "Ele, this is beautiful and all for me. You've no idea how wonderful it is. This brings joy to my heart. You're so kind. You didn't need to."

"Yes, I did. You and Roger...I owe you both so much. What you did after Beth—"

"What we did was what any good folk would do," Joan said with the most energy Ele had seen since she'd arrived. "We were proud to be there for you and grateful that you let us."

Ele was humbled and took hold of Joan's hands. "I love you both so much. You know that, don't you?"

"Oh, humbug." Embarrassed, Joan rose from her chair. "Why don't you let me put the kettle on and make you some tea?"

It had always been tea and sympathy with Joan. She would plant a pot of tea between them, and then tell Roger to disappear and "go fix something" while the two of them would chat. In the old days, it was always Ele who talked and Joan, kind Joan, who listened.

Now their roles were reversed, and Ele hoped the magic pot of tea might let Joan open up. But she didn't, and Ele chose not to push. They ended up discussing all manner of things, but never anything regarding Joan's ill health and her nightmares.

"Will you do another book?" Joan asked.

Ele nodded.

Joan's face lit up again with avid interest. "Not the kingfishers?"

"I think so," Ele whispered as if they were hatching a scheme not yet to be spoken of. Joan slapped her hands in front of her in delight.

"I'm still in the research stage and haven't written anything yet, but I've started the watercolors." Ele found it so wonderful to be talking to someone who loved a hobby as much as she did.

"Can I see them sometime?"

The only time Joan seemed like her old self was when she was talking about birds. Ele was happy to encourage this. Maybe Joan would open up to her at another visit, after another pot of magical tea. "I'll pop down soon, weather permitting, and show you what I've done."

As she waved good-bye to Joan, she was overwhelmed with sadness. Joan was one of those people she really cared about, one she didn't see enough of. She would change that and start visiting again more often. She was also aware that Roger was praying she might be able to nail what was bothering Joan, and to banish his fears. Ele had not managed to do either.

## CHAPTER TWENTY

The Neville Arms public house sat out in the middle of the English countryside nestled between Alcester, a small ancient Roman market town, and Droitwich, once famous for its spa. There weren't many houses around, and it was one of those places that never looked too busy and yet it had a healthy trade, due in no part to its location at a main road intersection and the fact it had added good pub food to increase its clientele.

Ele sat in her car in the pub car park and waited for Kier. She studied the quaint old country building with its external floodlights on, pushing the night darkness away. It had been a while since she'd last been here, but it hadn't changed much. It still appealed.

She fiddled with the car keys in her lap and knew she was uptight. She had done a lot of self examination since she'd last seen Kier. It reminded her that her life was safe, but she had nothing to show for it. As things were, Beth would never let her down. Was that enough anymore? She was recognizing that safe was nice, but not good.

Kier's car pulled in, and Ele couldn't stop smiling as she walked briskly over to her and linked her arm with affection in hers. She'd spoken to her once on the phone since leaving Kier's, and though friendly, she still sensed she was holding back.

As they moved toward the back entrance, she chattered away about the excellent food the pub served. In particular, the fish and chips that arrived on the plate wrapped in faux newspaper.

All the time, her heart leapt. She had been looking forward to this for days, counting the hours till she saw Kier again. These last two days she had been lonely, and memories of Beth had not filled the gap.

They sat in a corner away from the main throng of patrons. She could see Kier had missed her too and she hoped they could move on, that she could put right what she had said that dreadful night.

A waitress arrived and took their order as Kiernan asked her how she'd discovered the place.

"I was still doing my early morning show, and we were running a series about English towns and their heritage. Droitwich Spa was on the list, and I came here to interview historians and some locals about the place.

"I fell in love with the town straight away. It's nothing special to look at, but its small size appeals to me, and there are some very old medieval houses around. You can smell its history. Did you know Droitwich is sat on a massive deposit of salt?" she asked.

"That important fact has slipped me by."

Kier's feigned shock of surprise, her wide open eyes, brought Ele relief. The welcome return of Kier's penchant for humor meant things couldn't be too bad between them. Could they? The tension she'd felt before Kier's arrival began to seep away, and she continued her account. "Its brine contains ten times more salt per gallon than seawater, rivaled only by the Dead Sea. Not bad going for a small town. The Romans occupied the area, as salt was their prized commodity."

"Clever Romans. Isn't this fascinating?"

"Oh, stop it." Kier was playing with her now, talking as if Ele were describing ditch water. "I think it's interesting, even if you don't."

"I never said that."

"I can tell what you're thinking."

"And you called me a geek!"

They smiled. "Anyway," Ele said, "I brought Beth here to visit, and we found this pub."

The minute she said that she saw a strange shadow cross Kier's face. It was gone before she could blink, but she knew she'd seen it. Kier changed the subject.

"Any strange happenings?" Kier seemed relaxed again as she rested her chin on one hand.

Ele shook her head as their drinks arrived. "None at all, and I'm not complaining. I've needed this respite to get my nerves back in order."

"And are they?"

Ele sipped her wine. "Yes, until the next John Stafford moment." Though her answer was lighthearted and given with a smile, she couldn't keep the apprehension out of her voice. Her nerves were finitely balanced, and she knew the slightest oddity at home would throw them out of kilter again. By nature, she was a strong-minded, independent woman not given to nervous disposition. She hated how vulnerable the haunting made her feel. She felt a warm hand cover hers.

"I know. Maybe I shouldn't have spoilt the evening by reminding you."

Intense eyes full of compassion stared at her, and the caring remark reminded Ele that her ghost, while he robbed her of calm, had brought her Kier. In some small way, perhaps she should be thankful to him. "It's good to talk, and if I can't talk to you about this, then who?"

Her words resonated in her head and she knew they meant more than face value. They were true. Kier wasn't just anybody. She was special. She was the only person Ele wanted to share her innermost thoughts with. The only other one she'd done this with in her life had been Beth. It didn't feel so wrong now that she might want to do this with someone else—with Kier. She looked across the table and saw Kier's eyes flicker. Ele dared to hope she understood the subtext of her message. But the moment was broken as the waitress returned with their food. Kier removed her hand. Ele missed its warmth, its quiet connection, and support.

For the next half hour, their discussion was on the quality of the food, of what they thought of the house wine, and of the pub. Ele ordered another wine; Kier declined. Maybe it was the drink and the fact that Ele was calmer that other plaguing thoughts kept vying for her attention. Try as she might, she could not push them from her mind entirely.

"You seem worried," Kiernan said. "If your ghost is behaving himself, has something else happened?"

What was it about Kier and her ability to read her mind? She acknowledged Kier's astuteness with a raised eyebrow and then thought about what she said next. She did not break people's confidences, and certainly not Roger's, but she knew she needed to talk to someone, to share her worries. She made a conscious decision to talk to Kier about Joan.

"It's very upsetting to see Joan like this, so unlike her usual self. She was my shoulder when Beth died and would listen to me for hours. We grew close, and still are. I was hoping she'd open up a bit and talk to me, but she didn't."

"And no one knows what's causing her problems? Doctors?"

Ele shook her head. "Roger is convinced she's losing her mind. I think she believes this too, and that possibility is making everything worse. She tried so hard to hide it from me, Kier, but she looked drained and lost. It would help if she could get a decent night's sleep. When she tries, she has nightmares. Roger is beside himself with worry, and I can see why. Joan's whole life is changing."

"It could be one of those winter depressions people get. You know, not enough sunshine and vitamin D. I hear it sends some people loopy. They have to sit in front of those special lights for hours a day to combat the blues," Kier said.

Ele appreciated her compassion. "I wish it was that simple. The awful thing is that she doesn't have anyone she can talk to—

that she *wants* to talk to—not like I have with you." She paused as she saw that strange look in Kier's eyes again. A look that said she'd spoken something she shouldn't? "But thank you for listening." The topic was heavy and she had said enough. "What did you think of the hoarfrost?"

Kier's face brightened. "Stunning. I grabbed a camera, hopped in my car, and drove around taking photos most of the day. The view from my place was incredible. I wanted to phone you and tell you to get over."

"Why didn't you? I'd have come, you know." She couldn't hide her disappointment. For a moment, she thought Kier looked disappointed too, as though she had missed something special.

"If I'd done that, it would have stopped you seeing Joan, and that was more important," Kier reasoned. It did not make Ele feel better. "Besides, I thought the drive over might be dangerous. The roads were covered in black ice."

"And yet you drove around taking photos," Ele said as Kier forked a piece of fish and ate it. She changed the subject. "How did your business appointment go today?"

"Appointment?" Kier looked at her blankly.

"The one you said you had over here today, which is why you didn't need me to give you a lift?"

Kier frowned and looked down at her plate awkwardly. "Oh, that. It went okay." Kier seemed preoccupied with what little food was left on her plate. Ele probed.

"What is it about?"

"Nothing much. It's a possible photo opportunity next year."

"Something interesting?" The more she asked, the less Kier wanted to talk about it. She wasn't imagining it. Kier was uncomfortable, and the intense eye contact present until now, disappeared.

"No. It's more a private thing…for one of the groups. They don't want me to say too much. You know how private some of these folks can be."

Kier was being evasive, and Ele knew it. There had been no meeting. She had sensed this the other day and couldn't understand it.

"This was a wonderful idea, Ele. You were right about the food. I'm so glad we've come here."

Ele recognized Kier's abrupt change of subject. "It was the least I could do after all your hospitality. I hope I didn't overstay my welcome." Had she? But the answer she received was swift enough, and Kier seemed at ease again.

"You did not. I can't think of any better houseguest, Ele. And if anything sinister reoccurs at the house, you know there's always a bed for you."

"Thank you."

The waitress returned and removed their empty plates. She asked if they wanted drinks. Ele went to order another wine, but Kier interrupted, sending the waitress off for two coffees.

"Best not have another. You're driving. I'd hate anything to happen to you on the way home." Kier placed her hand over hers again. Small electric shocks ran through her body.

"Like what?" she said.

"Like being breathalyzed and charged with drunk driving."

"Nothing more?" Ele couldn't hide her disappointment. She didn't know what she wanted Kier to say, but this wasn't it.

"Or being wrapped around a tree."

Still not the answer Ele might have preferred—something more intimate, like not wanting to lose her—but it would do. It showed Kier's concern for her safety.

In no rush to leave, they continued talking as if they had not seen each other for months, and time sped by. It was the sudden quietness of the pub and the fact they were the last couple there that made Kier indicate they should go.

As they moved through the deserted narrow passageway that led back out into the car park, they brushed against each other, and Ele thought she sensed Kier slow. Instinct laced with desire made her reach out and pull Kier toward her, touching the side of her face with a hand. It was a bold move. Kier didn't resist.

Ele leaned in and kissed her. This time she knew it wasn't impulse. Kier responded as the warmth of their lips and their tongues intermingled. Kier moaned. "Beth," Ele whispered before drawing back, horrified. Kier stiffened like a statue. In the subdued lighting, Ele saw the look of hurt on Kier's face before she turned and walked toward her car.

Ele ran and caught her by the arm, forcing her to look at her. "Kier, I'm sorry. It was a slip."

"I can't do this, Ele. Not again." Kier's voice was raw.

Ele was mortified, she felt sick. How could she have said Beth's name? "It's the wine," she tried to explain, but its reasoning was weak and valueless. Kier looked crushed, and it was all Ele's fault. The evening had gone so well and now she had ruined it. Kier's initial distance had faded and Ele had sensed them drawing closer. And now she had done this?

"Ele, you called me Beth."

"It was a stupid slip, that's all."

"No, not all." Kier looked tormented. "I won't lie. I'm in love with you. But—it's Beth." Ele saw the misery in her eyes as she tried to explain. "You kiss me tonight, but tomorrow you'll change. Like before."

"Before?" Ele didn't understand.

"That kiss. The one after we left Dot's. It was so good. We connected, but after, it was as if you wished you hadn't kissed me. You became detached. And then at my place, you told me you acted on impulse."

"But—"

"You blow hot and cold, Ele. And I understand. It's Beth and her memory. You're stuck in the past with someone I can't compete with. Even tonight…" Kier pointed to the pub. "This is where you brought her. She's still part of you, and she comes between us. I feel her all the time." Kier looked exasperated. "It's not your fault, or mine. It's just life. But I can't do this again. I can't keep waiting and hoping you're going to change. I won't play second fiddle again. With Chrissie, it was her career. With you, it's Beth." Kier let out a huge sigh as she opened her car door and climbed in. "I'm sorry," she said before she drove away into the darkness.

For a few minutes, Ele stood not knowing what to do. When the cold started to bite, she pulled her coat tightly around her, climbed into her vehicle, and started the engine. She didn't drive away immediately. She sat, fiddling with a ring on her finger, listening to the motor whir. She looked down. It was the ring Beth had given her.

❖

Kiernan drove like a lunatic down narrow country lanes that were a shortcut home. Loud music filled her car, but Kiernan wasn't listening. It was there only to stop her thinking. God, what had just happened? The music wasn't working so she turned the volume up to its maximum capacity.

She rounded a bend and felt the back wheels skid as she hit a straight piece of road and drove faster. The car's temperature gauge showed it was below freezing outside, but Kiernan already knew this, her breath was crystallizing inside the still cold vehicle.

On the side of the road, she saw the yellow box on a pole—a speed camera—but she didn't care and didn't slow down. As she passed it, she looked in her rear mirror to see if the box flashed, the sure sign she would get a fine through the post within a few weeks. But it didn't. She scoffed. All the cutbacks from councils struggling in the recession; not many speed boxes actually functioned these days.

A little too cocksure, she entered a bend at the bottom of the straight road too fast and skidded again. This time her luck deserted her, and she felt her control of the car go. The car skewed wildly.

The back wheels hit the grass verge first, and the car slid sideways off the road. Kiernan shut her eyes from the inevitable. The car bumped and banged beneath her. She waited for the big hit. But it never came. Seconds later, the car was at a complete halt. She opened her eyes and saw a huge oak tree in front of her.

Kiernan staggered from her car, slowly, unable to stop shaking. Using the bonnet for support, she edged toward its front. There was not room for a human hair between her car and the tree, but neither object was touched.

She drew a hand up to her mouth and breathed out, hearing the unnatural panting sound she made. To her left was a huge field hedge, and before it, a deep ditch. She had avoided the latter by less than an inch and now the car rested precariously on the edge. Moving around the vehicle, she saw no damage and furtively looked up and down the road to see if anyone had seen what she'd done. The road was dark and quiet, an eerie stillness to it.

Carefully, she climbed back into the car and turned the key. She half expected it to be a dead engine, but it didn't let her down and she couldn't hide her joy when the car started. She placed the gear in reverse and was amazed when the car moved back. Less than ten seconds later, she was back on the road and driving at a more sedate speed.

Back home, the first thing Kiernan did was go into the kitchen where she poured herself a large, neat whiskey. Despite the car, in time, pushing out a huge amount of heat, she was still unable to stop shaking. Just how close had she come to having a nasty accident and possibly one she might not have walked away from? The answer was too horrid to contemplate.

She threw off her fleece and walked over to the large glass window at the bottom of her sitting room, allowing the warmth of the drink and home to saturate into her bones. The lights of the streets and houses lit up against the darkness of the night. It was such a pretty view. But her attention was on her reflection. There was a strange look on her face that she didn't recognize. It should have been shock, but it wasn't. It was because of what had happened at the pub.

Her body had reacted to Ele's kiss, her skin turning sensitive, her desire instant. But then Ele had called her Beth. Kiernan hung her head and groaned. Her heart ached for how much she loved Ele. What was not to love? But the cruelty was that Ele loved someone else. Someone untouchable. Someone perfect. An entity she could not compete with. Ele still wore a ring on her wedding finger. She kept seeing the pain on Ele's face as she had withdrawn from her embrace and run into the night air. "Oh, Ele. I can't—won't—make the same mistake I made with Chrissie."

All the emotions she'd felt with Chrissie, when she knew the woman she loved would never commit to her, surged back. It had cut her to the core. Everything had been so right between them. It was that final step that Chrissie wouldn't take.

Whatever seeds of romance now hinted between her and Ele, she thought it was like an old Hollywood movie. Same sad tale, just a remake with different characters and back story.

Kiernan knew it was over. She downed what was left of her drink and went to bed. She wondered why she was bothering. She would not sleep.

❖

*Ele heard someone call her name, and she walked outside into the brilliant sunshine. She could feel the heat on her back as she looked around, but no one was there. Then she heard her name called again, and this time, she glanced across the lawn in front of her house. Beth was standing there, the other side of a tennis net, holding a racquet.*

*"Hey, Slim," Beth called out. "You going to play or what?"*

*"Beth?" Ele couldn't believe she was here. It had been so long. She started to run toward her, but her feet hurt. She glanced down and saw she was shoeless and still in her pajamas. The*

gravel was cutting into her feet. If I can just get to the grass, she thought. And then inexplicably, she was on grass.

"I've got no shoes on," she said. She couldn't seem to remember why she hadn't seen Beth for so long. Had she been away? But seeing Beth now, her heart felt like it would burst with joy.

"Your adoring public isn't here now. They don't care." Beth was laughing and looking at her feet. "Just hit the ball back!"

But Ele didn't want to hit the ball back. It had been so long since she'd seen Beth. She wanted to reach out to her and hold her in her arms. She ran toward her again, but the net that divided them grew tall and strong, out of all proportion, and it blocked her.

"Beth, I can't get to you." She was desperate. She pushed against the net, but its steel mesh was rigid. Beth was still laughing as she hit the ball over it. When had Ele returned it? She couldn't remember.

Then Ele stood at the back of the lawn court again, near the gravel. There was a racquet in her hand.

Beth was taunting her. "Pick the ball up, Slim. Put it back in play."

Slim. It was the nickname Beth used to call her. It sounded so familiar, so good to hear it again—to hear it spoken by Beth. No one else called her that. "I can't see the ball," Ele shouted. "It's lost."

"Nice try, Ele. You can't get out of this game like that. Just because I'm winning. It's over by the gazebo." Beth was swinging her racquet in front of her, as if practicing.

Mystified, Ele turned to the gazebo, but couldn't see the ball. She walked toward it, but as she did, she could see a woman standing inside it. She looked familiar. She heard Beth shout, "I'm waiting."

As Ele approached the gazebo, the woman turned. It was Kier. She'd been crying.

"What are you doing here?" Ele asked.

*"I'm waiting for you."*

*Ele saw the hopelessness in Kier's eyes and wanted to reach out to her, but she was assuaged with guilt. What if Beth had seen? She looked over at the lawn, but Beth was no longer there. She heard the gravel crunch behind her. Beth was here?*

*She turned expecting to see her. Instead, she saw—John Stafford. She couldn't breathe. He was right behind her with his awful piercing eyes bearing down on her.*

Ele awoke with a shout, and Featherstone darted off her bed and out of the room. It took her a while to realize that she'd been dreaming. She held the bedcovers close to her, waiting for her racing heart to calm. Beth had been so real. If she'd been able to cross the net, Ele *knew* she could have touched her. She had looked so good. And then she had seen Kier. Her dream had been of the two women in her life that she loved. Its aftereffects left her dazed. Her longing to see Beth again was fulfilled. But her emotions and wants were refocused on Kier. Kier was the memory that lingered. The sadness on her face. She'd been crying. Ele's heart ached.

Featherstone jumped back on the bed and started meowing. He wanted food. He wanted it now.

Ele got up.

## CHAPTER TWENTY-ONE

L ater that morning, Ele sat in her car outside Kier's home. Her fingers tapped the steering wheel as she gathered her thoughts. She knew Kier was in. Her sports car was parked next to hers.

The dream still played in her mind. It had produced a cocktail of emotions. The joy at seeing Beth again. So tangible. Ele had experienced her *alive* again. Beth had looked young and full of vitality, not like she had in the last months after her stroke.

Ele had also experienced terror. Seeing Stafford almost face-to-face and staring at her with those burning eyes. It was that image that had woken her, that had made her cry out.

But the overwhelming emotion that continued to dominate, above all others, was that of guilt. No longer guilt at betraying Beth, but guilt because of what she had done—was doing—to Kier. The dream had awakened her past, but had it also shown her a future? It scared her. She saw now that not trying to move forward meant losing everything—losing Kier.

Twice, she had held—and kissed—Kier. Twice, she had known what it was to hold someone close again, to feel that intimate connection. She had dated others, after Beth. She had even kissed one or two of them, but none of them evoked the passion and longing she had for Kier.

This was her moment. This was her chance to have a life again, not a memory of a life. She prayed it wasn't too late.

❖

Kiernan was nervous as she waited for Ele to climb from the bottom of the stairs up to her door. This was unexpected, and she had no idea what Ele wanted. She wondered if she might be about to reprimand her for leaving so abruptly last night, for not being more understanding of what Ele was going through.

Ele stepped through the door and gently closed it behind her. Kier could see she looked tense, too. They held each other's eyes and tried to smile. It didn't work.

Kiernan invited Ele to step into the room and sit down, but she politely refused.

"I keep turning up at your door unexpected, don't I?" Ele's hand rose to push hair out of her face. Kier saw her hand shake. She didn't answer; she didn't know what to say. She hadn't slept last night, and she felt numb.

Instead, Ele filled the short awkward vacuum of silence. "I wanted to say I'm sorry, Kier. What I did—said—last night was dreadful. I don't know why I said Beth's name, but I can understand how you felt. I've been trying to work out why that happened. Beth's been gone for so long, it's like some startling Freudian slip."

Kiernan was frozen, unable to make any soothing noises to make this easier for Ele. She wanted to. Ele looked so vulnerable.

"It's just that Beth has been on my mind so much, of late. I realize it's because of you."

The declaration astonished Kiernan. Ele saw it did and nodded.

"You're right, Kier. Beth is always around. It's like the two of you are competing. And I've felt like I'm betraying her, thinking of replacing her with you—"

"I understand, Ele, I do."

Ele cupped her hands in front of her. "I'm scared, Kier. I've only just found you, and I don't want to lose you. I don't want us to stop—not that I've given us a chance to start." She took a deep breath. "I know Chrissie hurt you, and now you don't want to be hurt again. I know you're protecting yourself. I can't understand that sort of pain because I've never been through it. Beth and I never experienced it. We were first time lovers who never needed to find anyone else. People tell me that's unusual. Rare."

"I don't want to make the same mistakes again," Kiernan said.

"No. Of course you don't. And I don't want you to make those mistakes again."

Kiernan felt awkward. What was Ele trying to tell her?

"Please help me, Kier. Please give me one more chance. Last night, what I did, how I felt after you drove off. I've done a lot of soul searching. I'm ready, Kier. I'm ready to take a chance, if you'll let me. You make me *feel* again. We've only known each other a short time, but already, I know. I know that when you're not around, I miss you. And I think about what you're doing. I count the hours until I can see you again. I dream of you." Ele's hands fell to her sides. "This is powerful stuff, Kier. Let's not walk away from it, back to our own little positions of safety where we can't be hurt anymore. Give me one more chance?"

Kiernan *heard* her, but didn't think anything had changed. Not really. She saw the ring on Ele's finger and couldn't hide the pain she felt. It was pointless to dream. Ele must have read that in her face. She turned to leave, her head bowed as if in defeat. As she placed her hand on the door handle, she faced Kiernan.

"Just so you know. I kissed you last night, at the pub, after fish and chips, in that hallway—because I love you. I want you to know that."

"Oh, Ele." Kiernan knew she must be strong. She didn't trust that Ele was able to move on, even if she thought she might be. It felt terrible not being able to respond to Ele. But if you were going to finish something, wasn't it better to do it now? At the beginning—before it went any deeper? Before they really hurt each other.

"Just think about it, Kier. Just do that for me, please." Ele opened the door and had stepped through it before she poked her head back inside.

"I nearly forgot. Dot Harding rang to say she's home and has found some old photos her father took of the Staffords and of the house. I've arranged to go and see her tomorrow morning at ten o'clock. I would love you to join me, but I'll understand if you can't."

Ele then left, and Kiernan listened as her footsteps echoed down the stairs and into the distance. Kiernan heard a car start and drive away.

She didn't move. Now that Ele was gone, her home seemed empty. She breathed in deeply and slowly exhaled. She realized she'd been holding her breath all the time Ele had been here.

Everything was surreal. Kiernan had felt detached as Ele had laid everything out in front of her. She had told her she loved her, for heaven's sake! But she had not responded. She'd done nothing at all. What must that have felt like to Ele? Kiernan loathed herself for not behaving differently; for not acting like an adult. It was only now that she realized how much Chrissie had damaged her. She was still raw. Would she have been this cautious before her?

The real question was whether she was strong enough to give Ele her second chance. Was she willing to take another risk so soon?

Kiernan didn't know the answer.

## CHAPTER TWENTY-TWO

The next day, Kiernan parked outside Dorothy Harding's house. She looked up at the sky. It was an intense blue this morning and the sun shone down on the overnight frost, but there was no heat to it. The frost would linger, unthreatened. A small memory cut across her mind of something her grandmother once told her. White, crisp frost that stays too long will be waiting for the snowfall. It didn't look like snow, but then you could never tell with the whims of the British weather.

Ele drew up and parked a few yards ahead of her. Her heart flipped as she recalled the last few days. She was struggling. One minute she was so damn sure she should walk away from Ele before either of them got hurt. Another, that she should put everything behind her and brave a chance of something wonderful with her— however that might turn out. She internally slapped herself. She'd accused Ele of blowing hot and cold, and here she was negotiating swings and roundabouts. Why couldn't life be a little simpler? Was that too much to ask?

Kiernan wasn't sure what she wanted and she'd made no decision. No. That wasn't quite true. She had made one decision. That was that she wouldn't make a decision until some time had passed with her dilemma. She would put an air gap in to allow thoughts to cogitate more freely. She owed herself, and Ele, that. After Ele's robust and heartfelt sharing yesterday, she could do no less. She wouldn't let any decision she made be hasty and down to Chrissie's influence. She hoped Ele wouldn't want any answers right now for she had none to give.

As they approached each other, Ele watched her intently, a strange unreadable expression on her face. Kiernan braced herself as she pressed her hand down flat on her stomach and breathed in deeply.

"Good morning, Ele." It seemed pointless to add surface conversation like what a nice day it was, had she had a good journey, and so on.

Ele smiled, but Kiernan knew she was on edge. "I wasn't sure you'd show."

Ele sounded calm enough as Kiernan tilted her head to the side. "I may have a few things to work out," she said, "but letting you down in time of need is not one of them."

"We're still friends, then?"

"Yes, we are." Kiernan wanted no doubt between them. "And I want to thank you for coming to see me yesterday, for sharing how you are feeling. For telling me that you love me. That means a lot."

"Is it enough?" Ele's smile disappeared. Her question was earnest and important.

Kiernan needed to be honest. "I don't know yet, Ele. I'm thinking about it. Is that okay?"

"Take your time, Kier. I think time is something we both need right now. At least we know we love each other. Any decisions made will be based on that understanding."

Kiernan agreed.

The awkward moment over, they turned in unison and walked up to Dot's front door.

Dot was expecting them this time and opened the door almost before the echo of the first knock disappeared. Settled inside, she took no time in showing them some old black-and-white photos.

"My daughter dug these out while I was in Bewdley." She scattered some dozen photos across the same table they had sat around on their last visit. "I knew we'd kept my father's photo albums, but I'd forgotten we had these. He took them during the time the Staffords lived at your place. I think I told you he'd just bought his first camera and was obsessed with it."

They looked at the faded, sepia toned photos that were taken at the vicarage. They were outside shots of the main house, its garden, and some of the outbuildings. Most of them had people in them.

Ele lifted a photo from the table and scrutinized it closely. She held the photo with care so as not to damage it. It was a shot of the front of the house showing a long flowerbed running all the way in front of it and a quaint trellis framework around the main door. All this was long gone and the gravel of the drive now went right up to the sides of the house.

"My father helped Mr. Stafford put that trellis up," Dot said. "Mrs. Stafford always wanted roses around the door, but I don't think they ever grew."

She swapped the photo in favor of another that showed the old stable buildings.

"They never had a horse," Dot said as she held a photo showing a group of people standing in the garden on a well-manicured lawn. "This is my father." She indicated a man in a Sunday suit with a starched collar and looking very formal. He stood next to a relaxed couple who were smiling into the camera. "Those are the Staffords." Dot pointed them out. "I don't know who took the photo, but I suppose it was Mother since she isn't in it."

It was the first time Kiernan had seen a photo of Harriet Stafford, and she thought how like Ele she was, for she was tall and lean. Her dress and deportment were elegant and epitomized what a lady would have looked like in those days. She was pretty, and her dress fell to mid shin level. Her light colored hair was whipped up into a loose bun favored during those times, and her large dark eyes seemed to sparkle as her arm rested on John Stafford's. His hand caressed hers with obvious affection.

"That lawn's gone now," Ele said. "The garage is there."

Kiernan nodded. It was where a double garage now sat. She also recognized the gazebo in another photo and said so, but was corrected.

"No, it's not the same one. When we moved in, the original was still there, but in very bad condition. There was no way we could repair it so we replaced it with something as close to the original as we could. We loved it and kept it in the same spot." Ele's tone changed to amazement. "Good grief." She picked up another photo. "I never realized it was that old. I thought it had been put there by more recent owners."

"What, dear?" Dot turned Ele's hand so she could see.

They all looked at a large garden seat cut out of something like Portland stone. The curved seat was about four and a half feet long, with fine scrolled seat supports and strong, study legs to hold the weight. Circling it was a small rose garden, located down from the stable block and in view of the kitchen.

"It was their love seat," Dot said. "Mother told me how they sat there on summer evenings and talked endlessly. They idolized each other and were so in love." Dot took the photo from Ele. Her eyes narrowed and then brightened as she remembered.

"They had this pact," she said. "They enjoyed this delightful habit of sitting outside most summer evenings and partaking of a glass of sherry. Mother thought it so endearing, she started the habit with my father, who I suspect would rather it had been a beer. Anyway, it's a tradition I have carried on too. I always have a tipple of sherry at lunchtime." Dot's eyes glazed, lost in her memories.

"What was the pact?" Kiernan asked.

"When Mr. Stafford volunteered for the front, they had an understanding that at a certain time of the day, Mrs. Stafford would sit on that seat, regardless of the weather, and she would raise a glass of sherry and think of him, wishing him the Lord's protection.

No matter where he was or what he was doing, he would know that at that certain time of the day she was thinking only of him."

Kiernan's eyes watered. It was the sadness of it all that drew her tears.

"Mother would often see her do this. It was something Mrs. Stafford kept doing even after they told her he was dead. She never believed them. It upset Mother to the end of her days. It still upsets me. Of course, I never knew them, and yet I feel I did because of everything I was told. Mother was so very fond of them, and they were wonderful employers. She said she never worked for people as nice as them again. It was all very sad."

"And Harriett always knew he was alive, but never saw him again," Ele whispered.

"Oh, that influenza, as if the war hadn't done enough." Dot rubbed her hands. "My father was very worried for my mother. When Mrs. Stafford became ill, he feared she might contract it. She refused to stay away from the house and insisted on continuing to work there, even though the doctor warned her it was unwise. But she never fell ill and carried on working for Mrs. Stafford right up to the day her family came and took her home to die. They kept Mother on afterward to look after the house. Not so many hours of course, but then, when Captain Stafford returned, she resumed her full duties and was glad of it. Work was difficult to find in a small village like Pegmire. Neither she nor Father had a vehicle. Couldn't afford one."

"Did I tell you that I found out they were buried together?" Ele said. Dot looked shocked. "I found out that John Stafford was buried in Pegmire churchyard, and that later, Harriet's family exhumed her body and brought it here to rest with her husband."

"Oh, how marvelous!" Dot was overjoyed. "I've often thought how sad it was that they were never reunited in life. I hope Mother knew that they were buried together, though she never said. You see, what happened to Captain Stafford on his return haunted my mother to her dying day."

It was the word haunted that drew Ele's and Kiernan's immediate attention. They both looked eagerly at Dot.

"What happened?" Ele asked. "I thought he died of complications from his war wounds?"

Dot scoffed. "That would have been the coroner's conclusions. My mother's were entirely different. She found him, you know."

Kiernan's hungry anticipation was matched by Ele's. Both leaned in closer to Dot, waiting.

"I'll never forget what Mother told me. Every time she talked of it, my blood froze and I had nightmares. I'm not too keen thinking of it now, and I hope it won't upset you, dear," she said to Ele as she leaned back in the chair and patted her hands on the table.

"My mother said that John Stafford returned home a very sick man. He'd been blown up while in the Somme trenches, and while he'd not died, I think they'd been unable to identify who he was until his condition improved and he was able to tell them himself.

"As you know, by the time he returned home, his beloved Harriett had died. Mother always said he was a broken man. She caught him crying occasionally. I know it upset her dreadfully. Every morning, she would go up to the house and set the fire in the sitting room in time for when he arose and came downstairs. She would then prepare his breakfast as she always had for them both. Sometimes, if my father wasn't working, he would go and sit with Captain Stafford for an afternoon, just to give him companionship.

"It was into nineteen nineteen, and one particularly brutal winter's morning, my mother went up to the house, lit the fire, and then went into the kitchen to prepare breakfast. There, she happened to look outside the window across the yard. That's where she found him. Dead. He was on the stone seat they had called their love seat, and he was frozen to death. Beside him was a half-empty glass of sherry. Mother reckoned he had been out there all night. He was stiff and covered white with frost. She said his eyes were still open, and he had the most pitiful, sad look on his face.

"My mother never believed he died of his wounds. She said he died of a broken heart, and she thought he chose to die on that seat because that was where he felt closest to his wife after she had gone. It held such special memories, you see."

Kiernan did see. The tale of the Staffords was even more tragic than she'd first imagined. It was a touching, distressing story of two lovers lost, and it chilled her to the bone. She looked across at Ele to see if she was as affected as she was, but what she saw surprised her.

Ele didn't seem upset. Instead, she was frowning, and there was a quizzical look on her face as if something curious crossed her mind. Something was worrying her.

"I think that's all I know, girls," Dot said. "Has any of it helped you?" She placed a bony hand on top of Ele's. Ele placed her other hand, with affection, on top of Dot's.

"Perhaps." Ele's voice was soft before she spoke with more gusto. "Would you mind if I borrowed a few of your photos for just a day or so? I promise to let you have them back."

Dot did not object and produced a small brown envelope to place them in.

Kiernan waited until they stood outside and Dot had closed the door. "What's wrong?"

Ele looked at her in the strangest manner. "I don't know. It may be nothing; it may be everything, but I have this feeling…"

Intrigue gripped her, and she grabbed Ele by the arm, almost pushing her to her car. That Ele didn't object only implied how absorbed she was by something and Kiernan longed to find out what that was. There was no whisper of the personal issues that rested between them as she sat in the passenger seat of Ele's car and asked her to explain.

Still engrossed in thought, Ele opened the envelope containing the photos and pulled out two that showed the stone seat. For a few very long seconds she just stared at them, her eyes full of confusion, before she placed them on her knees so Kiernan could see.

"I may be wrong," she said slowly.

"It's something to do with the stone seat?" Kiernan studied the two photos.

"I think so." Ele was introducing a new piece of evidence into her calculations, like some evolving murder mystery.

"It was still at the house when you bought it?" Kiernan was impatient to discover what was going through Ele's mind. They had waited so long for the answer to the haunting. Had Ele solved the riddle?

She heard a whispered "yes," and she swore she could hear the cogs turning in Ele's brain.

"What happened to it?" *It isn't there now.*

"I had it moved."

"Moved?" Kiernan's mind searched the grounds at Ele's. Had the seat been placed elsewhere? She couldn't recall seeing it.

"It was in the wrong place." Ele's attention remained fixated on the photos. "The stables were being converted, and I wanted to open up all of the area down past the kitchen toward the front of the house, get it all cobbled. I could then drive up to the kitchen, unload shopping, wash the car, way more convenient." She raised a hand to her chin. "I had the seat moved."

"You said that." Kiernan couldn't hide her exasperation. Normally, Ele cut to the chase, but now, was she ever going to say what was bothering her? Something clicked in her mind and a disturbing thought materialized. "Where did you move it to?" Something in the way she asked made Ele swivel and look at her, her eyes wide.

"I never liked the seat and wanted it gone, so I gave it away."

"Who did you give it too?" Kiernan knew the answer.

"I gave it to Roger." Ele was ashen. "As a gift for—"

"Joan," they said in unison. A bolt of cold fear ran through Kiernan's body like an iceberg shaft landing on the deck of the Titanic.

"Joan often admired it, so I told Roger to give it to her as a gift from me. I wanted to give it a good home." Ele brought her hands to her face. "Oh, God, Kier. How could I have missed it? Joan's feelings of being watched—her paranoia. It's been staring me in the face."

Kiernan couldn't move. She watched Ele mentally kick herself, but it was so easy to see the obvious once it was presented. She thought back to everything Ele told her at the pub, of how ill Joan was. The thought that the haunting extended beyond the vicarage was almost too chilling to contemplate. She'd be careful buying antiques in the future. Who knew what unexpected surprises might come with them?

"Kier, Joan's illness, her terrible nightmares…is it because of that seat? It can't be this simple. Can it? I moved John and Harriett's love seat and I shouldn't have?"

"Let me see those." Kiernan reached out and took the photos from Ele's lap, studying them closely. "Stafford is pointing in the area of the seat."

"Yes, and that day when the leaves went mad and I thought I saw a face in the wind…" Ele didn't have to finish. Kiernan knew. "And Feathers, he sits on the cobblestones where the stone seat once was." Her face drained as she begged the question. "What have I done?" Her hands went to her face and covered her mouth.

Kiernan leaned across and wrapped Ele in her arms. She wasn't sure who was comforting whom, for she was trembling. "What are you going to do?" she asked.

It took Ele's mind a few seconds to spring into action as she pulled back. "I want to get copies of those photos and return the originals to Dot. Then I need to go and talk to Roger again. I've got questions that need answering."

Kiernan volunteered her help. "I can duplicate the photos back home and then I'll drop the originals back off with Dot. Do you want me to come with you to see Roger?"

"No, this is something I have to do alone. I'll ring you later and let you know what I find."

How Kiernan wanted to go with Ele, to see if her hunch was right. But she could see why Ele needed to do this alone. There were Roger and Joan to consider. They wouldn't take kindly to a complete stranger bumbling into their personal affairs. She would have to wait—patiently—while Ele pursued this line of investigation. Patience was not something she felt she had in abundance. She'd have to be content to sort out Dot's photos. But this sudden turn, that Ele might have stumbled on what had started the haunting, was a bizarre lead. But then everything sinister that was happening was bizarre.

As she climbed out of Ele's car, she squeezed her hand. "Please phone me if you need me. I am here for you." She was. It occurred to her that a ghost was keeping them together at the moment. She was grateful.

"Wish me luck."

Kiernan gave her hand one final squeeze. "Always."

## CHAPTER TWENTY-THREE

Ele stared at the house in the middle of Pegmire village that resembled a building site and looked for Roger. He was doing a home extension, and she hoped to find him and have a talk. But for now, all she could see was a landscape of mud, a small middle-aged man going up a ladder with roof tiles, and two younger laborers working to the side of the property. It crossed her mind that Roger would not be too far away, as he would be keen to complete the roofing work before the dreaded winter weather put in an appearance. Once that arrived, work would stop and stay that way until well after Christmas. Winter was a bad time for builders. She carefully negotiated her way around pools of wet mud, skipping onto rare islands of dryness.

"Ele!" Roger limped toward her, his hands waving in the air. "You daft woman. Are you mad? High heels on a building site?"

Glancing down at her feet, she realized her footwear was out of place and grinned at him. He was laughing as he wrapped his arms about her. He guided her back the way she had come and to relative safety where the mud was less on the walkway.

"You looking for me?" He wiped his hand across his face, removing building dust.

"I came to see you about Joan. How's your foot?" She couldn't ignore the limp.

He grimaced as he gingerly balanced on one foot while lifting the other off the ground and rotating it in small circles. "Could be better I suppose, but it's healing. This damp air makes it stiff and it aches like hell, but I'm coping."

"You ought to be resting it. You moan at me being in high heels, but you messing around on a building site with poor balance isn't helping. You could hurt yourself."

"Not going to happen. Building sites are like second homes to me. And frankly, it's safer here than at home with Joan. I can't do anything right at the moment, and she never hesitates to let me know."

"How is Joan?"

"Full of you, love. She was thrilled about the book, and it's lifted her spirits a bit."

"But she's not much better?"

"Nah, not really. What did you make of her?"

"That's what I came to talk to you about. Do you have a few minutes?"

"Always got time for you, love, especially after everything you've done for us."

It never ceased to amaze Ele how grateful Roger and Joan always seemed toward *her*, and yet she had done nothing to deserve it.

Roger guided her toward his van. "It'll be warmer and drier, and we can talk without any interruptions. Hang on a mo." He paused and shouted across the site to one of the younger men. "Steve, tell Andy that when you're both done, you're to give Norman a hand on the roof. Get some more tiles up there."

The lad raised his hand in acknowledgement and then shouted across to the unseen Andy who was at the back of the property. "Andy! We gotta give Stormin' Norman a hand on the roof when you're done."

"Stormin' Norman?" Ele asked as she got into the van and closed the door. Roger raised his eyes in discomfort.

"It's what the other lads call him. I don't like it and have said so, but the name's stuck. Trouble is, Norman is older and moves at his own pace, which can be a bit slow sometimes. When you talk to him, you're always itching for him to get the next word out. But his work is first-class, and I wouldn't lose him for the world, not if I had to lay off all the other lads first."

"That's a bit of a golden compliment, Roger. What's so special about Norman?" Roger glanced down at his hands uneasily. Ele felt he was struggling whether to tell her something.

"He's a bloke with a huge heart, although you'd never believe it to talk to him. And he knows how to keep his mouth shut about things...things that are private." Roger looked across at Ele, his huge dark brown eyes locking onto hers. "You see, a few months ago, something happened—happened here, and Norman, well, he took care of it." Roger's entire body language oozed discomfort.

"I was away picking up some stock I'd ordered. Anyway, one morning, Norman found Joan wandering around here looking frenzied and distraught, her hair unkempt, and she was still dressed in her slippers and dressing gown. She was covered in mud. She'd run out of the house, which as you know is a good half mile away, and come straight here to try to find me. At first, Norman couldn't get any sense out of her, but she eventually told him that something had scared her at home.

"Joan told him she'd heard tapping on the window pane at the back of the house, but when she'd peeped behind the curtain, no one was there. But the tapping continued. Norman put his tools down and drove her home. Once there, he went into the garden and scoured it thoroughly for a sign of any perpetrators, but he found no one and nothing. Then he cleaned Joan up and sat with her in front of the fire with a cup of tea until I got there.

"He managed to convince Joan—maybe—that it was the crows making the tapping noise. You see, crows have a habit of tapping windows if they can see their reflection in it. Years ago, a cheeky crow used to tap the windowsill because Joan hadn't put food out. Anyhow, Joan was more her old self when I got home. I've a lot to thank Norman for. He's never mentioned it since, to me or any other. He's a good, decent chap."

Roger took a deep breath. "I'm glad you're here to talk about Joan. I did come looking for you at your place, but you weren't in."

"I've been away for a few days." Ele was glad that Roger brought the conversation back to Joan's problems. They seemed distressing on so many levels.

"I'm so glad Joan likes my book." She removed her brown leather gloves. "It was good to see her again. We spent a good couple of hours talking. I can see she's not well, and I've never seen her look so tired." She got straight to the point, and Roger seemed grateful. "I tried to talk to her about all this, but the opportunity never arose, and I didn't want to say anything that would tip her off that you and I have spoken."

"I understand." Roger looked conflicted, and Ele knew he was disappointed, but also feeling guilty for betraying his wife's trust by talking to others about personal family matters.

"But I've left it open to go back and see her in a few days. She wants to see the water colors I've done of—"

"The kingfishers." He smiled. "Bless you. It's all she's been talking about these last few days. She's looking forward to your next visit." He briefly touched her shoulder. "Thank you for bothering."

"Don't be daft, Roger. You and Joan are so dear to me. You're my friends. Hopefully, Joan might open up more next time I see her, but I need to ask you a few questions, something to help me understand more." She saw he was agreeable. "When do you think Joan's troubles started?"

"That's easy. It was when she stopped being able to get a good night's sleep."

"And when was that?"

Roger sucked air through his teeth. "Not sure I can really plot it, but some good long months ago."

"Well, was it before you did the work for me, during it, or maybe after it?" This was a crucial question for Ele. Its answer would reveal much.

He scratched his head. "Joan went to see her sister, Marjorie, after her husband died suddenly. That was before your job. She was all right then. I remember her bringing my lunch up to your place when I left it on the kitchen table one morning. She was all right then. I remember I did a quick job on Bob Price's roof, after your job. Joan wasn't all right then.

"It would be just after I finished your job. It started with some sleepless nights and then her thinking someone was watching her when she was in the garden. I was concerned. I was doing that roof job for Bob, and I wasn't happy leaving Joan alone in the house. At the time, I thought someone was stalking us."

Ele cringed. This all sounded so familiar. "And it's become worse?"

"It has. She won't go in the garden, and that seems to be her key obsession now. It's what fuels her anxiety and strange behavior. I told you, she won't go out and top up the bird feeders anymore, and I expect you notice how she keeps the curtains drawn all the time."

Ele remembered how dark the house was on her last visit. At the time, she had started to worry that Joan's problems were something deeper than a serious attack of insomnia. She had considered that the doctor's thoughts on agoraphobia might have been right. But now?

She altered her line of questioning. "What did she think of the stone seat?"

Roger cringed, and something told Ele she was on the right track. "She doesn't like it, does she?" It was written all over his face. Roger all but crumbled in front of her.

"Oh, Ele, I hoped you wouldn't ask me about this. Joan was over the moon when I took it home. Me and a couple of the lads took ages to maneuver it into the garden and place it over by the little water feature. It weighs a ton! Joan never stopped talking about how wonderful it was and admiring how lovely it looked in the garden. At first, she spent ages out there, sitting on it and enjoying the summer. But that was before her illness."

"Go on." Ele could tell Roger was hiding something. She stared at him, willing him to continue.

"To tell the truth, Ele, she doesn't like it anymore." His eyes begged an apology. "At first, it was her pride and joy, but then her illness kicked in. She started saying she didn't like sitting on it anymore because she never felt alone, like someone was always there with her—watching her. It gave her the creeps."

His eyes watered and he looked away from Ele. "I feel bad telling you this, because I know how much joy you got giving it to Joan, and under normal circumstances…" He drew breath, unable to continue for the moment. "I love that woman, Ele. She's everything to me. Please don't be upset. She doesn't like anything outside now, so it's not just your seat." Roger visibly shivered as he turned to her and asked a question. "Do you think Joan's losing her mind?"

Ele pursed her lips in thought before answering. Roger's expression changed. It was as if he read an unspoken yes on her face. She had to sort this out and get her answers quick. "I don't know, Roger. Tell me about these nightmares. What are they about?"

"Oh, stuff and nonsense." His voice was dismissive and his expression eased.

"Tell me, please? It's important."

"It's pretty much the same dream. Some stranger, a man, is in them in one way or the other. Often, she can't see him, but knows he's there. There on the seat. When she does see him, she always wakes up screaming."

"Often she can't see him, but sometimes she can?"

"She won't talk about it too much, but from what I can gather, it's always the same chap. Bit of an old-fashioned bloke with awful piercing eyes. He's always watching her."

*Oh dear God.* It was the key answer she sought. Ele felt like the last piece of a difficult jigsaw had slotted into place, and she fought to keep her composure. But as she realized the implications of what a simple gift to an old friend had brought about, she felt her shoulders involuntarily sag. She was so sure now that Joan's problems rested on the awful fact that she had given her the stone seat. A sigh from Roger drew her attention.

"My precious Joan."

Roger was convinced that she thought Joan's condition was serious. Ele reached out and grasped his arm. "Roger, I need to ask you something. It's a little odd, but I wouldn't ask this unless I thought it would help. Can I have the seat back?"

Roger frowned, dumbfounded at the strange turn of conversation. Ele couldn't blame him. One minute, they were talking about Joan and her illness, and now about replacing a seat.

Ele tightened her grip. "I know this sounds peculiar, and I can't explain it, but I'm sure it's the stone seat that's causing Joan's problems. Things have been happening at home that you wouldn't believe. I have very strong reasons for believing it should never have been removed. *Please*, will you bring it back?"

Roger looked shocked. He scrutinized her so closely she wondered if he was going to ask her to leave his van. Was she making everything worse for him? He continued to look at her hard until he started shaking his head in disbelief. When he next spoke, she could hear what sounded like relief in his voice.

"I've known for a while that I need to get rid of that seat. I've had my suspicions that it's behind Joan's strange behavior. But how do you explain that? And it was a gift from you." He looked like none of what he said made sense before adding, "You're actually taking a weight off my mind."

The more she heard, the more Ele knew she was on the right track. "Bring it back, Roger, as soon as you can. I want you to put it back exactly where it was. I've photos that will help."

He drew his hands down his face, never once taking his eyes off her. Then his expression turned puzzled. "But that'll mean digging up some of the cobblestones to seat it in again. After all that fuss you made to have them laid in the first place."

"Roger! Stuff the stones." Ele was amazed how he could be so concerned over her cobblestones at a time like this. *Typical man.* "I know, but it's what I want. You're going to have to humor me." Another thought crossed her mind. "By the way, how did you say you broke your foot?"

He eyed her suspiciously. "I didn't. But since you ask, I did it in the garden. I tripped over the seat. I shouldn't have because there was no reason to, but I did."

Ele said nothing, and Roger fidgeted uncomfortably. "Ele, I don't understand any of this, but since you're asking, you might also want to know that the dog won't go anywhere near the seat either." He squirmed some more. "I don't know what we're talking about here. I don't believe in mumbo jumbo stuff, but this is downright creepy. When do you want the seat back?"

"Yesterday."

"I'll need a couple of strong blokes to help, and I'll see if I can borrow a truck with a hoist." Roger looked across the site to where Norman was going up the ladder again. "Norman might help." He scratched his head again. "I'm not sure I understand all this."

Ele looked him straight in the eyes. "Nor me."

He stared back. "Is this going to help my Joan?"

"I hope so, Roger. I really hope so."

"How's your asthma?" Dot asked as Kiernan sat in her kitchen drinking tea.

Kiernan had duplicated the photos and then driven over to Dot Harding's to return them. Dot had insisted she come in for a warm drink and Kiernan had sensed she wanted the company. Truth told, Kiernan wanted it too. Anything to stop her thinking about Ele and what she was going to do.

"It's fine, Dot. I now make sure it's on me all of the time, especially in winter." She reached into a pocket and pulled an inhaler out as proof. She saw the laughter lines crinkle around Dot's eyes.

"Glad to see it," Dot said. "Ele was very worried. You shouldn't frighten her like that."

"Yes, I'm sorry. It's a mistake I won't make again." Kiernan couldn't help laughing. Looking back, her desperate moment of struggling for breath had not been without humor. Dot had revealed her own unique way of showing sensitivity.

"You two been together long?"

Kiernan was sipping tea and the liquid caught on the back of her throat. Yes, Kiernan thought, Dot had all the sensitivity of a sledgehammer. She coughed. "No. Not long." She wasn't ready to start explaining the precise relationship she and Ele had.

Dot looked surprised. "It's just that the two of you seem so comfortable together. You have that ease that suggests you've been around each other a long time. That normally takes a while to grow."

Kiernan was taken aback that Dot might be asking her about personal relationships. She wasn't shy in stepping forward. Also that she seemed so open to a same-sex relationship. The older generation wasn't always so accepting and certainly not comfortable talking about it openly. Dot had none of those inhibitions.

Dot read her face. "I may be old, but I'm not narrow-minded. My granddaughter in Bewdley is a lesbian. Took a bit of getting used to. Far too much women's underwear over the radiators, and the house too clean. But she's had a partner for years now. Lovely woman. Loves scuba diving," she added as if it was important. She sipped her tea, then continued. "My son's been married twice. Still not right. Looks like it's all going wrong again. I smell a divorce. He seems to want utopia and the perfect woman. Well, that doesn't exist." She leaned back in her chair. "You grab happiness when it comes, and from whatever direction, and you take the ups and downs, too. That's my philosophy. Don't you agree?"

Kiernan went to answer, but Dot gave her no chance.

"You're very lucky. You're obviously right for each other. I'm pleased. Good for you two." Dot paused before asking, "Do you scuba dive?"

Kiernan left Dot's earlier than she wanted to. She liked Dot a lot, and her conversations were—different. But it had started snowing as she'd arrived there, and as the afternoon had progressed, it was coming down thicker and heavier. Kiernan wasn't sure how bad the roads would be. Her sports car didn't do well in snow, and it was already dark.

She made a conscious decision to drive over to Ele's. She knew she could have gone home and then phoned her to find out how the talk with Roger had gone, but she needed to *see* her. Suddenly, that was crucially important.

It was like a penny dropping. Everything seemed clear to Kiernan. Maybe Dot's no-nonsense approach to life—her philosophy—was rubbing off on her. She saw now that Chrissie's inability to commit was after years of going out with her. Kiernan was being unfair to Ele. They'd only known each other a short time, and yet, she was demanding Ele show her more of a declared intention. Kiernan was looking for a relationship, up front with a guarantee. How stupid. If Ele was willing to risk loving her, after years of entrenched devotion to a memory, why couldn't she be brave?

## CHAPTER TWENTY-FOUR

It was dark by four o'clock, and Ele watched as one small inconsequential snowflake fell outside her sitting room window as she went to close the curtains. By the time she went upstairs to fetch her slippers and a warm jumper, the ground was already white and the air thick with flakes. All afternoon, the man on the radio warned that a big storm was coming in and that Oxfordshire could expect at least four inches of snow by early evening, and then more overnight. He said that if the warm front met the cold one, and if the expected easterly wind came in from across Europe, then people should expect blizzard conditions. He warned that the early morning commute tomorrow would be treacherous.

Ele clapped her hands together with glee. She loved snow. Christmas was less than a week away, and it never felt right without it. There was something wonderful about a warm fire crackling, blazing away in the hearth, while everything outside was deep, and crisp, and even. Her adoration of snow was dampened only as she realized Roger would not be able to return the seat until the weather improved. Her thoughts turned grim. What if she was wrong about the stone seat? What if she was trapped in the house by the snow where she could not get out, and no one could get to her? What if the haunting continued? She would be alone with a ghost. She shivered. She had not thought of this. Maybe the snowfall was not so wonderful after all.

It was gone seven o'clock as she sat downstairs. She had been reading the newspaper in front of the fire, but now her head was tilted back, and she was resting in the armchair Beth always favored. She heard the fire pop and it occurred to her that this was the same fireplace that Beatrice Lavish, Dot's mother, once made up for the Staffords. Had they sat in front of its warm embers as she did now? Of course they had. What memories old houses held of their past.

She closed her eyes in comfort and enjoyed the still and quiet surrounding her. Unexpectedly, her peace was broken as she heard a muffled crunching of gravel.

❖

Kiernan stepped into the house with more haste than she wanted to show. It was bitter cold outside. She rubbed her hands. She'd had the car heater on the highest setting as she had driven over, and stepping out of her warm chariot into the cold night air was not enjoyable. Ele bolted the door at the top and bottom.

"You're sure those bolts are across?" It was a night for keeping ghosts out, and heat in.

Ele glanced back at her. So, they were both still nervous.

"You shouldn't have driven over in this," Ele said, but Kiernan heard the genuine joy in her voice. It reassured her that what she had come here to do tonight, was right. She crossed over to the fire, thrusting her hands close.

"I'm amazed you managed to get up the drive." Ele's sweet voice stopped her meditation.

"So am I." Kiernan was amazed too. The drive had been okay en route to Dot's, but coming back, it had been awful. There were times when she thought she wasn't going to make it. She'd never taken much notice of how many hills and slight inclines there were on the roads over here—not until she had to drive up them in snow. She dug a hand into her coat pocket and passed Ele an envelope containing photos. "These are the copies. I've returned the originals to Dot."

Ele looked impressed. She took Kiernan's jacket and hung it over the back of a chair. "Would you like a drink? I was about to have a sherry."

They looked at each other, aware of the significance of that drink in this house's past.

"Please."

Ele moved gracefully across the room and extracted two glasses from a sideboard. Kiernan watched as her hand, covered with the slightest smidgeon of paint, poured sherry from a decanter standing on a silver platter atop a fine piece of furniture.

"You've been doing your water colors," Kiernan said.

"Wrong. I've been *trying* to do my water colors." Ele handed her a sherry, beckoning with her eyes for her to sit down. "Somehow, working in my studio has lost its allure."

"Ghosts will do that," Kiernan said as she sipped her drink and watched Ele drop onto a sofa.

"It only takes one," Ele said more to herself.

Kiernan couldn't imagine how Ele was able to return home after all that had happened. She admired her tenacity and inner strength. It prompted her to find out how the rest of Ele's day had gone. "I was wondering if you managed to have your chat with Roger."

Ele recounted all, and Kiernan listened with fascination. Maybe—just maybe—they were on the right trail.

"This may be a false lead," Ele said, "but my instinct tells me it isn't. Anyway, I suppose I won't know that answer until Roger delivers the seat."

"That isn't going to happen anytime soon, looking at this weather front moving in." Kiernan immediately wished she had kept her mouth shut. Her comment made Ele look miserable.

Neither spoke for a while and the silence only broke when Ele chipped in, "I don't suppose you looked at any of your photos again and have had any thoughts about the stone seat?"

Kiernan thought of Stafford's pointing finger. "I did, but there's nothing new to add except to agree that his focus is drawn to the general area of where the seat once was. I think you're on to something."

"I can't believe this might all be something as simple as my removing an old stone seat." Ele clearly found her discovery incongruent and uncomfortable.

"But it isn't just any stone seat." As Kiernan spoke, Ele regarded her curiously. "It's a piece of stone, true enough, something cut out of a wall of rock and given an attractive shape. It started life as inanimate matter, something lifeless and inorganic, but then it came here and became saturated with love, hope, sadness, and loss. It became the key focus where two young people expressed their feelings of love, and the bitterness of parting, and where they made a promise to each other that they would think of the other every day while they were apart."

Kiernan had also thought of this as she'd driven back from Dot's. "We talk about places holding memories, of houses too. I talk to my car because, to me, it's an important part of my life. I wonder if this inanimate piece of stone became sentient as it listened to a young woman praying for the return of her lover, and then crying for his loss. If that's true, did it grow lonely when that woman no longer sat on it every day, and would it have understood where she'd gone? Why it rested there alone? If it was conscious, how did it feel when John Stafford passed away on it, grieving for his wife?"

Ele's eyes glistened. "You're quite the poet, you know."

"I'm Irish; it's in our blood," she said softly, unable to take her eyes off Ele. No, she thought, I can't let you go.

"Do you really believe that memories linger in places, in objects?" Ele asked.

The way it was said, Kiernan knew a serious answer was sought. She held the top of her glass between two fingers and studied the color of its contents like a forensic scientist. "I didn't believe in ghosts a few months back, Ele, but I do now."

She looked up and caught Ele studying her like she did her sherry. Something passed between them, and in the corresponding silence, Kiernan knew the time was right, to say what had brought her over to see Ele—the key reason. Everything had suddenly made sense to her as she'd left Dot's. It was something that couldn't wait. "I think it's my turn to apologize. I'm sorry, Ele. I've been a complete idiot trying to push you away."

"No. I've been the idiot. You accused me of blowing hot and cold, and it's true. I called you *Beth*." Ele shook her head in disbelief.

"I know, but we're not giving ourselves time, are we? We can't expect our pasts to disappear in a puff of smoke. Whether we like it or not, I have to get over Chrissie, not let what happened between us ruin *my* future. You have to learn to let Beth go—"

"I am ready, Kier. I know I am."

Kier smiled. "We deserve a shot at love. We should be listening to what John Stafford is telling us. Lost love—it'll haunt us all our days if we don't try."

"Are you ready?" Ele asked.

"Yes, I am." She couldn't tear her eyes from Ele's. It was as though there was a secondary communication going on between them. Some subtext that spoke of distorted things straightening. She noticed Ele's finger no longer wore the ring. Ele caught her look and silently gestured its significance. "If we can sort Stafford out, I'm sure *we* can work something out." Ele's eyes watered. Kiernan crossed over to the sofa, sat beside her, and took her in her arms.

"I've been so scared, Kier." Ele's voice sounded muffled against her shoulder. "After the pub when you drove off, and then yesterday, what you said—"

"Didn't say," Kier said. How could she have been so hard as to not respond to Ele's heart renderings?

"I thought I'd lost you."

"But you haven't, Ele." They hugged tighter.

"What changed your mind?"

Kiernan drew back, starting to laugh. "Dot Harding."

"Dot?" Ele looked puzzled.

"It's a long story, and one I'd rather tell you later. But let's just say the old bird has got a great philosophy in life." She relaxed back into Ele's arms, pulling her close and feeling the welcoming warmth of their bodies together. This felt so right. To think she'd almost let Ele go. What a fool she'd been. "We'll have to tell her, you know."

"Eh?"

"Tell Dot," Kier said. "Tell her what's been happening. She deserves that. I mean, if this all works out, it'll be because of her."

"We'll have to have her over here."

Kier nodded. "She'll love seeing this place—where her mother had such memories. I wonder if she's ever been here?"

Ele shook her head. "No idea, but we'll ask her over for dinner."

"You'll cook?" Kier said.

"I will. She's a friend!"

They embraced for a long time before Ele drew back, taking Kiernan's hands in hers. She sighed as she glanced over to the window.

"Kier, I don't think you'll be going far this evening, not given the weather." She looked down at their hands. "I want you to stay the night."

"But?" Kiernan heard something unspoken.

Ele looked at her. "I love you, and I want nothing more than to express that love, to be with you. But I hope you understand why I can't, not here in this house, not yet."

"Memories? A house that remembers?" This was the house where Ele and Beth had loved, where they had kissed, and where their lives had grown closer together like a climbing rose up trellis. Ghosts existed in many forms, and Beth's was somewhere here, either in the air that moved around them, or burrowed forever in

Ele's mind. Kiernan knew that to ask Ele to make love to her here, for the first time, it wouldn't be right.

"We can wait, darling." There would be a time when they would make love within the walls of this house, but not yet. There was a time for everything if you were patient. "Will Beth allow a kiss?"

The expression in Ele's eyes said it all, and Kiernan leaned in. She started with a gentle, chaste kiss. Ele responded, and Kiernan kissed her harder. The passion and heat grew as their tongues danced. Ele moved even closer to her. Kiernan savored how good it felt to be so near to Ele this way. She longed for more, but pulled back. She would honor Ele's request.

"Another sherry?" Ele's breath was labored.

"Another sherry," Kiernan said.

That night, the snow fell deep, and a north wind blew. She and Ele slept in the same bed, spooned together. Ele had decided that Beth's ghost could accommodate them sharing a bed. Kiernan silently thanked Beth.

She slept a deep and satisfying sleep. She only woke once, to the sound of distant tapping. She ignored the noise and wrapped Ele's arms closer around her. Sleep reclaimed her and she thought no more.

## CHAPTER TWENTY-FIVE

It was the morning before Christmas Eve as Ele moved around in her kitchen. She glanced across at Kier who was eating toast and drinking coffee. Weeks earlier, consumed with guilt, Ele had longed for this. Now her repressed dreams had come true. She was deliriously happy. They had spent several days together, trapped in the house by the weather. Ele thanked the snowfall.

They had not made love in all this time. Kier continued to respect Beth's memory. Ele loved her for this even though her body cried out for more. Yet such a bond had grown between them. They slept together and touched each other liberally. They embraced and kissed as often as their lungs would allow.

Making love was important, but sometimes Ele thought it overrated, as if it was the pinnacle and "must have" of any meaningful relationship. She didn't doubt how essential it was, but it wasn't everything. She and Kier spoke of this. Both agreed that while making love was natural and fueled by desire, intimacy was more important. It was the revelation of mind and spirit coming together, a deep bonding of souls. When the sex receded, as it often did over time, it was what remained of intimacy that was crucial. They had laughed one night as, both frustrated, they concluded that intimacy between them was now firmly established. They were ready for the next stage.

Ele felt an incredible closeness to Kier, and the way Kier looked at her, she knew she felt the same. She edged up close behind her and stole the toast that was half eaten in her hand.

"Hey, that's mine."

"What's mine is yours, and yours, mine." Ele finished the toast.

"I call it theft." Kier moved around and hugged Ele. "It's just as well I'm going home today or I might starve." This morning, she announced that as the snow had stopped and the sunshine reappeared, she needed to return to her place, as there was something she had to do. Ele licked the butter from her fingers. Kier had asked her to spend Christmas at her place and she had accepted.

Kier stood in the hallway about to leave when a heavy rumbling sound reverberated from outside the house. Its noise sent Feathers darting up the stairs. When they looked, they saw a truck turning in the driveway and backing up by the side of the kitchen.

"It's Roger." Ele was surprised. She grabbed a heavy jacket and gloves and rushed out the kitchen door with Kier close behind. Roger and two muscular men vacated the truck.

"Delivery," Roger said, smiling at Ele. He glanced toward the back of the truck and she saw the stone seat sat beneath a winching device. "Where would you like it placed?"

"I didn't think you'd be able to do this before Christmas." Ele was unable to hide her elation.

"Neither did I, but with this break in the weather I thought we should take every opportunity to get it up here. I won't be able to remove any cobblestones and seat it in firmly until better, warmer weather arrives, but we can at least put it where it needs to go."

She took no time showing Roger and his team an old sepia photo to help them pinpoint the seat's former position. Then with Kier, she watched as a coordinated effort between the three men began. They lifted, swung, and painstakingly moved the stone seat as Roger checked the photo continually to ensure accuracy. He seemed to sense its importance. Twenty minutes later, the truck and the men left.

"So this is it, then," Kier said, looking at the seat, sat in a ray of sunshine, snow all around it. "There's no denying that it's a handsome piece of stonework."

"This is it." Ele stood back and studied it as Kier brushed up behind her and placed a reassuring hand on her shoulder. Ele tilted her head until her cheek touched the hand. "I wonder if this is what it's all been about—a missing love seat."

She left the warmth of Kier's hand and moved slowly around the seat, regarding it closely. "When the better weather comes, I'm going to plant some little rose bushes around it...make it look like it used to."

Wanting to show Kier what she meant, she darted over to the garden refuse area and extracted two dead rosebushes, ones she had planned to put in the borders by her wisteria. They were in large black plastic pots and resembled a collection of lifeless twigs rather than the glorious roses once envisioned. She positioned them either side of the seat. "I'll do something like this, maybe have half a dozen around it."

"It'll look pretty."

"I think it will. Isn't it funny? I never liked this seat before, and yet now I can't believe I ever wanted to let it go." She ran her hand across the top of it. "You know, Kier, I have the strangest, strongest feeling that I've done the right thing." She edged forward and sat on the seat, gently testing its balance on the uneven cobbled brickwork and thick snow. It held firm, and she relaxed.

"Wait there, and don't you move." Kier dashed inside. She reappeared moments later with a camera. "You have no idea how stunning you look with the sun bouncing off your hair and catching the color of your eyes. This is a picture in a million."

"Oh, really..." Ele blushed and looked down into her lap, embarrassed, but adoring every minute.

Kier pointed the camera and turned it to get the desired angle. "If you date a photographer, you'll need to get used to this."

Ele stared patiently into the camera and allowed Kier her moment of indulgence. When Kier looked at her again, she saw nothing but love in her eyes. These last few days, cocooned together as if on an island of snow, they had grown so close. It was another thing she knew was right. It crossed her mind that she had known this from the first moment she met Kier.

Kier rested a hand on her hip. "Now I really need to be on my way. Things to do." Her eyes narrowed in secrecy.

"What are you up to, Kier?"

"That's for me to know and you to find out later."

Ele rose. She studied the seat one final time before following Kier back into the house. "How will I know if this is what John Stafford has been trying to tell me? And what if it isn't?"

Kier turned and ran a hand down the side of Ele's face. "I'm sure he'll find a way. And if you're wrong, he can't be too angry with you because you're lovely and he'll know how hard you've been trying."

"You're besotted."

A few minutes later, as Kier sat in her car, she cast a warning eye at Ele. "Do not arrive at my place before five o'clock. I want to make sure everything is ready."

"What?" Ele splayed her arms in front of her. She hated surprises. What plan was Kier hatching?

"Patience, Ele." Kiernan touched the tip of her nose. "Everything comes to those who wait." She waved as she drove off.

The green sports car disappeared down the drive, and when Ele could no longer hear it accelerating down the country lane beyond, she sighed.

She stood for a while and looked at the glorious view before her. The snow transformed everything, making it all look virgin pure and clean. Snowdrifts had given bushes and sheds new shapes, and the sunlight bounced off the trees in a peculiar fashion that made her think of fantasy lands. The sound was different too, deadened and muted. It was how she felt now, quiet and empty. Kier's absence existed like a huge void, and Ele couldn't wait until she saw her again this afternoon.

As she walked toward the house, she smiled. Kier had a natural playfulness about her. She loved that. She thought of Kier's touches, sensuous and gentle. She ached for those again, and she longed to join Kier at her home. There she would have no memories to defile. Her wanting was becoming urgent. Despite their civilized discussions of intimacy versus sex, civilization was losing its battle.

Featherstone was inside the door watching her. He wouldn't come outside; he didn't like snow. It made his precious paws wet. She bent and patted him as she closed the door behind her. Apparently satisfied she was now inside, he moved up the stairs. Ele knew he headed for a back bedroom where sun streaked in through a window and onto a chair; it was one of his favorite spots.

She followed him. She needed to tidy up and then pack a few things for Kier's. There was also something else she wanted to do.

Ele had done a lot of talking to ghosts lately, and yet Beth had never felt like one to her. All through the years since Beth had died, Ele had continued to talk to her and share with her what she was doing and how she felt. When she had thought about converting the stable buildings into a studio, she had sat and *talked* to Beth, asking her opinion. Of course, Beth never spoke back, but Ele sensed her approval. Others might call it madness, a sign of someone caught in a bereavement cycle, unable to break free and move on. But it was her way of honoring Beth, of letting her know she was still in her heart, in her mind, still cherished. Now she needed to tell Beth something important.

"I miss you, you know." Ele sat on the edge of her bed, the one she had shared these last few nights with Kier. "And I don't want you to ever think I'll forget you." Her eyes smarted. "But I think I've met someone special, Beth, somebody who makes me feel inside like you used to." She wiped her eyes with a tissue and grinned. "I expect you're already eyeing Kier up and making sure she's good enough for me.

"It's why I won't be here for Christmas this year. I've never wanted to leave you before, but now I know it's time to spend it with someone else, and I hope you'll understand." She crossed over to the dressing table and placed Beth's hairbrush and perfume in a drawer, close to where she'd placed her ring earlier.

"You will always be my special girl, my first love." Her tears fell. "Merry Christmas, Beth."

## CHAPTER TWENTY-SIX

E le finished climbing to the top of the stairs as Kier opened the door.

"Close your eyes," she said, removing her small overnight bag and setting it on the floor. Kier took her hand and lead her into the sitting room before maneuvering her around, an arm about her shoulder. "Now you can open them."

Ele opened her eyes to a colorful festive sight. Wrapped around every corner of the room were minute twinkling lights and garlands of green and red. Sparkling tinsel generously covered every surface and object. Tiffany lamps added to the subdued ambience. Their colored stained glass pushed warmth in small circles around couches and chairs that had now acquired varying sized cranberry, red, yellow, gold, and green cushions. Her gaze was drawn to the far end of the room. The huge ugly plant with big leaves that once sat near the entrance had been moved and now rested by the floor to ceiling glass pane. It was covered in decorations and fairy lights.

"You've moved the tree," she stated the obvious.

"You said it would look better here."

"It looks so handsome." Ele was impressed at how it responded to so little attention. Like us all, she thought. She could feel Kier's breath on her neck and it resonated deep within her, speaking to a need. "Oh, Kier, it's like the Christmases we used to have at home. My parents would go to such lengths to make it magical. I'd forgotten how wonderful this can be." She heard the awe in her own low voice. This was what Kier was planning. She was touched, for it was so personal and intimate. It was all done for her.

"Mine too, but I've never bothered before, but I wanted to. I want to make this Christmas wonderful." Kier's voice sounded hoarse and gravelly, the way Ele liked it. Sexy.

Ele swiveled around into Kier's body involuntarily and kissed her. The kiss was nothing like the one at the pub; a quick, nervous one praying the other would respond. This transcended that, as her entire body reacted to this one kiss that exploded inside her.

Her animal desire was mirrored in Kier. Every nerve in her body escalated as she felt Kier's tongue enter her mouth, and arms push inside her coat to circle her back. Kier pulled her close as a wet tongue snaked toward her ear.

"If I knew a few Christmas decorations were all that were needed…" Kier breathed as she brought a hand to Ele's hair, pushing her head back. Ele saw desire in her eyes. "I won't deny I want you, that I want to take you to bed and make love to you, but I don't want you to do anything you don't feel like doing. This isn't what it's all about."

Ele didn't need Kier's compassion and understanding. She needed something else. She smiled seductively at Kier as she stepped back from her to slip her coat off, letting it fall to the floor. She moved back close, pushing her hips into Kier's. She nuzzled up against her neck, smelling her scent. She was hot and aroused.

"Seduce me, Kier." She bit and pulled at Kier's earlobe, panting. "I need you now. Make love to me." She took Kier's hands and placed them low around her. Her encouragement was rewarded as Kier pushed them hard into her bottom, thrusting their pelvic areas closer. Kier gyrated her hips and Ele was instantly wet. She felt as if every nerve in her body was exposed and she longed for Kier to bring a hand forward and slip it into the front of her jeans. She arched her back and opened her mouth as Kier's tongue sought reentry. She moaned, aware that she was being guided to the wall behind her for support. Kier must have read her thoughts; a hand now attacked the belt on her denims.

Kier broke the kiss and Ele saw her look down as she tugged at her belt. Her physical excitement grew as Kier pulled her jean buttons open and slipped her hand down past her navel toward her sex. Ele could barely stand as she parted her legs to allow Kier better access. Her mental faculties dimmed and surrendered to the desires of her body as Kier's fingers manipulated her clitoris, playing in circles. Each slow rotation drove Ele crazy. She was ready now and needed no foreplay. Pushing herself down onto Kier's hand, she begged, "Yes."

But Kier stopped and moved her hand away. She tugged Ele along the open hallway and toward her bedroom. Once there, Ele cast off her top clothing as Kier's hand retraced its way back past her mound and to her sex. Never had wearing jeans felt so good. Ele shook as Kier's wet lips encircled her left nipple and sucked as fingers served her clitoris. Her legs weakened.

Ele was pushed back onto the bed. As she lay there, she saw Kier desperately stripping off her clothes, the excitement hot in her eyes. Ele saw the trim, toned body before her as she somehow managed to push the shoes from her own feet. She was attempting to discard her jeans when Kier frantically pulled them off her in one move before yanking her back to the edge of the bed, leaving her legs dangling over the side.

Kier pushed herself down on top of her. Their naked bodies rubbed together as Kier started moving up and down her rhythmically. Ele responded, the ache between her legs almost unbearable. Tongue to tongue, breast to breast, sex to sex, she heard Kier's heaving breathing and felt her wetness on her.

"Now, Kier. Now."

She guided Kier's hand between her legs again and felt the electricity as fingers played with her, the occasional teasing brush against the entry of her wet vagina. She pushed down, enticing

Kier to go where she badly needed her. A double joy of stimulation, she felt a wonderfully wet tongue snake its way down to her breast, and then lips and teeth pull and bite a nipple, as playful fingers finally pushed into her and started the rhythm she ached for.

The bed moved with them in unison, its little creeks announcing to the world that their crescendo was building. Kier started the pace slow, her thumb caressing Ele's clit. Ele raised her hips in time with pushing fingers that searched for depth. She felt a chill on her nipple as Kier pushed back up her and returned a seeking tongue into her mouth while simultaneously manipulating one of her legs to open Ele's wider. The intensity within Ele mounted as she rocked back and forth with Kier, their speed increasing as forceful fingers pushed deeper with every thrust. Her breathing was labored. She groaned and whimpered. She moaned. Her body arched one final time as it trembled and her muscles strained as the climax hit her. Seconds later, she heard Kier cry out. They continued to rock until both stopped in exhaustion.

Ele moved up the bed and lay still. She grinned as Kier crept with her and curled up beside her. Sated, she placed a hand on thick auburn hair and turned over onto Kier's sweating body. "I love you," she whispered. She heard the words returned.

Kiernan sat close to Ele on her cream couch, surrounded by multicolored cushions of every size. Her arm was around her and she listened as Ele spoke. She wasn't sure what she was saying, and really, she didn't care. She was content to listen to her beautiful accent and admire her in her state of semi undress.

They had showered and eaten. Now they were sat together relaxing, Ele wearing a white cotton dressing gown that was several sizes too small. She didn't seem to mind. Neither did Kiernan as they drank wine.

Kiernan sat with her feet tucked beneath her and wished she could save the moment forever. Music played softly in the background as she listened to Ele talk enthusiastically of the Oxford and Cambridge boat race, and why she always supported the former. Kiernan knew little of the race other than it was an historic annual rowing contest between two rival universities on London's River Thames every April. She understood its importance to Ele who chose to support Oxford because it was Beth's alma mater.

It no longer worried her that Ele spoke of Beth, and those moments seemed to grow less frequent now they were together. But in many ways, Kiernan was thankful to Beth. Whatever existed in their relationship, it had left Ele the person she was, warm and decent, loving and nurturing. Kiernan accepted with ease that Beth would always be a part of Ele, but now, she was too. Everything was balanced.

"Let's go next April and see them race." Ele's zeal was contagious as she spoke like a teenager going to her first rock concert. "It's a great day out, and the race itself is less than twenty minutes. We could go into London and take in a show or something."

"I'm for that." Ele could have asked her to go to a sewage farm, and she wouldn't have said no. She could deny her nothing. Any time with Ele was time gloriously spent. What would she have lost if she'd backed away from her? She listened as Ele spouted dull facts about which team had won the most races, and she silently nodded in support, aware that the statistics could have been water volume through her mythical sewage works. She didn't care. All she cared about was Ele. Kiernan was in love.

As she listened, she massaged Ele's shoulder with her hand. Kiernan wondered if she was happy too. She smiled as she thought of their lovemaking and knew her question was redundant. There was too much passion to not believe Ele was as head over heels in love as she was. Kiernan thought how she would make it her objective to love and nurture Ele, and to never let her regret leaving the sanctity of Beth's memory.

"Where have Chrissie's CDs gone?"

Ele had noticed the clear expanse of floorboards where the pile of discs had once sat.

"I packaged them up this afternoon. I'll post them on to Chrissie after Christmas," Kiernan said. She no longer wanted them. It was time to close the very last chapter.

The change of subject awoke a thought in Kiernan. She sprang off the couch, explaining she still had photos of Ele taken by the stone seat. She hadn't had time to download them, and now she was keen to see how they had turned out. She reached for her camera and laptop off a nearby table and returned to sit by Ele. She slipped the small disc from her camera into the computer and manipulated keys. All the time, she felt Ele leaning over her, her breath on her neck. She knew neither of them would get much sleep tonight. She could handle that. But for now, she forced herself to concentrate on her task.

She opened the folder, and seeing three shots, clicked the one that looked best. There appeared little to choose between them, such was the abundant beauty of her subject. Yes, she was in love. As the image filled the screen, it satisfied her photographic standards. She had caught the right amount of light, and the setting was well configured. The expression on Ele's face was perfect, and she was pleased with the results. But as she enlarged the photo to show Ele, she blinked hard. She could no longer trust what her eyes saw. The photo morphed and became something impossible. She gasped, and Ele shifted closer to look.

"What's wrong?" Ele knew enough to know that photos taken at the old vicarage had a tendency to surprise. Kiernan's heart plunged. She hoped there would be no more photos like these. But she was wrong.

At fleeting glance, it was a picture of Ele alone on the seat, staring with affection at Kiernan. But before their eyes, an image of a man materialized—John Stafford—looking young and happy, sitting close to her, his arm around Ele's shoulder. Fear gripped Kiernan. What happened next made her question her sanity. Ele's face began to fade out, and slowly, another's profile appeared. A familiar face grew recognizable, more delicate and lean, hair darker and its style of an age long ago. She knew they were looking at the face of Harriett Stafford.

Kiernan felt Ele's hand on hers as they watched the screen. They drew breath at the same time as the next alteration occurred. The photo began to oscillate, and as it did, it moved slowly—impossibly—as if it were a piece of film footage. John Stafford was looking lovingly into the eyes of his wife, but then he and Harriett looked toward the camera and smiled. In their eyes, Kiernan saw the unmistakable look of gratitude. The image held for several seconds before fading into nothingness and leaving only the original photo of Ele. Alone.

Neither of them spoke. Nor did they move. Their temporary paralysis stayed with them until Ele managed to find words.

"Did you just see—"

"Yes."

"They smiled," Ele whispered.

"Yes," Kiernan said.

Ele put steepled fingers to her lips. "What does it mean? Is it over?"

Kiernan didn't know and said so. She looked at the other two photos, but they appeared simply as they were, photos of an attractive woman in her late thirties sitting amidst a winter backdrop with sunlight in her hair. Nothing disturbing happened.

"I need another drink." Ele stood and Kiernan, without words, thrust her empty glass toward her.

As she waited for Ele to return, a thought crossed her mind. She accessed the other photos she had taken, the original ones where she had first captured John Stafford and his pointing finger.

She didn't find it surprising that as she opened each photograph, they were the same. Every single image of Captain

John Stafford was gone. He was no longer in any photo. It was as if he had never existed at all.

Kiernan put the laptop down and followed Ele into the kitchen. She stopped at the door jam. "Ele, you asked how you would know if you'd done the right thing, if replacing the garden seat would stop the haunting."

Ele looked at her, her eyes wide.

"I think the answer is yes."

"How do you know?"

"Because in every photo I took of John Stafford, he's now gone."

Kiernan had to show Ele each photo to prove it, that Stafford had really disappeared.

"He's gone, Ele. I think he's at peace, at last."

# CHAPTER TWENTY-SEVEN

John Stafford was not alone in finding peace.

When Ele returned home with Kier some days later, she felt changed and different. She felt electrified, as if she'd been in a dormant state, but was now pulsing with life. She was happy and knew everything from now on would change irrevocably. With Kier, she would never be alone again. Everything was becoming as it should.

En route home, she and Kier had food shopped at the out-of-town supermarket. They had bumped into Roger who told them how well Joan was, that she was sleeping better, and seemed more her old self. She was feeding her birds again, and the curtains were open. All were hopeful signs.

Ele felt sure that John Stafford was at peace as she stood in the kitchen putting groceries away. Though it would take her some time to stem the nervousness she still felt when outside, her heart told her he was gone, and the haunting over.

She bent to stroke Feathers as she fed him, and then crossed over to the sink to top up his water dish. As she did so, she looked out onto the courtyard to gaze at the stone seat. At first, everything looked normal, but something drew her attention back to the plastic pots, the ones containing the dead roses she had dragged off the garbage and placed by the seat to show Kier her future plans. Was she imagining it, or could she see tiny buds on them?

She crossed to the back door and went outside. Both plants clearly showed signs of life. There were small buds breaking out on them. The roses were alive.

"This is impossible," she said to herself.

"What is?" Kier had followed her out.

She pointed to the roses, allowing Kier to make her own diagnosis.

"They were dead." She watched Kier touch each bud before looking at her in confusion.

Ele walked to the refuse area and inspected the other four discarded roses. They were still dead. She held one up to show Kier. Only the two plants she had placed by the seat showed signs of growth.

"This is impossible, Kier. These plants were dead, but now they're not."

"Maybe it's a mistake," Kier said. "Maybe they weren't completely dead, and when you moved them, they got the sun?"

Ele knew that didn't make sense. "Roses do not start to bloom in winter, and neither do they bud this quickly. Just days ago they were snap dry twigs." Ele examined the roses again, doubting her eyes.

They stared at them for a minute. "What does it mean, Kier?" A lump rose in her throat as she feared the haunting wasn't over. But Kier stepped up close and smiled. A reassuring arm went around her and Kier smiled. Kier tugged her closer before she spoke softly.

*"Live not your life with bareness grim,*
*Nor block the light to stem a love,*
*Or hinder by winds fierce blows.*
*But nurture it with shining sun,*
*As this that will give the rarest rose."*

She looked at Kier as she tugged her closer again.

"Ele, this is John Stafford's way of thanking you. He's given you a gift of the rarest rose."

# EPILOGUE

*Four months later.*

Ele woke.

For a while, she lay still and listened, vaguely aware that something had stirred her from sleep. She heard nothing, only the stillness of the night, and saw the usual shadows that filled her bedroom in the half-dark.

Nothing happened when she thrust her head back into the welcoming thickness of her pillow. It seemed she was awake now, and her body wasn't inclined to return to sleep, not just yet. So she rose quietly and, putting her slippers on, walked out onto the landing to search for what might have disturbed her.

Moonlight streamed through the bathroom window, and she wandered into the room, captivated by the mesmerizing brightness. She caught her reflection in the mirror and grinned. *Drop dead gorgeous, not!* Her hair was wild and skewed, her face full of sleepiness. She grinned and rubbed her eyes.

As she was leaving, she thought she heard something in the courtyard below, a brief sound of laughter. She crossed to the small window that overlooked her studio and peered out. Though still dark outside, the moon cast its eerie, incandescent light, and she saw nothing untoward.

An owl screeched and drew her attention to treetops in the distance. Perhaps that was what woke her. It screeched again, and its shrill cut loud through the quiet night. But as she turned away from the window, her eyes registered something that told her sleepy state it was not right. Had she seen two silhouetted shapes on the stone seat below, shapes of a man and a woman sitting close, their arms around each other? Ele stared at the seat, this time alert, but whatever she thought she saw, it was gone. All she saw was an empty seat surrounded by an abundance of blooming roses.

She stood and watched for several minutes more, but apart from her noisy owl, nothing else happened, and eventually, she crept back to bed.

As she pulled the covers over her, she felt movement at her side and a sleepy Irish voice said, "You laugh in your sleep."

She knew she didn't, and cuddled up to Kier's back. "Did I wake you, my love?" No answer came. Ele wondered if Kier would remember what she'd said in the morning. She doubted it; the woman slept like a hibernating bear. She nuzzled up closer and felt the heaviness of sleep finally approach.

In her last conscious thoughts, she considered how happy she was, and how happy the ghost of John Stafford. This was simply a *happy* home, filled with love on so many levels.

She fell asleep, smiling.

The End

# About the Author

I. Beacham grew up in the heart of England, a green and pleasant land, mainly because it rains so much. This is probably why she ran away to sea, to search for dry places. Over the years, and during long periods away from home constantly travelling to far away places, she has balanced the rigidity of her professional life with her need and love to write. Blessed with a wicked sense of humor (not all agree), she is a lover of all things water, a dreadful jogger and cook, a hopeless romantic who roams antique stores, an addict of old black-and-white movies, and an adorer of science fiction. In her opinion, a perfect life.

# Books Available from Bold Strokes Books

**The Rarest Rose** by I. Beacham. After a decade of living in her beloved house, Ele disturbs its past and finds her life being haunted by the presence of a ghost who will show her that true love never dies. (978-1-60282-884-1)

**Code of Honor** by Radclyffe. The face of terror is hard to recognize—especially when it's homegrown. The next book in the Honor series. (978-1-60282-885-8)

**Does She Love You** by Rachel Spangler. When Annabelle and Davis find out they are both in a relationship with the same woman, it leaves them facing life-altering questions about trust, redemption, and the possibility of finding love in the wake of betrayal. (978-1-60282-886-5)

**The Road to Her** by KE Payne. Sparks fly when actress Holly Croft, star of UK soap Portobello Road, meets her new on-screen love interest, the enigmatic and sexy Elise Manford. (978-1-60282-887-2)

**Shadows of Something Real** by Sophia Kell Hagin. Trying to escape flashbacks and nightmares, ex-POW Jamie Gwynmorgan stumbles into the heart of former Red Cross worker Adele Sabellius and uncovers a deadly conspiracy against everything and everyone she loves. (978-1-60282-889-6)

**Date with Destiny** by Mason Dixon. When sophisticated bank executive Rashida Ivey meets unemployed blue collar worker

Destiny Jackson, will her life ever be the same? (978-1-60282-878-0)

**The Devil's Orchard** by Ali Vali. Cain and Emma plan a wedding before the birth of their third child while Juan Luis is still lurking, and as Cain plans for his death, an unexpected visitor arrives and challenges her belief in her father, Dalton Casey. (978-1-60282-879-7)

**Secrets and Shadows** by L.T. Marie. A bodyguard and the woman she protects run from a madman and into each other's arms. (978-1-60282-880-3)

**Change Horizon: Three Novellas** by Gun Brooke. Three stories of courageous women who dare to love as they fight to claim a future in a hostile universe. (978-1-60282-881-0)

**Scarlet Thirst** by Crin Claxton. When hot, feisty Rani meets cool, vampire Rob, one lifetime isn't enough, and the road from human to vampire is shorter than you think… (978-1-60282-856-8)

**Battle Axe** by Carsen Taite. How close is too close? Bounty hunter Luca Bennett will soon find out. (978-1-60282-871-1)

**Improvisation** by Karis Walsh. High school geometry teacher Jan Carroll thinks she's figured out the shape of her life and her future, until graphic artist and fiddle player Tina Nelson comes along and teaches her to improvise. (978-1-60282-872-8)

**For Want of a Fiend** by Barbara Ann Wright. Without her Fiendish power, can Princess Katya and her consort Starbride stop a magic-wielding madman from sparking an uprising in the kingdom of Farraday? (978-1-60282-873-5)

**Broken in Soft Places** by Fiona Zedde. The instant Sara Chambers meets the seductive and sinful Merille Thompson, she falls hard, but knowing the difference between love and a dangerous, all-consuming desire is just one of the lessons Sara must learn before it's too late. (978-1-60282-876-6)

**Healing Hearts** by Donna K. Ford. Running from tragedy, the women of Willow Springs find that with friendship, there is hope, and with love, there is everything. (978-1-60282-877-3)

**Desolation Point** by Cari Hunter. When a storm strands Sarah Kent in the North Cascades, Alex Pascal is determined to find her. Neither imagines the dangers they will face when a ruthless criminal begins to hunt them down. (978-1-60282-865-0)

**I Remember** by Julie Cannon. What happens when you can never forget the first kiss, the first touch, the first taste of lips on skin? What happens when you know you will remember every single detail of a mysterious woman? (978-1-60282-866-7)

**The Gemini Deception** by Kim Baldwin and Xenia Alexiou. The truth, the whole truth, and nothing but lies. Book six in the Elite Operatives series. (978-1-60282-867-4)

**Scarlet Revenge** by Sheri Lewis Wohl. When faith alone isn't enough, will the love of one woman be strong enough to save a vampire from damnation? (978-1-60282-868-1)

**Ghost Trio** by Lillian Q. Irwin. When Lee Howe hears the voice of her dead lover singing to her, is it a hallucination, a ghost, or something more sinister? (978-1-60282-869-8)

**The Princess Affair** by Nell Stark. Rhodes Scholar Kerry Donovan arrives at Oxford ready to focus on her studies, but her life and her priorities are thrown into chaos when she catches the eye of Her Royal Highness Princess Sasha. (978-1-60282-858-2)

**The Chase** by Jesse J. Thoma. When Isabelle Rochat's life is threatened, she receives the unwelcome protection and attention of bounty hunter Holt Lasher who vows to keep Isabelle safe at all costs. (978-1-60282-859-9)

**The Lone Hunt** by L.L. Raand. In a world where humans and praeterns conspire for the ultimate power, violence is a way of life...and death. A Midnight Hunters novel. (978-1-60282-860-5)

**The Supernatural Detective** by Crin Claxton. Tony Carson sees dead people. With a drag queen for a spirit guide and a devastatingly attractive herbalist for a client, she's about to discover the spirit world can be a very dangerous world indeed. (978-1-60282-861-2)

**Beloved Gomorrah** by Justine Saracen. Undersea artists creating their own City on the Plain uncover the truth about Sodom and Gomorrah, whose "one righteous man" is a murderer, rapist, and conspirator in genocide. (978-1-60282-862-9)

**Cut to the Chase** by Lisa Girolami. Careful and methodical author Paige Cornish falls for brash and wild Hollywood actress Avalon

Randolph, but can these opposites find a happy middle ground in a town that never lives in the middle? (978-1-60282-783-7)

**More Than Friends** by Erin Dutton. Evelyn Fisher thinks she has the perfect role model for a long-term relationship, until her best friends, Kendall and Melanie, split up and all three women must reevaluate their lives and their relationships. (978-1-60282-784-4)

**Every Second Counts** by D. Jackson Leigh. Every second counts in Bridgette LeRoy's desperate mission to protect her heart and stop Marc Ryder's suicidal return to riding rodeo bulls. (978-1-60282-785-1)

**Dirty Money** by Ashley Bartlett. Vivian Cooper and Reese DiGiovanni just found out that falling in love is hard. It's even harder when you're running for your life. (978-1-60282-786-8)

**Sea Glass Inn** by Karis Walsh. When Melinda Andrews commissions a series of mosaics by Pamela Whitford for her new inn, she doesn't expect to be more captivated by the artist than by the paintings. (978-1-60282-771-4)

**The Awakening: A Sisters of Spirits novel** by Yvonne Heidt. Sunny Skye has interacted with spirits her entire life, but when she runs into Officer Jordan Lawson during a ghost investigation, she discovers more than just facts in a missing girl's cold case file. (978-1-60282-772-1)

**Murphy's Law** by Yolanda Wallace. No matter how high you climb, you can't escape your past. (978-1-60282-773-8)

**Blacker Than Blue** by Rebekah Weatherspoon. Threatened with losing her first love to a powerful demon, vampire Cleo Jones is willing to break the ultimate law of the undead to rebuild the family she has lost. (978-1-60282-774-5)

**Silver Collar** by Gill McKnight. Werewolf Luc Garoul is outlawed and out of control, but can her family track her down before a sinister predator gets there first? Fourth in the Garoul series. (978-1-60282-764-6)

**The Dragon Tree Legacy** by Ali Vali. For Aubrey Tarver time hasn't dulled the pain of losing her first love Wiley Gremillion, but she has to set that aside when her choices put her life and her family's lives in real danger. (978-1-60282-765-3)